IT WAS A MODULATED ELECTRONIC BURST THAT LASTED NO MORE THAN A SECOND....

Captain Spock remained perfectly still, wondering if he would hear it again—and he did, a moment later. The third time he heard the sound, he was certain that he recognized it.

Phaser fire!

As quietly as possible, Spock rose. His ears told him that five assassins were creeping through the lodge, intent upon killing him and Teska. Armed with phasers, they could vaporize the bodies and leave no trace at all....

STAR TREK®

MIND MELD

JOHN VORNHOLT

POCKET BOOKS
New York   London   Toronto   Sydney   Tokyo   Singapore

An *Original* Publication of POCKET BOOKS

POCKET BOOKS, a division of Simon & Schuster Inc.
1230 Avenue of the Americas, New York, NY 10020

ISBN: 0-671-00258-9

First Pocket Books printing June 1997

10 9 8 7 6 5 4 3 2 1

For Dan

Historian's Note

This story takes place shortly after the events portrayed in *Star Trek VI: The Undiscovered Country*.

MIND MELD

Chapter One

AN OLDER MAN with a saturnine face, sallow complexion, dark hair, and angular eyebrows pulled his hood over his pointed ears and stared down into a dripping cesspool. His long tapered nose did not contract at the odors of the reservoir, which relieved the great city of its waste. He was intent upon his mission, and his only means of reaching the shuttle-craft field undetected was through this sewer.

He gazed at the ceiling of the cavernous tunnel, with its network of baffles and vents for removing harmful gases, then he looked down at the intricate system of tanks, gutters, and reclamation pools. It was a marvel of engineering that no one ever saw. His people were master builders, renowned throughout the galaxy, but they were also master destroyers.

"Father, I want to go back," said a small voice beside him.

Wislok stared into the eyes of the seven-year-old Hasmek, a smaller version of himself. He could not be angry with the child. Hasmek looked wide-eyed at their gloomy surroundings. Like most children of the Pretorium, he had experienced only the finer things in life. Work in the sewers was restricted to the plebians.

"Why can't we go in a hovercraft?" asked the boy. "Or walk in the sunlight?"

Wislok frowned. "There are times when subterfuge is called for, and this is one of those times. Haven't I made the plans clear?"

"Yes, Father. But I don't understand why I have to . . ." Hasmek gulped. "I mean, no other boys go through this ritual."

"Not on Romulus," answered Wislok patiently. He had explained this all before, but the boy needed reassuring. "On Vulcan, all children go through *koon-ut-la* at your age, when they meet their future mate. You volunteered for this experiment, and you have to be brave. There's nothing in the ritual that can harm you."

He certainly hoped that was the case, but he had to admit to himself that he was guessing. Vulcan rituals relied upon a combination of mysticism, biology, and collective consciousness that he didn't pretend to understand. Perhaps it was time to tell his son the truth. Wislok took a deep breath and began.

"The reason we're doing this is Pardek. He's always two steps ahead of everyone else, with friends in every corner. This connection with the Vulcans is brilliant—it could be the excuse for a new government, with *us* as the leaders. The Vulcans are so literal-minded that they have to see proof that our races are related. *You* are going to be that proof."

"Why don't we just conquer them?" asked the boy.

"That is the thinking of many, but when you destroy a thing, you never learn its worth. With Pardek's plan, we can usurp them and all their knowledge of the Federation and science without firing a torpedo. If we fail, there is always the option of war."

The boy looked down. "What will she be like?"

Wislok could only shrug his broad shoulders. "She comes from the family of Sarek and Spock, and Pardek assures me they are very important." His chin jutted into the air, and his angular eyebrows lifted. "I hear something. Get down."

Without hesitation, he and the boy jumped into a deep drainage gutter and crouched against the grimy wall. Wislok motioned for silence and listened to the sounds of footsteps jumping off a ladder and landing on the catwalk with a metallic thud. He waited to hear more footsteps, but there was apparently only one person. With any luck, thought the Romulan, it would be a maintenance worker, and he would take his readings and leave swiftly.

"This is the Civil Guard!" announced a stern voice, which echoed importantly in the sewer tunnel. "Who is down there?"

Wislok muttered an oath under his breath. They

could not ignore a member of the Guard, even the lowly Civil Guard. At least there was only one of them. "Remain hidden," he whispered to his son.

He stood up, located the guard on a catwalk about fifty meters away, and addressed him authoritatively. "I am Wislok, Chief Surgeon to the Proconsul. I was taking water samples to check on a report of liptherum bacteria."

The young guard snapped to attention and lowered his disrupter rifle. "Yes, my liege, I recognize you." He looked thoughtful. "You set off an alarm. Do you have clearance for this project?"

"Of course," answered Wislok with the put-upon air of the upper class. "At the highest levels. I can't imagine why the prefect didn't turn off the alarms." He started to climb out of the gutter but pretended to slip.

Helplessly, he held out his hands. "I seem to be mired in my work at the moment. Could I trouble you to come down and see my permit?"

The guard nodded, although he wrinkled his nose at the pungent odors emanating from the cesspool. Wislok watched him descend the stairs, waiting to see if he would use his communicator to alert the centurions. When he didn't, Wislok relaxed. He didn't smile at the man; that would have been too familiar with an underling, but he assumed an air of patience.

The officer approached, and Wislok fumbled in his equipment belt. "I have the document here." He produced a fiber scroll with one hand and a tubular device with the other, then he pretended to slip backward, forcing the guard to come even closer.

4

From the corner of his eye, he saw Hasmek pressed against the grimy sewer wall, his dark eyes wide and unflinching.

As the guard bent over the gutter to get the scroll, Wislok lifted his laser scalpel, applied pressure with his thumb, and generated a pinpoint laser beam thirty centimeters long. He slipped the beam into the guard's left ventricle before the man even felt the pain. The guard stared wild-eyed and gasped, and Wislok grabbed his son and dragged him out of the way an instant before the man tumbled into the sewer. His body jerked and rolled over, then it began to float away with the refuse.

"He died swiftly," Wislok assured his son, putting his laser scalpel away.

The boy gulped. "Did you have to kill him?"

Wislok's patience began to snap, and he turned angrily on the seven-year-old. "Stop behaving like a . . ." *A what,* thought the father guiltily. *A child?* He put his hands over his weary eyes for a moment, and then he began again. "This is a meaningful experiment, Hasmek. The risks are high, but so are the rewards."

The boy nodded solemnly, and it wasn't a mechanical nod. *He is truly wise beyond his years,* Wislok noted with renewed hope of success. It would take wisdom, perseverance, and ruthlessness to complete this experiment—an experiment that would require two decades to yield results.

Wislok gently lifted his boy out of the sewer and set him on the catwalk, then he dragged himself out. Their brocaded suits were filthy, and he hoped that Pardek had left them clean clothes in the shuttlecraft as planned. Wislok sighed. He realized that he might as well be honest with himself. He wasn't worried about Pardek so much as he was worried about their Vulcan "allies." Even though Pardek knew Sarek and Spock personally and vouched for them, Wislok was putting his son's life in the hands of strangers from the dreaded Federation. He had good reason to be concerned.

Fortunately, the Romulan had three older sons, so he could afford to endanger the youngest on a risky venture such as this. He pushed the boy along the narrow catwalk. "No more talk. We must hurry."

James T. Kirk sat on the bridge of the submersible sport-fishing boat *Cataluna,* watching his float bob upward through turquoise water that shimmered in a porthole above his head. If he had wanted, he could have plunged his hand into the water, which was held at bay by forcefields and air pressure, but he was content just to fish. The twenty-meter-long vessel was constructed of a translucent material, so they were surrounded by sun-streaked water and majestic schools of sea creatures.

Kirk looked down and could see not only his instruments but also the deck below him. In the bow, Uhura and Spock were operating the sounding device and fish locator, which were tasks they found more interesting than actually fishing. Dr. "Bones" McCoy was sitting in the stern of the ship, doggedly fishing through a hole in the bottom of the boat, even though he could have fished through the hull or the upper deck. Only Kirk had caught anything big enough to keep—two plump raylike fish with three eyes topside and two mouths on the bottom—and he intended to eat them both.

He could see Bones glancing his way and looking grumpy, and he figured the good doctor would pay him a visit on the bridge very soon. Sure enough, Bones rose to his feet, careful not to stick his head through a pool of suspended water, and stepped gingerly upon the ladder.

Kirk smiled at his friend's approach. "You'll never catch anything but bottom-feeders that way."

McCoy pointedly ignored the comment as he stepped onto the clear deck. He looked disapprovingly at Kirk's line suspended above his head into the wavering water. "This is unnatural. Why can't we use a surface boat?"

The captain shook his head with amusement. "Bones, you live in a ship surrounded by an endless void, and a little water makes you nervous?"

McCoy's attempt to suppress a smile was only partially successful. "I am accustomed to *that* void, Captain," he said with a false pomposity that immediately deflated. "I just can't get used to this one."

"Doctor, may I remind you that this is supposed to be rest and recreation." Kirk tugged on his line to give his lure a bit of movement.

McCoy sunk into the co-pilot's seat. "Well, I'm neither rested nor recreated. It's not easy to relax when we don't know what's going to become of us. Are we going to be kicked out, or given medals? What about the *Enterprise*—is she going to be scrapped?"

Kirk's face drooped at the last suggestion, and he looked most of his sixty years. "I don't know, Bones.

I'm not sure I want to run around the galaxy anymore, but I don't want to see the *Enterprise* floating in a junkyard either."

"It seems to me like we're hiding out down here," grumbled McCoy, casting a jaundiced eye at the captain. "You know, Jim, Pacifica is a big planet—there are cafes, concert halls, and restaurants. If Starfleet won't give us anything to do, can't we at least have a look around?"

The captain shook his head. "There are too many reporters on the islands, and all they want to talk about is Khitomer, the trial, or those damn whales. But you go topside if you want to, Bones. It's not fair to keep you cooped up with me, if you want to go out on the town."

"By myself?" Bones scowled and shook his head. He took a flask out of his hip pocket and smelled its contents before he took a sip. "It's not fair. They get you out of retirement, run you ragged, then want to put you back on the shelf."

The doctor offered the flask to Kirk, but he waved it off. "Remember what MacArthur said about old soldiers never dying—"

McCoy nodded somberly. "Yes, I remember. And I can tell you right now that I'm nowhere near ready to fade away."

"Hear, hear," said Kirk with an affectionate smile. A moment later he grew serious. "If we started fading away, would we even know it?"

He heard Spock's footsteps on the ladder and turned to see the Vulcan pass through the translucent hatch. "That is an illogical metaphor. Humanoid life forms do not fade away—energy is always converted into another form of energy."

"And you should know," said McCoy with a smirk.

Spock ignored him. "There are only two states—active and inactive."

"And this feels like inactivity, doesn't it?" asked Kirk. "Let's find ourselves a better fishin' hole. Dr. McCoy, turn off the forcefield anchor, will you?"

"Aye, aye, sir!" McCoy capped his flask and bent over the co-pilot's instrument panel. "Anchors aweigh."

"Captain!" called Uhura from the lower deck. "Don't forget the fishing lines!"

Kirk nodded gratefully. "Thank you, Commander. Would you please reel in Dr. McCoy's line—you're the closest."

"Certainly, Captain." The serene dark-skinned woman hiked to the stern of the boat and reeled in a few handfuls of line to get the hook off the bottom. Then she turned on the automatic winch, and the fishing line reeled slowly into a receptacle.

Suddenly the line went taut, and the ship jerked. McCoy was thrown off his feet, and Kirk gripped his armrests instinctively. It felt as if they were back in space, except instead of stars, Kirk saw a leviathan rise from the depths and become engulfed in an eruption of sand. The beast was as big as the submersible, twenty meters long, and it looked like a flounder—flat except for a frill of delicate-looking fins.

The sea monster appeared to be moving slowly,

but its pace was deceptive. It curled upward, dragging the ship, and the crew members were knocked off their feet once more. Uhura had the presence of mind to stop the winch and release the line, but it couldn't unreel fast enough. The giant fish hauled the submarine upward, and a splash of salty water hit Kirk in the face. He looked up to see water churning in the porthole above his head.

"Close all ports!" shouted Kirk. "Drop anchor!"

Spock took over at the co-pilot's instrument panel. "I am unable to reapply the forcefield, Captain, but I am closing the ports."

The porthole above Kirk snapped shut, shearing off his fishing line. He looked around and saw that all the portholes were closed, except for the active one, and the ship was listing badly.

"Get out of there, Uhura!" he shouted down to the lower deck. She scurried up the ladder, and upon reaching the upper deck she slammed down the hatch and twisted it shut. Kirk turned on the engines and threw the ship into reverse. He'd be damned if he'd let some big fish drag his boat around the bottom of the ocean.

McCoy sat up and grinned at him. "Let's see if you can reel him in."

Kirk scowled. "If you think I'm going to bring that fish in, you're crazy!" He blinked at Spock. "How long would it take?"

"It would take at least an hour to subdue that creature," said Spock, "with a high probability of failure."

Out of breath, Uhura slumped to the deck beside them. "The line will run out if we don't lock it."

"If we move toward him, we'll put some slack in the line," said Kirk, wrestling with the controls. At that moment, his wrist communicator chirped.

"Blast it," muttered Kirk. "Spock, take over."

The Vulcan dutifully slid into the co-pilot's seat and grabbed the stick. "Orders, Captain?"

"Follow the fish," echoed Kirk, "and keep some slack in the line." He lifted his arm and spoke into his communicator. "Kirk here."

"Brace yeself, Captain," said Scotty in his clipped accent. "We've gotten orders from Starfleet."

Kirk bolted upright in his seat, and McCoy blinked at him. Uhura moved, and Spock listened as he deftly piloted the submersible in pursuit of the giant sea creature. "You've got our attention," said Kirk, "what are the orders?"

"The *Enterprise* is relieved from active duty, but she is assigned for special duty to the diplomatic corps, under the direction of Ambassador Sarek."

Kirk glanced at Spock, who cocked an eyebrow at the news that his father was now their superior.

Scotty went on, "Ambassador Sarek is on his way to brief us, an' he wants to be met by just yourself and Captain Spock. But he's not comin' alone—he has spare parts and a crew of forty-two, all for us! It's not a full complement, to be sure, but it's enough to keep the boilers stoked. We may not be the flagship of the fleet anymore, Captain, but we're still in business!"

The captain could hear the excitement in Scotty's voice. "How soon will Sarek be here?" asked Kirk.

"Inside of two hours."

"Good, we've got time to pilot this bucket back to

shore. Stand by to beam us up in one hour. Kirk out."

"Get closer!" said McCoy, leaning over Spock's shoulder. "We've got to *reel* him in. I'll get the line."

"Belay that order," snapped Kirk. "Back up slowly and let the line run out." Spock said nothing as he reversed the craft.

McCoy stared at Kirk in astonishment. "You're going to let him get away, aren't you? *My* fish!"

"Just think, Bones, when you tell them about the one that got away, your arms won't even be long enough." He slapped his friend on the back, but McCoy still looked glum.

As Spock piloted the submersible on a gradual course of withdrawal, the majestic creature faded from view. Kirk looked down through the clear deck to watch the reel unwind in fits and starts. Finally the line snapped off and disappeared into the sun-drenched turquoise sea.

"Closing the stern porthole," said Spock. "Would you like me to set course for shore?"

"Go ahead," said the captain, taking a breath.

McCoy shook his head with disappointment. "There was a time, Jim, when you would have reeled him in."

Kirk gave his old friend a wistful smile. "We all have to grow up sometime."

Captain Spock snapped to attention as his father materialized on the transporter platform aboard the *Enterprise NCC-1701-A.* He understood that Sarek was not coming to visit him, per se, but was there in his official capacity, and Spock could easily sep-

arate these two distinct roles of the Vulcan states-
man. He stepped out from behind the transporter
controls and nodded cordially. Spock would treat
their distinguished visitor with the same respectful
attitude that he would show any representative of
the Federation.

Captain Kirk was much more ebullient as he
stepped forward and held out his hand. "Ambassador, good to see you again!"

"Captain Kirk," said Sarek with as much warmth
as he could muster, which wasn't much. "I am glad
to see that you are well and recovered from your
recent travails."

Kirk smiled. "I'm never turning myself over to the
Klingons again."

"Those were unfortunate circumstances," said
Sarek. "However, you admirably demonstrated that
the needs of the many outweigh the needs of the few.
Thanks to the actions of you, Dr. McCoy, and your
crew, a disaster was averted."

"All in a day's work."

At last, Sarek turned to his son. Except for the
graying hair, he was little changed from the man
Spock had known his entire life. A handsome,
robust man, Sarek was only 138 years old, still in the
prime of life for a Vulcan.

"Captain Spock," said Sarek in a cordial tone. "I
have not fully thanked you for your part in saving
the conference at Khitomer."

Spock cocked his head. "It was only logical to
make peace with the Klingons."

"And do you believe it is equally logical to seek
peace with the Romulans?" asked Sarek. The ambas-

13

sador turned to Captain Kirk, whose mouth was dropping open.

"First the Klingons, now the Romulans?" he asked. "Are we going to make friends with *everybody?*"

"In essence, Captain, that is precisely what we are doing. In a way, your new assignment is more important than a mere treaty, because it will set in motion events that will eventually lead to the unification of Vulcans and Romulans."

Silence greeted Sarek's remark. Spock quickly looked over at Kirk, who appeared anxious to question the ambassador further. The Vulcan nodded slightly in the direction of his commanding officer and friend and was gratified to see an expression of understanding on Kirk's face. They would talk later. But now Spock had questions of his own for his father. "Have our discussions with Pardek yielded results?" he asked.

"Possibilities," Sarek replied. He looked around, as if doubting that the transporter room of the *Enterprise* was secure enough to contain this conversation. "These matters must remain secret for a time, as few Romulans can risk discussing the theory that both our races are descended from the same ancestors."

Spock nodded. "One can understand why; the data on our common ancestors is mostly apocryphal. Genetic tests have also proven inconclusive."

"Yes," agreed Sarek. "We need a stronger test, one that will convince the Vulcan Science Academy to back our plans. With the Vulcan Science Academy on our side, we can proceed to the next logical step;

without them, we will not even receive a hearing. We need proof that goes beyond mere biology—to the core of what it means to be a Vulcan."

The ambassador's expression changed slightly, not so much that Kirk would notice, but Spock realized that they were about to discuss something personal.

Sarek gazed at his son. "I asked the two of you to meet me alone, because we have both family matters and ritual matters to discuss. They directly affect this mission. Normally, outworlders would not be privileged to hear this information, but Captain Kirk participated in your *koon-ut-kal-if-fee,* and the *fal-tor-pan* which restored you to us. He has demonstrated his respect for our traditions."

"Ambassador Sarek, I appreciate your confidence," said Kirk, "and since you have placed so much trust in me, I feel I must speak frankly. I don't think you should make any kind of deal with the Romulans. They may *look* like Vulcans, but your cultures are quite literally worlds apart."

Sarek smoothed a wrinkle out of his robes. "That remains to be seen, Captain. We were once much like the Romulans—brutal, treacherous—until we learned to control our emotions."

He looked intently at Captain Kirk. "We have a unique opportunity. High Priestess T'Lar has agreed to perform the *koon-ut-la* ceremony between a Vulcan female and a Romulan male. If these children go through *pon farr* in the seventh year of their adult life, we will know that the similarities between Vulcans and Romulans are far deeper than appearance. The Vulcan Science Academy will be forced to give serious attention to our theory, and so will open-minded factions on Romulus and Remus."

Spock suddenly realized why he and the *Enterprise* had been chosen for this assignment. "Teska," he said.

"Yes, your niece."

Spock bowed to his father. "I will be honored to perform my duties as *pele-ut-la.*"

"What is that?" Kirk asked warily.

Sarek replied, "The role of *pele-ut-la,* or chaperone, is a traditional duty for an uncle. But since the child has no uncles, I have arranged for Spock to serve instead. One complication is that Teska's parents are dead, and she is living with her grandfather, Sopeg, who teaches geology at Starfleet Academy. Spock must accompany Teska from Earth to Vulcan with a stop on the way, and he needs the *Enterprise* for that. The boy and his father are coming to Vulcan by a circuitous route, and we must be ready when they arrive."

"Wait a minute," said Kirk, holding up his hands. "You're betting the whole idea of reunification between Vulcans and Romulans on whether these two children, who have never met each other, go through with a marriage when they grow up?"

"There are significant risks," Sarek acknowledged. "If they fail, our cause will be set back decades. Perhaps Vulcans and Romulans will never be unified, because we may never have a priestess with the stature of T'Lar who is willing to officiate."

He continued, "If a Romulan suffers the effects of *pon farr,* it would convince Romulans, Vulcans, and even doubtful humans that we are biologically similar. We are depending upon you, Captain—this ceremony must take place."

Kirk scratched his chin and looked at his old friend. "What do you think of this, Spock?"

The Vulcan answered slowly. "As we are all aware, a *koon-ut-la* ceremony does not guarantee a successful partnership. In my case, it was unsuccessful. Therefore, I would be most impressed if the ceremony resulted in a successful marriage. It would prove the viability of unification."

"The probability of success is unknown," said Sarek. "However, the presence of T'Lar will afford the young couple the best possible opportunity. As you and few outsiders know, Captain, it is the high priestess who must fuse their minds in a ceremony that will, at the proper time, drive them to *plak-tow*, the blood fever."

"I am familiar with the blood fever," said Kirk quietly. If Spock were not Vulcan, he would have winced at the memory of the blood fever that gripped him during his first tour of duty aboard the *Enterprise*. Kirk had risked his career, then his life, to bring him through the turmoil of *pon farr*. Most of it was a blur to Spock, except for the memories of helplessness, anger, and rejection, followed by despair when he thought he had killed his captain. The only thing that was always clear to Spock about that terrible time was that he owed Jim Kirk his life.

"Captain, you may want to attend their marriage," Spock told his friend. "It could be the beginning of the most important event in Vulcan and Romulan history."

Kirk smiled. "I'll check my schedule and see what

I'm doing in twenty-one years." He grew more serious. "I take it we shouldn't tell the crew about this mission."

"I would prefer you did not," answered Sarek, "unless it is necessary. As cover for this mission, you are also transporting a group of Rigelians who have been involved in talks on Earth. Taking the Rigelians home to Rigel V should not inconvenience you, and it will allay suspicion."

Kirk smiled. "I see. Rigelians also look a lot like Vulcans, and you're counting on the girl blending in with them."

"Yes," agreed Sarek, "and there is another matter. The Rigelians are under investigation for practices that are forbidden under Federation laws. If these charges are true, we will not renew their trade agreements, and their membership in the Federation may be revoked. This delegation did not get the reassurances they sought, and they may be agitated. I do not wish to involve you in these matters, but I feel it safe to warn you—the Rigelians are not as reserved as Vulcans, and they may seek your aid."

"We'll stay neutral," said Kirk. "And we'll keep our eyes open."

The venerable Vulcan nodded. "I must take my leave. There are more negotiations with the Klingons at Camp Khitomer, even talk of a Klingon settlement there. Shall we beam your new crew members aboard?"

"Please," said Kirk crisply. "The old crew members are just itching to delegate a little work."

Sarek nodded and turned to Spock. His face remained immobile, but Spock could feel a oneness with his father as he held up his right hand in the traditional, open-handed Vulcan salute. "Live long and prosper."

"May our paths soon cross again," replied Spock with the same salute.

As the ambassador climbed upon the transporter platform, the Starfleet officer strode behind the controls. For years, diverse interests and careers had kept father and son apart—now they saw each other more frequently, often working for the same causes. Over the years, Spock had become something of a diplomat, and Sarek had become as much a representative of the Federation as he was for the planet Vulcan. Remembering the years when they hadn't spoken to one another, Spock took considerable gratification in the meshing of their lives and careers.

"Energize when ready," said Sarek.

"Yes, Father." Spock's deft fingers worked the controls and converted Sarek's molecules into a column of sparkling lights. A moment later the renowned diplomat was gone.

Chapter Two

A CHIME SOUNDED over the ship's intercom, and the captain's precise voice followed: "To all hands, the *Enterprise* is now in standard orbit around Earth. My commendations to the new crew members for a job well done on our first journey together. I wish I could give you all shore leave, but we will only be here long enough to pick up passengers. The Rigelians have been involved in difficult trade talks, so let's make sure they have a quiet trip with lots of privacy. Captain Spock, I will meet you in the transporter room."

Spock nodded automatically, although he was alone in his austere quarters. He looked back at the computer screen on his desk to see the visage of a seven-year-old Vulcan female. Her face was impish, elflike, and her ears appeared large, even for a

Vulcan. Shiny bangs pointed the way to luminous black eyes, which showed a marked degree of intelligence.

He had seen Teska twice in the four years she had lived on Earth. Now he regretted not spending more time with the girl, although his life had been rather eventful of late. He should have remembered that her *koon-ut-la* was coming soon—even without the Romulan involvement, he would still have served as her chaperone.

Putting these concerns out of his mind, Spock turned off the computer screen and looked in the mirror. He saw a Vulcan male of middle age—tall, gaunt, and stern. There was no indication whatsoever that he was half-human, which suited Spock; only he knew the trials it had taken to achieve that state. The Vulcan straightened the collar of his maroon uniform jacket and headed toward the door, which opened at his approach.

A few minutes later Spock walked into the transporter room and found Captain Kirk and Commander Scott waiting for him. Scotty was in his usual place behind the transporter controls, and he gave Spock a jovial smile. "Good day, Captain Spock."

"Mr. Scott," replied the Vulcan with a nod. "I presume from your demeanor that you are satisfied with the performance of the crew."

"An' right you'd be. They've got a lot of silly theory in their heads, but we'll soon replace it with practical experience. The Academy is still turnin' out a good grade of officer."

"They seem awfully young to me," said Kirk wistfully.

"You are about to meet someone even younger," replied Spock as he climbed upon the transporter platform.

Kirk stepped on after him. "Yes, I'm looking forward to it. I haven't met many Vulcan children."

"Neither have I," answered Spock. "Not since I was a child."

"Your party is waiting for you on the campus green," said Scotty. "I've entered the coordinates."

"Beam us down," ordered Kirk.

Spock felt a slight tingle as his molecules were scattered and rearranged, and the view in front of him changed from the sterile surroundings of the transporter room to a lovely commons area in the center of the Starfleet Academy campus. The smooth lines of the Academy buildings surrounded them, yet the buildings were dwarfed by the skyscrapers of San Francisco and the vast ocean beyond. It was a cool day in March, and the air was bracing and salty. Several cadets and instructors hurried past them, paying little attention to two people materializing in the middle of the green.

From the midst of the scurrying pedestrians, two people walked slowly toward them—a thin Vulcan male about the age of Spock's father and the seven-year-old, Teska. She was smaller than Spock imagined she would be, but he reminded himself that Vulcan children seldom had a growth spurt until they reached their teen years. He was more accustomed to seeing human children, who were often quite tall by the age of seven. Teska's demeanor was properly reserved, and Spock nodded with approval at her approach.

"Pele-ut-la," said the girl in a lilting voice, "we meet in the appointed time and place."

"Koon-ut-la," replied Spock, "possessor of the flame which burns from the time of the beginning, I am your servant." He bowed reverently, and the girl bowed back.

Now that the official greeting was over, the older Vulcan turned to Captain Kirk. "I am Sopeg, a teacher here at the Academy."

"Captain James T. Kirk," answered the human, "of the *Enterprise.*"

"Curious," said Sopeg, "I thought you were promoted to admiral."

"I was for a while, but they came to their senses." Kirk turned to the little girl and smiled. "And you must be Teska."

"Obviously," she agreed. "I have been reading about your exploits, Captain Kirk, and it is an honor to meet you. You are very courageous."

"I'm glad to meet you, too," answered Kirk. "But I'm not sure I would have the courage to do what you're about to do."

Sopeg looked thoughtful. "It is unusual for an outworlder to know about our ceremonies."

"Captain Kirk has made many important journeys with me to Vulcan," said Spock. "He is not an outworlder, but a friend."

"I understand," said the elder Vulcan. "I know much more about Earth and its customs than I ever thought I would know. Just two days ago, I attended a hockey game. Very enlightening. Captain Kirk, could I have a few moments to talk privately with Spock?"

Kirk checked the chronometer on his wrist communicator. "I don't see why not. The Rigelians were supposed to meet us here by now, but they're running late."

Spock replied, "You will find that Rigelians are not as punctual as Vulcans."

"Who is?" answered Kirk. "Take as much time as you need. Teska and I will chat."

The two Vulcan men ambled down the sidewalk about twenty meters and stopped. Spock waited patiently for Sopeg to tell that which needed privacy to be told.

The elder Vulcan glanced over his shoulder at Teska and Kirk. "She is a bright child," he began, "and she does well in her studies. I have done the best I can these past four years to see that her training is adequate, but she spends many hours a day with non-Vulcans. She has been exposed to more outside influences than a typical Vulcan child of her age."

Spock raised an eyebrow. "Are you saying that her training has been corrupted?"

"As you can see, she knows how to behave correctly, but she also knows how to behave incorrectly. A few times, I have caught her mimicking humans, quite well, I might add. I am aware of what she does in my presence, but I am unaware of what she does around others."

"I see." Now Spock glanced over his shoulder at the middle-aged captain and the young Vulcan. Indeed, the two of them were chatting quite amicably, and it was clear that Teska had little of the reticence typical of her race. Around humans, a typical Vulcan child would behave more or less like a statue. But Teska had spent her formative years among humans; like himself, she had a special bond with them.

Spock turned to the elder Vulcan. "Sopeg, we do not see one another often, but you are my kinsman. Therefore, I can speak frankly. The task that Teska is being asked to perform is so difficult that it requires an exceptional person, and the probability of failure is quite high. It was Sarek's decision that she partake in this great experiment, and her experience with other species will serve her well."

Sopeg nodded solemnly. "I see much of your father in you and your reasoning. We must be tested to the fullest if we are to achieve greatness. I can see why you have accomplished so much."

"As the humans say, I was often in the right place at the right time. This is one of those right places and times, and we must proceed without hesitation. Does Teska know she is marrying a Romulan?"

"I have told her," answered Sopeg. "I am not sure if she understands the full ramifications of that decision."

"Decades will pass before we complete this work," observed Spock. "In the meantime, we must be concerned about Teska's long-term development. Is it possible that she could remain on Vulcan after the *koon-ut-la?*"

"I have thought about this," answered the professor. "Our family is small and widely scattered, and there is no one presently on Vulcan. I know you could have your choice of assignments, and Teska could remain with you if you were to stay on Vulcan."

Spock lifted an eyebrow. "My plans are not finalized, but I will give it consideration. Is there no one else?"

"No. But there is always the *pak-or-tuk.*"

Adoption, thought Spock, translating the term into the Federation equivalent. Of course, many families would accept a child of Teska's heritage, but adoption was a very difficult procedure on Vulcan, requiring perfect harmony within the family and the ministrations of a high priestess such as T'Lar. It was nearly as tricky as the ceremony they were about to undertake.

"We can delay that decision until after the *koonut-la,*" said Spock. He lifted his hand in the Vulcan salute. "Live long and prosper, Sopeg, and thank you for your diligence on behalf of Teska."

"I did what was necessary," the older Vulcan replied.

Spock and Sopeg strolled back toward Kirk and Teska, who stopped their conversation to wait for them. Spock looked for signs of emotion on the face of the girl, who must have known what was coming next. The only adult caretaker she could remember was about to hand her over to an obscure uncle, who was about to hand her over to a stranger from another race.

In some respects, she was following in the footsteps of Sarek, who had taken a human wife and pioneered intimate Vulcan-human relations. But

Sarek had made that decision as an adult, after his first wife had died; Teska was a child who had been volunteered by her family. Her sacrifice made Spock somewhat uneasy.

Teska's face remained impassive as Sopeg held up a withered hand in the well-known salute. "Granddaughter, live long and prosper."

Teska held up a smooth little hand which trembled slightly. "The same to you, Grandfather. When shall I see you again?"

"That is unknown," answered Sopeg. "Obey your uncle." He turned on his heel and walked away, never looking back at his young charge.

Spock watched Teska carefully now. An outward show of emotion would demonstrate that her early training was considerably corrupted. The girl's face remained impassive, but her lustrous dark eyes looked downcast. Then she lifted her chin with determination and cast off the fleeting emotion.

Spock was satisfied with her behavior.

"I'd suggest we get going," said Kirk, "but our other passengers aren't here yet. Teska, are you aware that we're traveling with a group of Rigelians?"

"I have been told this," answered Teska, "but not the reason."

"Well," answered Kirk, glancing around, "we're not going to lie and say you're one of the Rigelians, but we're not going to dissuade anyone from that notion either. Do you understand?"

"Subterfuge," answered Teska.

Spock pursed his lips. "Indeed."

John Vornholt

Kirk cleared his throat uncomfortably. "Uh, Teska, you'll like seeing the Rigel solar system—it has a—"

"A blue giant sun," Teska finished. "From Earth, it is visible with the naked eye in the constellation of Orion."

"Cute kid," muttered Kirk. He peered into the distance. "I think I see our passengers."

Spock followed Kirk's gaze and saw an odd band of black-suited, sallow-skinned humanoids come strolling around the corner of a building. They looked lost and uncertain, until one of them—a voluptuous woman wearing a form-hugging jumpsuit—spotted Kirk and led the way. Spock counted four men, four women, and four children. This symmetrical number was due, no doubt, to the Rigelian fascination with numerology. Each member of the group wore simple black clothing. The outfits differed only slightly in style.

At a glance, the Rigelians did appear to be identical to Romulans and Vulcans, but there was something alien about them—perhaps the way they carried themselves. They possessed none of the discipline common to Vulcans and Romulans. Like humans, they were not afraid to look foolish.

"They have children," said Kirk. "That's handy."

"When my father makes arrangements, they are usually quite thorough," observed Spock.

"I have read that Rigelians believe in group marriage," said Teska.

Spock nodded, impressed by her knowledge. "Yes, most Rigelians practice group marriage. Three of

28

the women, two of the men, and all of the children are from the Heart Clan, who represent the rural craft guilds of Rigel V. However, the most important person in the group is Ambassador Denker, the man on the left."

Kirk smiled. "Who's the gorgeous woman in the lead?"

"That would be Vitra, a wealthy industrialist." At Kirk's grin, he added, "And former prostitute. In fact, she prefers to be called Madame Vitra."

The captain shook his head. "The Rigelians aren't much like Vulcans, are they?"

"No, they are not," answered Spock. "Physically we are similar, but the Rigelians have demonstrated no appreciable telepathic abilities. They are superstitious, emotional, and deeply rooted to an agrarian lifestyle and precious-metal economy. They are what humans would describe as 'earthy.'" Kirk looked surprised. "No offense intended," Spock added.

"None taken," replied Kirk with a smile.

The party of Rigelians strolled haphazardly along the sidewalk, with the children lagging behind. A slim woman wearing a flowing black skirt dropped back to round up the children. The children hopped swiftly at her urging and were soon at the front of the pack, so she turned her attention to the young women in the group. She had them tying back their long hair as they approached, which was the sort of preening a Vulcan woman would never do. The woman's actions reminded Spock of an alpha mare in a herd of horses, nipping and prodding the others into obedience.

Captain Kirk smiled charmingly, sucked in his stomach, and made a beeline for the woman in the clinging jumpsuit. "Madame Vitra, I presume?"

"Yes." Her black hair flowed in an unruly mane from a face that wasn't young but was heavily altered by cosmetics. "Are you the famous Captain Kirk?"

"I am," he assured her. As the others caught up, Kirk turned to the leader of the delegation. "Ambassador Denker, we are honored."

The ambassador was a rugged-looking man in a tailored black suit, and he was not as quick to smile as the others. "Captain Kirk, I appreciate your willingness to take us home, but can we make the introductions short and get right to our cabins? I'm tired, and I have a report to write."

"Of course," answered Kirk, nonplussed. "This is Captain Spock and his niece, Teska."

Denker nodded curtly. "A pleasure. You have met Madame Vitra, and this is her champion, Mondral." Spock looked at the tall muscular Rigelian hovering behind Madame Vitra and realized that "champion" was a euphemism for "bodyguard." The impassive expression on Mondral's face would have suited any Vulcan or Romulan.

The ambassador motioned to the family huddled behind the others. "This is the Heart Clan—Hanua, Dilni, Espera, Rassero, Hemopar, and their children."

The slim woman whom Spock had observed earlier looked directly at him. Their gazes connected for a moment, and he was surprised at the carefree mirth in her dark eyes. Unlike Madame Vitra, her complexion was healthy and natural.

"It is our immense pleasure," said Hanua with a smile. "We never dreamed we would be traveling in any ship so grand as the *Enterprise*."

"After what she's been through," said Kirk, "the *Enterprise* is not so grand anymore. But she still does the job."

A female Rigelian child stepped warily toward Teska. "Where are you from?"

"I am from Vulcan, although I live here on Earth." Teska glanced at Spock. "Perhaps it is more accurate to say I *lived* here."

"I like it on Earth," said the Rigelian girl with a grin. "They have pretty birds that sing a lot. I'm Falona."

"Teska," answered the Vulcan.

"We should be going, Captain," Spock said.

"Yes, yes," answered Kirk. He made a quick head count and tapped his wrist communicator. "Kirk to *Enterprise*. Fifteen of us to beam up."

"Scott here," came the welcoming voice. "We kenna take you all at once, so we'll beam up the children first. Locking on to their life signs."

The children huddled around Hanua, who gently lined them up. "Space yourselves out, there's nothing to fear. First Starfleet Academy, and now the *Enterprise*—what a day you've had!" With her reassuring voice ringing in their ears, the children stood calmly while their molecules were scrambled and beamed to the ship in orbit. Teska stood at attention until her slight form disappeared altogether.

Madame Vitra reached out to take Kirk's arm. "Captain, I trust you will be dining with us tonight?"

"Of course," he answered with a smile. "I wouldn't miss it."

"Captain," said Denker, "the passenger transport was four days getting here, with scheduled stops. How long will the journey take aboard the *Enterprise?*"

"Less than two days," answered Kirk.

Vitra batted her long dark eyelashes at him. "You can take your time, Captain. We're in no hurry."

"Speak for yourself," muttered Denker.

Kirk glanced at Spock and smiled, and the Vulcan could tell that his friend was amused to see people who resembled Vulcans bickering like humans. Spock, on the other hand, was uncertain that the Rigelians were a proper influence on young Teska, but he supposed she could survive a few days with them.

Scotty's voice chimed over the communicator. "I'm ready for the rest of you, Captain."

"Proceed," answered Kirk.

A few moments later Spock and Kirk stepped off the transporter platform, followed by Hanua, Vitra, Mondral, Denker, and the other four Rigelians. The members of the Heart Clan were instantly greeted by warm hugs from their children. Teska stood at proper attention and gazed at Spock. He could almost read her mind; she was questioning whether a little affection was such a bad thing. He knew it was. Vulcans had a savage history, which had remnants in their rituals. That history made it clear that Vulcans were once addicted to emotion and violence. For them, there was no such thing as a little bit.

Spock turned to find Kirk smiling at him. "Go on and escort Teska to her quarters. Take your time, Spock, we don't need you on active duty."

"Thank you," replied Spock. He motioned to the open door, and the seven-year-old started out.

"Teska!" called little Falona. "See you later?"

She glanced at Spock, then cocked her head at the young Rigelian. "Perhaps."

Uncle and niece spoke very little as they traveled the ship's turbolifts and corridors. Teska continued to deport herself with the correct demeanor, nodding politely but impassively at the crew members they passed. Still Spock could not get Sopeg's warning out of his mind.

"Will you have any difficulty sleeping alone tonight?" he asked. "My quarters are directly across the corridor from yours."

"I require little sleep," she answered.

"You will need to rest for the ceremony."

"Two days' worth of rest?" asked Teska. "Is it that hard?"

Spock cleared his throat, thinking that her turn of phrase was more colloquial for Earth than Vulcan, although it was a fair question. "You will be severely tested," he answered. "But much good will come of it. Here is your cabin."

She studied the door with interest. "My own cabin. That is more than I expected."

"Computer," intoned Spock, "record voiceprint of new occupant." He nodded to Teska. "State your name."

"Teska," she answered.

"Teska," repeated the impersonal voice of the computer. The door slid open with a whoosh.

Spock followed the child into the small but tastefully appointed crew quarters; the colors were mostly mauve and gray, with renderings of the Horsehead Nebula on the wall. Teska began to take in her surroundings, until her eyes fixed on the basket of thorns upon the desk. Inside was a pile of withered red fruit, sun-dried into shriveled pellets.

"Ah, tono'pak berries!" said Teska, not hiding her delight. She froze to the spot with a stricken look on her face, knowing she had slipped.

Spock adjusted his face to a frown. "The tono'pak berries are a symbol of the childhood that will shrivel and die, to be born again in the heart of a young woman. You must eat one every hour until the *koon-ut-la.*"

She turned to Spock. "I have many questions about this undertaking."

"I assumed you would," answered Spock. "I have taken the liberty of stocking the computer with selected readings from the *Meditations of T'Pau,* many of which pertain to your situation."

Teska shook her head. "Are you not equally qualified to answer my questions?"

"Certainly not as qualified as T'Pau," said Spock. He started for the door. "If you have any questions about this material, I will help you to further your research." The door whooshed open at his approach.

"What if it does not work?"

Spock froze in the doorway and turned around slowly, his hunched shoulders straightening to attention. "What if *what* does not work?"

"The ritual, everything." Teska paused as if searching for the right words to continue. "It sounds . . . unsettling—the blood fever, losing control, men fighting with each other. Uncle, I am aware that your *koon-ut-la* was unsuccessful. And it seems illogical to go through all of this for nothing."

Spock swallowed dryly and pressed the panel button, closing the door. He knew he was not going to leave this room anytime soon, so he pulled up a chair and sat across from the girl, who considered him with a frankness that was disconcerting. Spock's chiseled features drooped a bit more than usual.

"You know about my failed marriage?" he asked.

"I do, Uncle. I was urged to study the family histories. You fought the challenge over T'Pring, yet you did not claim her, as was your right. I do not understand."

Spock tapped his mouth with the tips of his index fingers. "You have asked several questions in one breath, and I will need several breaths to answer. The first thing to know is that the Vulcan way of marriage is usually successful. Failures like mine are rare. The Vulcan divorce rate is much lower than that of humans, for example, who theoretically choose their own mates and marry for love."

Spock continued, "Secondly, my situation was complicated by the fact that I was a Starfleet officer. For that same reason I was estranged from my father, and I did not return to Vulcan for several years. During that time I became rather well known as first officer of the *Enterprise,* and T'Pring did not want a husband who was an absentee public figure. Even then, I saw the logic in her position. My failure has nothing to do with your situation."

"But I am marrying outside my race," said Teska.

Spock's expression softened. "I can personally attest to the potential success of such a union. If you've read our family histories, then you are aware that my father is Sarek of Vulcan, and my mother is Amanda of Earth. I am the product of an inter-species marriage."

To her credit, Teska did not look perturbed by this news.

Spock took the opportunity her silence provided to redirect the conversation.

"Have you any other questions?"

"What is *pon farr* like?"

Spock rose, went to the desk, and turned on the computer screen. "I believe it is meditation sixteen, passage seven, of T'Pau's writings which describe the sensations and the theories. But I have always found every description to be lacking. And I expect that after it has happened to you, you still will not be able to describe it. *Pon farr* is the price we pay to achieve mastery over our emotions the rest of the time."

"I understand," said Teska, taking command of the computer screen. "I am glad you will assist me, Uncle."

"Yes," Spock answered thoughtfully. He had begun to suspect a secondary reason for the selection of Teska for this immense task. Himself. There was a high probability that the mental bonding with the Romulan boy would not be successful and would not produce the blood fever, let alone a lasting marriage. Because Spock did not marry his betrothed, Teska would not be totally surprised if such a thing happened to her. It was logical that they discuss this.

But before they could delve too deeply into the wisdom of T'Pau, Spock heard muffled shouts outside the door in the corridor. He jumped to his feet just as the chime sounded, rushed to the door, and pushed the panel to open it.

Uhura stood outside the door. "Captain Spock, I know you're off-duty—"

"What is it, Commander?"

She pointed down the corridor. "Two of those Rigelians—they're trying to kill each other in the recreation room!"

Chapter Three

As Spock and Uhura dashed down the corridor of Deck Six, Spock could hear the shouts emanating from Recreation Room Twelve. A knot of Starfleet officers were gathered in the doorway, forcing him to stop abruptly. Uhura cleared her throat, and the officers stepped back, looking sheepishly at the venerated Vulcan.

"Proceed to your stations," ordered Spock.

"Yes, sir!" They rushed off, although a couple of them stole glances into the recreation room, where two Rigelian women were circling each other, amid overturned tables and chairs. With cuts on their faces, torn clothes, and disheveled hair, they looked as though they were fighting to the death. Spock recognized one of the combatants as Madame Vitra, and the other was a member of the Heart Clan named Espera, who appeared to be several years younger than her foe.

Hanua, Mondral, and a few more Rigelian passengers were also present, and they were watching the scrap with disturbing calm.

"Shall I call for backup security, Mr. Spock?" asked Uhura.

"No, but stand by. We may need them yet." The Vulcan strode into the room and went directly to Hanua. There appeared to be no point in talking to the combatants.

"Please explain?" he said calmly.

Before she could answer, Vitra lunged for Espera and tried to rip her face off. The younger woman socked her in the thorax, and Vitra stumbled backward, gasping for breath.

"Not much longer," said Mondral.

"Am I going to receive an explanation?" asked Spock.

Mondral straightened to his full height, which was several centimeters taller and broader than the older Vulcan. "Don't interfere."

"It is the grief frenzy," explained Hanua. "We just received word that Vitra's husband died, and she is in mourning. The frenzy will burn it out of her. Don't you have such a thing?"

"Not connected with grief," answered Spock, "which we do not experience. Shall I have Dr. McCoy stand by?"

"No! No!" Vitra gasped as she staggered backward. "I yield! The grief is past."

Her foe nodded and slumped to her knees, breathing hard. Hanua instantly grabbed a pouch of medicines and rushed to her kinswoman's side. "You did well, my wife, now breathe deeply. Captain Spock, may we have more oxygen in this room?"

"Computer," said Spock, "increase oxygen content in Recreation Room Twelve by five percent."

"Increasing oxygen by five percent," answered the computer.

"Thank you," said Hanua, dabbing what looked like homemade ointment on a cut on Espera's face.

Mondral draped a towel around Vitra's shoulders and helped her to her feet. Spock now saw why she needed so much makeup—from the scars and bruises on her face, it appeared that this was not her first brawl.

Vitra wiped away a smear of olive-green blood under her eye. "I'm sorry we alarmed you, Captain Spock, but the death of my husband came as sudden news. I have sixteen more husbands, but I was particularly fond of Bonkuyo. He was one of my oldest, and richest, spouses."

She lovingly stroked Mondral's face. "Now I have an opening for a new husband. Or should I take a wife?"

"A good accountant would be a better choice," said Mondral dryly.

"Always so practical." She patted her champion's cheek and walked up to her opponent. "Thank you, Espera, for releasing my grief. May I contribute to the endowment of the Heart Clan in appreciation?"

"As you wish." Espera bowed in a servile fashion, and Spock had the unpleasant sense that she was getting paid for her role in relieving Madame Vitra's grief.

Vitra nodded to Mondral, and he escorted her out of the recreation room without further discussion. Uhura glanced at Spock, and he nodded; she promptly followed the pair of Rigelians down the corridor.

"We must seem like barbarians to you," said Hanua, as she picked up a chair and set it upright. The other Rigelians also began to straighten the room. One of them cleaned a few drops of green blood off the deck.

Spock picked up a game table. "No, I have seen barbarians, and you do not remind me of them. Vitra does possess a combative spirit, however."

"Yes," agreed Hanua. "Do you suppose Captain Kirk is safe with her?"

"I think the captain can look out for himself in that regard." Spock picked up a delicate three-dimensional chessboard and set it on the table, but the lower stand was broken, which made the board wobbly.

"I'm sorry we broke it," said Hanua. "Does it mean something to you?"

He looked up at her, wondering if his thoughts could be so transparent. Then again, he was holding the broken chess stand very gently, as if prizing it. He let go of it, and it fell apart in a clatter.

"When I was younger," said Spock, "I used to play three-dimensional chess for hours on end. There was a notable lack of worthy opponents aboard the *Enterprise* in those days."

Hanua began to reassemble the multilevel playing board. "Would you like to play? I believe I can repair this—I carry a fixative with me."

"We have other boards," said Spock.

"I insist," replied Hanua with a smile. "After all, we broke it." She opened the black pouch that hung from her skirt and produced a tube of fixative. Spock watched as she deftly glued the broken stand together. Within a matter of seconds, the three-dimensional chessboard stood ready for play. The other Rigelians finished cleaning the room and began to file out. Only Hanua stayed behind.

"I would like to play this game with you," she said. "Where are the pieces?"

"This would not be the most convenient time," said the Vulcan.

"Why not? I heard Captain Kirk say that you weren't needed on active duty. Are you afraid to play me?"

Spock cocked an eyebrow at the notion. "I am concerned about my niece, Teska. I left her waiting in her quarters."

"I'll wager that she's asleep," said Hanua. "She looked tired, and it's been an exciting day."

"She has more self-discipline than that. She is supposed to be studying."

"Sleep is a natural thing," said the Rigelian. "It's healthy for young children to give in to it. She looked tired to me, but if you're afraid to check, that's your business."

Spock furrowed his brow and looked at the slim Rigelian woman, who gave him a warm smile. If

Hanua were Vulcan, he would judge her to be about forty-five years old. She was still of child-bearing age, and she evidently knew a great deal about children. Spock had always thought that talking to an expert was the quickest way to increase one's knowledge about a foreign subject, so he resolved to sit with Hanua of the Heart Clan for a few minutes.

Besides, there was a possibility that she was a good chess player.

The Vulcan strode to the wall and pushed a button. A compartment opened, revealing a set of black and white chess pieces shaped like space vessels. Three-dimensional chess used the metaphor of space travel, because it also dealt in movement that was three-dimensional, not simply lateral.

"Can I be black?" asked Hanua, sitting at the table and tucking her black skirt under her legs.

"Certainly," answered Spock, sitting across from the woman. "Allow me to set the pieces. Do you require an explanation of the game?"

"No, I've played it. We are avid games players in the commune—every night there are a dozen games of various sorts going on. It's our reward after a hard day's work in the craft guild."

"How large is the Heart Clan?" asked Spock.

"I have fourteen children and fourteen spouses," answered Hanua with some pride. "I had more, but the marriage split last year into two separate clans. It was difficult but necessary with such a large number of people. A few of our younger folks wished to emigrate to the city. Our young often rebel against the rural life. Is it that way on Vulcan?"

"Few of our children rebel," answered Spock. "Of course, we have much smaller families, and our children receive an intensive education." He finished placing the last ship on the bottom level of the playing board.

"Is that why Teska is returning home?" asked the Rigelian. "To continue her education?"

"In a manner of speaking, yes." Spock was not about to discuss family matters or their ground-breaking mission with a complete stranger, however benign she appeared to be.

His wrist communicator chirped. "Spock here."

"This is Uhura. Our guests are safely back in their quarters. Shall I report this incident, Mr. Spock?"

"No," he answered with a glance at Hanua. "I trust it will not be repeated. Spock out."

Hanua frowned. "One never knows when tragedy will strike, and grief will claim us."

"The timing is unknown," agreed Spock, "but one may prepare oneself to fight grief."

"Or welcome it," said Hanua softly. "I believe it is your move. Traditionally, white goes first."

Spock raised an eyebrow and regarded the woman across from him. "Yes, let us maintain tradition."

Captain Kirk rose from his chair as Madame Vitra, Ambassador Denker, Mondral, and another Rigelian, Hemopar, entered the dining room. The statuesque woman led the three men past the gleaming galley toward Kirk's table. The captain tried to smile, even though he had been kept waiting for fifteen minutes—he would have to remember that

Rigelians were never punctual, at least not this bunch.

When Madame Vitra reached the table, Kirk noticed the fresh rouge on her face that didn't disguise a bruise under her eye. He tried to keep a poker face, but he was no Vulcan.

"Welcome, Madame Vitra, Ambassador, and your party," said Kirk cheerfully. "Has your stay been pleasant?"

" Yes," answered Denker with little enthusiasm. "The state rooms are small, but this ship runs quietly. I have gotten some work done." He pulled out a chair and sat.

"My stay has been rather eventful," said the woman in the form-hugging black jumpsuit. Vitra moved toward the table, and Kirk and Mondral both rushed to pull out a chair for her. She leveled Mondral with a glance, and he retreated to allow Captain Kirk to seat her.

"Eventful in the good sense, I hope," said Kirk, taking the seat beside her.

Vitra aimed her dark limpid eyes at Kirk. "Not entirely. My husband died, and I sought comfort in the grief frenzy. Rigelians believe that physical exertion is very important. So when we're upset, we fight . . . or have sex. Sex is crucial to Rigelians, as we believe it reduces our destructive impulses. What do humans think about sex?"

Several replies sprung to Kirk's mind, but he finally said, "We're for it. And I've always believed that taking action is better than sitting around brooding."

"Precisely," replied Vitra in a husky voice.

"May we have our food, Captain?" said Ambassador Denker impatiently. "I have more work to do on my report."

Kirk cleared his throat, but before he could reply, Mondral cut in. "Denker, you're supposed to be an ambassador. That requires . . . diplomacy."

The ambassador shot him a disgusted look. "I haven't got time for diplomacy, and neither do you."

Kirk was about to change the subject when an ensign appeared at his side. "Bring the appetizer, along with the *trijelian* tea. And hurry," he murmured out of the corner of his mouth.

"Yes, sir." The steward hurried off.

"Trijelian tea," said Vitra, nodding with approval. "You've done your research."

"I've also taken the liberty of starting off with *cargil* mussels, which I understand are a delicacy on Rigel V."

"A *passé* delicacy," said Denker. "It would be like serving caviar on Earth."

"I like mussels," said Hemopar with an embarrassed smile. "I haven't had *cargil* mussels in ages."

Kirk cast about for another subject. "You spent quite some time on Earth."

"Three weeks," muttered Denker.

"How did the trade negotiations go?"

"Fine," said Vitra in the same instant that Denker said, "Badly." The two Rigelians gazed at one another, and Kirk could almost touch the hatred between them.

Vitra gave him a snide laugh. "The Federation has the misguided notion that we are still dealing in illegal practices, such as prostitution and animal-skin trade. Nothing could be further from the truth. Oh, we have our history of being tolerant of many lifestyles, but that doesn't mean we have organized prostitution! Youngsters are no longer taken from their clans and sold to brothels in the city—that's in the past."

She tossed her mane of black hair. "Yes, it happened to me when I was a child—I was a prostitute at ten—but that was many years ago. Ancient history."

After that bold statement, Kirk scanned the faces of his guests. Each wore a different expression. Vitra looked sweetly innocent, as if it was perfectly natural to have been a child prostitute. Mondral looked mildly amused at his mistress's outrageous behavior; Denker looked disgusted; and Hemopar looked embarrassed.

None of the Rigelians were talking, so Kirk was forced to keep the conversation going. "I take it you can't get the concessions you want from the Federation until you clear up this matter."

"It's just a misunderstanding," said Hemopar with a glance at Vitra. "The rural craft guilds need the Federation credits from this agreement—we must make the extra effort to produce a study that will satisfy them."

Denker suddenly threw his napkin on the table and stood up. "I will not be a party to this facade any longer. Excuse me, Captain, I will dine in my quarters."

Mondral shot him a dark look. "Watch yourself, Denker, you have your position to consider."

"I've considered it, and it's not worth it." With that, the ambassador stalked out of the dining room, nearly knocking over the young ensign who was bringing tea and appetizers. The ensign seemed relieved that he managed to set the tray on the table before he dropped it.

"We'll be one less for dinner," said Vitra cheerfully. "And good riddance. Denker is such a stuffed-shirt—he pouts whenever things don't go his way. I'm beginning to think he's not the right person for the job of ambassador."

"Me, too," said Mondral. "But, of course, he can be removed."

"Politics is not the province of an honest man," said Hemopar thoughtfully. He picked up the teapot and poured everyone at the table a steaming cup of purple liquid. "Good," he said with glee, "scalding hot."

Vitra slipped a long painted fingernail into her tea and stirred it, while she gazed at Captain Kirk. "Have you ever known grief?"

"Yes, I have," answered Kirk. He thought about his son, David, and his tragic death on the Genesis planet.

"And did you take action?"

"Yes, I did."

Vitra lifted her cup to her bruised lips and blew the steam toward Kirk. "I like a man of action."

Teska lifted her chin off the desk with a start, not realizing until then that she had fallen asleep while studying the wisdom of T'Pau. Oh, what would her *pele-ut-la* think of her? She looked around the room, expecting him to be standing there, gazing at her with disapproval. When she realized she was alone, she calmed quickly. She knew that she wasn't the only one who found the stoic Captain Spock intimidating—she had seen the young crew of the *Enterprise* regard him with awe. And why not? The places he had gone, the things he had seen—they were enough to fill the logs of a dozen Starfleet officers. Spock was arguably the best-known Vulcan in the Federation, after his accomplished father.

These were her kinsmen, she reminded herself, but they existed more in reports and histories than in reality. She had not seen much of them in the flesh. Sopeg's old apartment in the Tenderloin district, her playmates at school, the crashing of the waves on the Embarcadero—these things seemed real to her. The idea of getting married on Vulcan, when the day before she had been playing hopscotch on Haight Street, was such a strange juxtaposition that it didn't seem possible. But Teska knew it was more than possible, it was going to happen.

In a matter of days, she would be married to a Romulan. The seven-year-old rose from her desk and paced the confines of her quarters. She was Vulcan, Teska told herself, even if her homeworld was nothing but a blurry memory. The *koon-ut-la* would have been her fate no matter what her circumstances, even if her parents had lived.

A chime came at the door, startling the girl from her reverie. Teska straightened her tunic, which was rumpled from sleeping, then called out, "Come in!"

The door slid open, and Spock entered, followed by Hanua from the Heart Clan. Teska bowed to them. "Uncle, I must report that I fell asleep while studying."

"Hanua predicted you would be asleep," said Spock. "I have been reconsidering my advice, and I believe you can best prepare for the ceremony by relaxing. Instead of studying, we will engage in recreational activities."

Hanua nodded. "My daughter, Falona, said she would like to play with you tomorrow. Shall we make a date, say, ten-hundred hours?"

Teska glanced at Spock, and he nodded in approval. "That would be acceptable," said the girl.

"Good," replied Hanua. "Well, I'll see you both tomorrow. I enjoyed our games of chess, Captain Spock. I'm sure it was just beginner's luck."

"No," insisted Spock. "You are an excellent player, and you beat me fairly. Your play was most unpredictable."

"Your play was a little *too* predictable," said Hanua with a smile. She backed out the doorway. "Good night." The door slid shut after her.

"You found a worthy opponent," said Teska.

"It would appear so," said Spock with a thoughtful nod. "Which activity would you prefer? Shall we take a tour of the ship or visit the exercise room?"

"I wish to practice the mind-meld."

Spock frowned. "That is not required for the *koon-ut-la*. You will have High Priestess T'Lar to guide you."

"I know," said Teska, working up her courage. "You asked me what I preferred to do, and I have told you. I wish to practice the mind-meld."

She turned away from Spock's stern gaze, but she never hesitated in her explanation. "I am Vulcan—I know this—but I have lived among humans for so long that sometimes I sense I am somehow disconnected. Perhaps if I mastered the mind-meld, I would feel more at peace with our rituals. Sopeg said I had a talent for it. On Vulcan, children my age practice the mind-meld."

Spock held up his hand. "That is true. However, it is also true that the mind-meld is mentally and physically exhausting. There can be unknown repercussions, especially if you perform it on non-Vulcans."

"I do not ask this lightly," said Teska. "I need to know what it means to be Vulcan."

Spock looked away from her and then finally spoke once again. "I can see the logic in your position—the path to freedom from emotion is too arduous without seeing the benefits. We will perform the mind-meld, if you wish."

Teska resisted any outward show of emotion over this decision. What she really wanted was to tap into Spock's solid beliefs in the Vulcan way, although maybe those convictions weren't as solid as they seemed. It was impossible to look at him and think he was half human. But now, slumped wearily on the edge of the bed, Captain Spock seemed more human than Vulcan. His face was still expressionless, but Teska sensed genuine empathy coming from him. He *cared* about her, and he *understood* what she was going through.

Spock suddenly reached out and grabbed her right

hand. He spread her fingers and studied each one, as if inspecting fine machinery. Teska held perfectly still.

"The *katra* is a stream," said Spock as if in a trance, "and it flows from one mind to another. Your fingers are channels to direct the flow, and your mind is a pool to be filled. Envision your hand reaching into my mind and drinking from the pool."

He lifted her hand to his face and positioned her fingertips at his nose, sinuses, and temple, and her thumb on his chin. Instantly, Teska felt a burning in her hand, which flowed like a surge of electricity along her arm until it reached her brain. She almost lost consciousness, but Spock grabbed her shoulder with his hand and held her upright. His touch seemed to complete a circuit, and the being that was Spock flowed into her mind.

The tears came unbidden to her eyes; she could do nothing to fight them, because they were not her tears. She realized Spock was more torn and incomplete than she would ever be. She saw his mother, his death, his father, his crew mates, bursts of laughter and joy, abject fear and horror—all at once!

Then the iron will asserted itself, and Teska saw the man pulling his disparate parts together into an amazing whole. Not a perfect whole; he had to work harder than most Vulcans. But Spock had found contentment. The bridge of the *Enterprise* was a constant in his life, even when he spent years away from it, and so was his friendship with Jim, Bones, and the others. His sense of righteousness and duty was as solid as the deck under her feet.

Spock pulled away, breaking the contact between them. Teska started to faint again, but she managed to catch herself on the bed and shake off the dizzying effects. She focused her eyes to find Spock staring numbly at her.

"Sopeg was right," he said hoarsely. "You have a natural ability. Of course, you will need to gain greater control of the initial impulses—they can be overwhelming. Unlike most children of your age, your training will focus on controlling your abilities, not developing them. You must *not*, I repeat, *not*, send your thoughts into someone else's mind, until you receive much more training."

Teska thought about the morass of conflicting desires and emotions she had seen within her uncle, a glimpse that was rare for a child. Spock knew far better than she what it felt like to be drawn toward humanity.

"Thank you, Uncle. I will not forget this."

He rose wearily to his feet. "However much you may admire other races, Teska, you are a Vulcan. Nothing will change that. We believe that wisdom flows from generation to generation, never to be lost but only expanded. Let my experiences guide you in the difficult years ahead of you. We are not dissimilar."

"Thank you, *Pele-ut-la*, I will."

The older Vulcan nodded curtly and headed for the door. "It is time for both of us to get some sleep."

"Can we continue to practice the mind-meld?" asked Teska hopefully.

Spock stopped at the door to consider the question. "We need a suitable subject, but I might know one. I will awaken you early."

"Thank you, Uncle."

"Until then, sleep well." Captain Spock stepped out the door, and it shut after him.

I will sleep well, thought Teska, *knowing that you are watching after me,* Pele-ut-la.

Chapter Four

DR. MCCOY GAPED at the two Vulcans. "You want to do *what?*"

The girl looked down, and McCoy wasn't sure but he thought he saw her smile. Even though she was a Vulcan, she had an impish quality about her that he liked. Still, he didn't really want her poking around inside his mind.

Spock merely regarded him with his usual obstinacy. "Doctor, I assure you, it won't be harmful. Teska is very accomplished for her age, and the meld will be unidirectional. This is my only opportunity to work with her, and I must see how accomplished she is before I recommend a teacher. There are no other Vulcans on the ship, and I know from first-hand experience that your mind is receptive to a mind-meld."

"Now you're trying to insult me," McCoy grumbled. One of his young medical technicians grinned with amusement, but McCoy's glower chased him out of the room.

"I would not allow this if there were any danger," said Spock.

"I know, I know. It's not dangerous," grumbled McCoy, "but it's also not my idea of a good time."

"Come," said Spock to Teska, "we can search the computer for a suitable subject."

Spock headed for the door, but the seven-year-old hesitated. "Perhaps we need to offer him a deal."

"A deal?" asked McCoy and Spock at the same time.

"Yes. I have found that humans favor a *quid pro quo* arrangement. If you want them to do something for you, you must do something for them."

McCoy grinned, thinking that he definitely liked this little girl. Anyone who stood up to Spock was okay with him. "Yeah, Spock, listen to Teska. Humans aren't all that hard to figure out."

"I am well aware that humans are often motivated by greed," said Spock. Was that a glimmer of amusement he saw in Spock's eyes, McCoy wondered.

"Not greed," offered Teska, "just fairness. What can I do for you in exchange, Doctor?"

McCoy scratched his chin. "Well, I don't know. We don't have any patients at the moment. If there was an emergency, I could think of all kinds of things I would ask you to do."

"I am very good at filing and organizing," said Teska. "Do you have anything that needs to be catalogued and filed?"

The doctor snapped his fingers. "We've picked up a lot of new supplies, like bandages and hyposprays. I haven't really counted them yet, so maybe you could go through the supply cabinet and do a quick inventory."

"I will start at fourteen-hundred hours after my play date," promised Teska. "Do we have a deal?"

"Sure," said McCoy, shaking her small but cool hand. He tapped a comm panel on the wall. "Hendricksen, you're in charge of Sickbay for a few minutes. I'll be in Examination Room One, doing some, uh . . . therapy."

"Yes, sir."

McCoy led his visitors to the examination room with its clear windows all around. As he approached the door, it opened, and lights came on inside the room. The doctor entered and found himself twisting his sweaty palms together. He tapped a panel which turned the windows opaque, so they would have more privacy, but it didn't help relax him. Besides, he had just thought of something.

"I've got to admit I'm a little nervous," said McCoy. "And I just realized—you're a little girl. I'm a grown man, and there are things in my head that are for grown people."

"I have studied human mating practices," said Teska neutrally.

Spock nodded in agreement. "We mind-melded last night, and she has shared all of my experiences as well. Of course, it will take her many years to understand them. Teska will obey the oath of confidentiality."

McCoy took a deep breath and let out a groan.

"Okay, I agreed, so let's do it before I change my mind. I should have my head examined." He groaned. That was exactly what was going to happen to him!

Spock pressed a panel and turned the examination table into a reclining chair. After it clicked into shape, the Vulcan guided the doctor into it. The metal seat felt cold against his back, which only aggravated his fear. *Damn it,* thought McCoy, sometimes it would be nice to be a Vulcan and avoid those rushes of terror to which humans were prone. Then again, sometimes terror was only your common sense telling you that you were doing something crazy!

Teska moved her tiny fingers toward him, and he wondered if she would be able to reach the important nerve synapses that Spock had told him about. But as soon as her fingers touched his cheekbone, he felt as if an immense claw had ripped into his face, and he jerked involuntarily. McCoy felt himself surging forward, like flood waters breaking through a dam. Then he rushed into a place of calmness, like an ocean. His muscles went numb, leaving him conscious but unable to move or react.

It could have been an eternity or a second before the claw disengaged from his face and he felt control over his body and mind returning to him. He touched his cheek and found to his surprise that he wasn't bleeding—his face wasn't ripped away. Then he saw the angelic pixie gazing at him, and he remembered that he wasn't in a nightmare.

"Doctor?" cut in a stern voice. "Are you all right, Dr. McCoy?"

McCoy jumped to his feet, filled with energy for no good reason. "Not bad!" he said in astonishment. "I think she's better at that mumbo-jumbo than you are, Spock."

"I am sure that is not the case," said Teska with a polite bow. "Thank you, Dr. McCoy. I believe it was a success."

He shrugged. "Maybe I should rent myself out to Vulcans for this type of thing on a regular basis. What do you think?"

"This is the doctor's idea of humor," added Spock.

"Well, at least I *have* an idea of humor." McCoy suddenly felt like scheduling the new crew members for physical exams, so it was time to usher these two out of his workplace. "I'm going to have lots of bandages for you to count later, Teska."

"Agreed," said Teska. She didn't smile, but she did bounce on her toes.

Spock turned to the girl. "Would you leave us alone for a moment?"

"Certainly, Uncle." Teska walked briskly out the door.

Spock turned and cocked an eyebrow at McCoy. "Doctor, it is highly irregular not to take inventory of a shipment of supplies."

McCoy scowled. "Oh, I know how many hypo-sprays we have, but I had to give her something to do. You won't tell her, will you?"

"No. In fact, I will make certain that she returns to work off her debt. She is gifted for such an early age—there is a chance that I could enroll her for training as a priestess. Perhaps even a healer."

"Yes, a healer," agreed McCoy. "She's got the touch—it just makes you feel better."

"Thank you for helping me."

"Helping *you?* I was helping *her!*" grumbled McCoy. "If the only mind she ever looked into was *yours,* heaven help the poor girl."

"My thoughts exactly," said Spock. He headed for the door and stopped. "When we deliver our passengers to Rigel V, we are beaming down for a courtesy call. Are you going with us?"

McCoy grinned. "Wouldn't miss it. I *love* the Rigel solar system. Did I ever tell you about these two dancers I met on Rigel II?"

Spock nodded. "Many times. Rigel V has a precious-metal economy, so if you would like a refreshment, I could bring enough local currency."

"Why, Spock," said McCoy in amazement, "are you—in some roundabout way—offering to buy me a drink?"

"Yes."

"As long as you let me pick the place."

"Agreed."

Spock started out the door, but McCoy called after him, "Before you leave, could I speak to Teska for a moment? In private."

"Certainly." The Vulcan went out of the room, and Teska entered. McCoy waited for the door to shut behind her.

"Yes, Dr. McCoy?"

He paced a few steps. "Teska, when you were inside my mind, did you, uh, find out anything about Spock?"

"I know you hold him in high regard and consider him a friend, as well as a loyal shipmate."

"Well," said McCoy, "I'd appreciate it if you didn't tell him any of that. I don't want him to get a big head."

Teska cocked her head. "As you wish. Thank you again, Dr. McCoy. I'll see you at fourteen-hundred hours."

"Good, I've got lots of inventory for you to count."

A tiny personnel shuttlecraft hurtled through Romulan space at warp one, but still it wasn't fast enough to suit Wislok. There were too many centurion patrols this close to the border—he needed a craft that was capable of outrunning them, capable of getting to Vulcan in days, not weeks. If Pardek failed him at this next crucial juncture, his life could be over.

The distinguished surgeon glanced at his youngest son, Hasmek, asleep in the co-pilot seat, shrouded in innocence. Wislok blinked his eyes and tried not to think about how weary he was, and how foolish he had been to make this mad trek with only a seven-year-old for a companion. He reached into his pack for a syringe-clip. He regretted having to give himself more stimulants, but he had to stay alert. Until they reached the rendezvous, it was him and the boy against the Romulan Star Empire.

Wislok was beginning to wonder what had possessed him to agree to this madness. When he and Pardek had begun to discuss Romulan-Vulcan similarities in hushed tones, it seemed a sensible experiment to see if Vulcan mysticism would affect a Romulan as well. Plus there were all the potential rewards in being at the forefront of a movement that could change history.

Volunteering his youngest son had seemed a reasonable progression, if somewhat cold-hearted, but Wislok hadn't realized how dangerous and lonely this act of treason would feel. He had always been a loyal retainer to the powerful and privileged, but now he was risking it all for what might be a mirage. Dangerous business indeed. The momentary burst of excitement had long since faded to a numbing dread.

He consoled himself with the fact that Sarek and Spock were offering up a child, too, for the great experiment. Vulcans were not conquerors, but they were ruthless in the pursuit of science and knowledge. Deep down, Wislok had to admit that he was risking his career and his son's life in a grab for greatness. His career as a high-priced toady would never land him in the history books, but this marriage could. Knowing Sarek and Spock could be very prestigious in a more enlightened future.

Wislok administered the syringe-clip to his neck and tried to calm himself as the stimulants kicked in. They always brought a momentary rush of panic, which seemed to be getting worse the longer he deprived himself of sleep.

He heard a soft moan beside him, and he turned to see Hasmek blinking at him. "Are we there yet?"

Wislok scowled. "To tell you the truth, I don't know. I haven't altered our course, so we're in the right sector, but I haven't had time to check our exact position. Besides, we're not supposed to stop—they're supposed to find *us*. If they don't, we'll turn back before we reach the Neutral Zone."

He struggled out of his seat, his legs feeling numb. "Hasmek, watch the indicators while I go to the stern."

"Yes, Father!" The boy sat up eagerly and studied the readouts and the view of the endless starscape.

After a trip to the head, Wislok had just started making himself some broth from a self-heating emergency ration when his son called out, "Father!"

He staggered to the cockpit, spilling hot soup all over his hand. "What is it?"

The boy pressed an earplug into a pointed ear. "It is a scout ship—they are hailing us, and they want to know our destination."

That is the correct question, thought Wislok, his heart thumping in panic. Of course, it might be a question that a *real* patrol ship might ask. He tried to stay calm as he whispered to the boy, "Narenz Marsh."

Hasmek blinked at him, unable to believe that he was supposed to give the code word, but he spoke it bravely and loudly. Wislok reached over his shoulder and pressed a button to put the conversation on the speaker.

"Prepare to be boarded," came the response.

Wislok let out a breath and nodded with relief. That was also the correct response, and it sounded like a familiar voice. If the centurions should be monitoring communications in this sector, their conversation would sound like a typical brush with authority.

He heard a crackling sound, and he whirled around to see two figures materializing in the stern of the shuttlecraft. One of them was tall and had to bend over to transport into the tiny craft, but Pardek had no such difficulty. He was rather short and stout for a Romulan, like a piston, with just as much energy. Wislok had come to depend upon his stocky reliability.

He rushed forward to grip Pardek's forearm. "Good to see you, my friend!"

His fellow conspirator smiled and grasped his arm in a viselike grip. "I can hardly believe we have come so far."

"Ah, but the worst is over," said Wislok with relief.

"Is it?" The expression on Pardek's face was troubled. "We must talk, but first, this is Dangoshal of Remus. He will pilot the scout ship."

Wislok noted the man's bronze uniform was of the Galactic Guard, an elite corps of long-range scouts. Unless the uniform was counterfeit, the man and his ship were an incredible asset to the cause. As usual, the depth of Pardek's connections in the government were a wonder to behold. With men such as this, their success was guaranteed.

"And this would be the groom," said Pardek, bending down to shake Hasmek's small hand. "You are so young to be a man of greatness, but you are. Your bravery will be talked about for millennia, and all you have to do is to marry a beautiful Vulcan girl."

Hasmek smiled brightly. "Is she really beautiful?"

"The promise is there, or so they tell me." Pardek turned to Wislok. "However, circumstances have dictated a change of plans."

The surgeon could feel his stomach wrench into knots. "A change in plans?"

"Yes. It seems that a member of the Civil Guard was discovered dead in the sewers near the shuttle-craft field, and there has been an inquiry. He was killed with a laser scalpel, an instrument usually possessed only by doctors."

Wislok put his hands on his head. "I had no choice, believe me."

"There is no case against you," said Pardek, "but there could be if you disappeared for several days. I'm afraid you must return to Romulus for the sake of appearance. Return the shuttlecraft, answer a few questions, and I'm sure that will be enough."

"Then we can delay the *koon-ut-la?*" asked Wislok.

"No," answered Pardek, "the Vulcans are await-ing us. I will continue on to Vulcan with the boy, while you return to Romulus. I'm sorry, but we must proceed this way."

Wislok looked sadly at his son, who pouted tear-fully at the news that they would be separated. He gripped the boy's shoulders and pulled him to his chest.

"Be brave, and do what Pardek tells you to do. You will be reunited with the whole family very soon." Wislok pushed the boy away and straightened his padded shoulders.

"Yes, Father," said Hasmek, fighting off tears.

"Why don't you go with Dangoshal," said Pardek, guiding the boy toward the taller man. "I have some final instructions for your father."

"Yes, sir." The boy stood beside Dangoshal, who turned on his communicator and informed the scout ship that two of them were ready to beam aboard.

"I'll be waiting to hear all about the ceremony!" called Wislok cheerfully.

The boy waved as he and the pilot were whisked away in swirls of shimmering lights. The smile drained from Wislok's face, and his normally stiff shoulders slumped. "I wish I didn't have to go back."

"But you do," insisted Pardek. "Give me that laser scalpel you used on the guard. It wouldn't be good for you to be found with it. We'll eject it into space."

Wislok sighed and reached into his equipment belt. He pulled out the scalpel, checked to see that it was turned off, and handed it to Pardek. "I need some sleep. I can't fly back with no rest."

"Get some sleep then," said Pardek. He studied the slim laser scalpel. "How do you turn it on? With this thumb dial?"

A thin purple beam shot from the device and attained a length of twenty centimeters. Wislok jumped back in alarm. "Be careful with that thing, Pardek! My nerves are already shot."

"You shouldn't worry, I know what to do with it." With that, he plunged the narrow beam deep into Wislok's chest.

The pain was like the fires of Volcaneum, and Wislok staggered backward and collapsed against the bulkhead. He gripped his chest and could feel his warm blood spewing all over the fine brocaded clothing that Pardek had obtained for him. Unfortunately, Pardek was not as skilled with the scalpel as the surgeon, and Wislok knew he might survive many minutes before he bled to death.

"Why?" he croaked. *"Why!"*

Pardek flicked the laser scalpel, and the beam retracted. "Did you really think the Praetor and his advisors knew nothing about this idea of reunification? They know about it, and they want to both outlaw it and control it. They didn't want *you* to become too friendly with Sarek and Spock, because that's *my* job."

In a haze, with his life seeping away, Wislok watched helplessly as his treacherous comrade took a small box out of his shoulder pack. He set it on the instrument array and pushed a button. Blurry numbers began to march across its display.

"A bomb." Wislok gasped. He reached for it, but Pardek lifted his boot and kicked him backward into the bulkhead. The doctor groaned and struggled to sit up, but his strength was almost gone.

"Also it is safer if the boy never returns to Romulus," said Pardek, straightening his tunic over his barrel chest. "This will give us a better chance of success. Thank you for being a visionary, Wislok. I shall glorify your name. In the meantime, I'll tell your boy you said goodbye."

Wislok tried to sputter something, but only frothing green liquid came from his mouth.

Pardek opened his communicator. "Beam me over. As soon as I am aboard, go to warp three."

"Yes, sir."

To Wislok, the entire cockpit of the shuttlecraft was whirling, and he could barely find Pardek's wavering image as the transporter beam converted him. A light blinded him for an instant, and he knew that the murderer had escaped. With great effort, Wislok focused his eyes until he spotted the small box sitting on the instrument panel. He lunged for it, but his insides convulsed with pain; he dropped to the deck with a howl.

While Wislok tried to collect himself, his tiny craft shuddered violently. Were they firing on her, too? No, he decided, it was just the larger scout ship going into warp, leaving him all alone to perish in space. No doubt Hasmek would officially perish with him, leaving no one to investigate his fate. It was a perfect plan, and he should have seen it coming.

Lie down with gatha, thought Wislok, *and you get up with stangmites.*

That was his last thought before the bomb rent the Romulan shuttlecraft into a billion silvery shards, which flowed outward from the explosion like a new sun in the void.

"Surak's philosophy of logic and pacifism turned us around," said Teska to a rapt Hanua and Falona, not to mention Spock, who appreciated hearing his niece expound on Vulcan history. She was an extremely bright child, one might say precocious, a trait which he planned to temper if given time. That *if* was up to him, and he knew it.

Dare he take on the responsibility of raising a

child? His contact with children had been rare indeed, and he had been like this child, forced to grow up quickly due to his unique circumstances. Vulcan childhood was not as carefree as human childhood—it was a time of learning and appreciation. Did he wish to be a teacher?

Spock looked up from his reverie and found Hanua gazing fondly at him. Hanua, Falona, Teska, and Spock had spent midday together, then reunited after Teska completed her chores for Dr. McCoy. Now it was late in the evening. It seemed to relax Teska to be with the Rigelians, and Spock found their company to be agreeable and nondemanding. Since he didn't wish to injure Hanua's feelings, he endured her mild flirting.

Teska went on: "Some believe that Romulans, and perhaps Rigelians, broke off from Vulcan during those turbulent times, before Surak began teaching. Or perhaps we had a common ancestor."

Spock cleared his throat in warning, and the girl glanced back at him. This was a topic he preferred she not expound upon at the moment, and she seemed to understand.

Falona shook her head in amazement. "I can't believe you're so calm about getting married in a few days."

"I have no choice," said Teska with complete logic.

"It is time for bed," said Spock, rising to his feet. "We dock early tomorrow at oh-seven-hundred, and there will be a reception for us."

"Can I go?" asked Teska.

"For a short time," promised Spock.

"Oh, you must!" gushed Falona. "Rigel V is so beautiful. I wish you could see our farm—we have lots of animals."

"Perhaps someday," said Teska. She caught her wistful tone and straightened to attention.

"Here!" Falona reached into her black pouch and pulled out a small silver locket shaped like two interlocking hearts. With a grin on her dark face, the Rigelian child put the chain around Teska's neck.

Teska looked back at Spock, and her eyes asked, "May I keep it?"

He nodded.

"We make these in our guild," said Falona proudly. "It's got a hologram inside with a picture of our farm, and the address. It's what humans would call a souvenir."

"Thank you," said Teska. Very carefully, she opened the locket, and a small scene sprang from the two halves and hung suspended in the air. Across the door of a picturesque lodge were trellises draped with thorny bushes and plump fruit, and banners waved in the breeze. As she moved the locket, the scene changed and became a signpost with the words: Heart Clan, Hermitage Township, Tanglewood Briar. Welcome!

"Wear it at your wedding," said Falona. Then she laughed.

"What's so humorous?" asked Teska.

"I will have *nineteen* weddings," said the Rigelian, "maybe more."

"Yes, but mine will be first," said Teska.

Hanua clapped her hands together. "Captain Spock is right, we should be getting to bed."

Since they were already in the quarters that Hanua shared with Falona, the younger Rigelian was already close to her bed. Hanua turned to Spock and said, "I'll walk with you down to Teska's quarters."

"That will not be necessary."

"I insist." Hanua appealed to him with a warm smile, and Spock nodded in assent.

"See you in the morning, Teska!" called Falona as she jumped onto her bed.

"Goodbye," said Teska as they stepped out the door.

The girl was still fingering the locket a few minutes later as she led Hanua and Spock through mostly empty corridors on Deck Six. With the *Enterprise* at one-fourth of its typical crew strength, there were no extra personnel—only Bridge, Engineering, and Life-support. When they weren't on duty, they were asleep, not roaming the ship.

Spock and Hanua walked a few paces behind Teska, and Hanua seemed more reserved than earlier. "Captain Spock," she said thoughtfully, "I understand that you could retire from Starfleet anytime you wish."

He nodded. "That is true. I have retired before and gone on extended leaves, only to be called back. They always seem to know where to find me."

"Your life is your own," said Hanua.

"Yes."

She gave him a fleeting smile. "That is good."

"Here we are," said the girl as they reached her quarters. "Teska," she announced to the computer, and the door flew open.

Hanua bent down and touched her delicate chin.

"Good night, Little One. I'm sure we'll see you tomorrow, but we may not have much time to talk. Listen to your uncle, and remember—there's nothing more important than family, whether it's a big one or a little one."

"I will remember." Teska clutched her locket and gazed into the slim woman's eyes. Without changing expression, she slipped into her room.

Spock folded his hands in front of him. "My room is also nearby. Good night, Hanua, and thank you for helping me entertain Teska."

She stepped toward him. "How would you feel about a quick game of chess?"

"I think not."

"Then five minutes of conversation. Please." There was something composed and businesslike in her expression that induced Spock to open his door and let her inside his quarters.

Hanua smiled as she looked around. "It seems like the place you would live, orderly and secretive." She pointed to his lyre hanging on the wall. "Is that a musical instrument?"

"Yes. I play it."

The Rigelian rushed to touch the lyre's polished frame. "I would very much like to hear you play it, Captain Spock, but not right now. I will be blunt with you. I sense within you a willingness to experiment, to search for knowledge. I believe you would make a worthy addition to our clan, and I'm asking you to marry into our family."

Spock raised an eyebrow. This infatuation was more serious than he had suspected. Before he could respond, Hanua held up her hand and said, "Your initial reaction would be to decline, which is why I suggest you take the night to think about it. Believe me, I do not toss these proposals about lightly. You are the first person invited into our clan since we split, despite the fact that we are still out of balance, numerically."

"I am flattered," said Spock. "But my answer will be the same in the morning. I must decline."

Hanua gave him a pained smile. "But I feel as if you are casting about for something, and perhaps we could offer it. I know your mating customs are different, and you would not be required to . . ."

"However tempting your offer might be," he interrupted, "my primary duty right now is to see that Teska is brought up as a Vulcan. I cannot deviate from my task to indulge in an experiment. Perhaps in the future, I will feel differently."

Hanua bowed and backed toward the door. "You are a gentleman, Captain Spock. Even in rejection, I don't feel rejected. Should our paths ever cross again, consider the Heart Clan your friends." The door opened, and the slim Rigelian woman exited, her black skirt flowing after her.

"Fascinating," said Spock to himself.

Chapter Five

THE NEXT MORNING, Captains Kirk and Spock strolled along a deck-three corridor on their way to the transporter room, ready to beam down to Rigel V. Teska followed them at a discreet distance. They had been discussing the Rigelian passengers, and she wanted to be close enough to listen but not close enough to inhibit their conversation. In the deserted corridors of the *Enterprise,* this was fairly easy to accomplish.

"What do you make of Madame Vitra?" asked Kirk.

"An interesting woman," granted Spock, "intelligent, determined, perhaps ruthless. Actually, I spent more time with Hanua, who is much different."

"Yes," said Kirk playfully, "so I heard. How many husbands does *she* have?"

"A sufficient number for all practical purposes, but Rigelian numerology demands a specific number of spouses in each clan, based upon many factors. They may be looking to add husbands."

Kirk nodded knowingly. "Good thing I declined a certain invitation last night. I'm getting smarter in my old age." He turned and glanced at Teska. "What did you think of the Rigelians?"

"I like them," answered the girl. "They remind me of humans."

Spock nodded in agreement. "An astute observation."

"Then we're all agreed, they're *wonderful!*" Kirk turned to his right and led the way into the transporter room, but he stopped abruptly upon finding the room already filled with Rigelians—the three females, two males, and four children of the Heart Clan.

"Hello!" said Kirk with surprise. "You're early."

"We are not all Madame Vitra," explained Hemopar. "We are usually punctual, but some Rigelians like to arrive late in order to make an impression."

Teska and Spock glanced at each other. They didn't have to exchange the remark, "Just like humans."

Captain Kirk turned to the transporter operator, who was another older officer. "Good morning, Kyle. Everything in order?"

"Good morning, Captain," said the officer. "Coordinates are laid in. It is twilight on the planet, and temperature and air composition are ideal for humans."

"I'm ready to go down," said Kirk, "but we're missing three passengers."

"As well as Dr. McCoy," added Spock.

Kirk nodded, glanced at his wrist communicator, and opened his mouth.

Before he could speak, Madame Vitra stalked into the transporter room, followed closely by her broad-shouldered champion, Mondral, and at a distance by Ambassador Denker. Both Denker and Vitra looked angry, probably with each other, and Mondral looked tight-lipped as usual.

"Captain," said Vitra with an icy steel in her voice, "thank you for your hospitality." She glared at Denker. "I wish more people would realize what the Federation is offering us."

"I am quite aware of what they're offering," said Denker. "It doesn't matter. We might as well be honest now rather than pay for deceit later." Without another word, the grim ambassador stepped upon the transporter platform and stared at the operator.

"We're all going down, Kyle," said Captain Kirk. "Will you arrange our party?"

"We can take seven more with the ambassador," said Kyle. "Captain, may I suggest yourself, Mr. Spock, and the children."

"Yes," said Kirk, leading the way. "Send the doctor down as soon as he arrives."

It was wise of Kyle to separate Denker and Vitra, thought the girl, as she jumped upon the transporter platform and stood on a glowing pad. Spock looked back at Hanua, who urged her brood onto the transporter platform, despite their misgivings over being separated from the adult members of the family.

"We'll get you down very quickly," promised Kyle.

"Thank you," replied Hanua gratefully.

As the three adults and five children stood at attention on the platform, Falona gave Teska a brave smile. The young Vulcan nodded back, then stared straight ahead.

"When ready," ordered Kirk.

As Kyle plied the controls, Teska's entire body began to vibrate. With concentration, she found that she could lessen the physical effects of the transporter beam, but she could do nothing about the strangeness of the visual experience. It was fascinating the way the transporter room of the *Enterprise* faded from view to be replaced by overgrown hills, covered with shadowy glades, vine-covered ruins, and low-slung lodges. Teska turned to see lush hills all around them, and she breathed in the glorious scent of wild flowers and fruit blossoms.

Although it was morning according to the *Enterprise*'s twenty-four-hour schedule, it was twilight on Rigel V, and the tip of a blue giant sun glimmered above the sylvan hills, bathing the scene with a bluish-gold tinge that was improbably beautiful. The sky was deep blue, shot with flaming-orange swirls of clouds. Teska had never seen anything like this place. This part of Rigel V was a paradise—a lush, overgrown, unkempt paradise.

She turned to see Captain Kirk smiling. "Very impressive, don't you think, Mr. Spock?"

"Indeed," said the Vulcan, opening a tricorder. "This valley is quite fertile."

The Rigelian children began to laugh and run around, chasing each other, as people on the hillside spotted them and waved. There came a tinkling sound, and Teska whirled around to see columns of sparkling lights transform into Hanua, Vitra, Mondral, the other Rigelians, and a grinning Dr. McCoy. In this overgrown glade, filled with the beauty of twilight, the glittering transporter beams seemed entirely normal.

"Yep," said the doctor, "it's as gorgeous as I heard. What did I tell you, Spock? You can't go wrong in this solar system!"

"Momma!" cried the children as they rushed to hug the adults. One thing Rigelian children never lacked, thought Teska, was physical displays of affection—they were hugged and kissed whenever possible. The young Vulcan wondered what that would be like.

People were now pouring out of the lodges and majestic ruins that hugged the overgrown hills. Teska could see the narrow steps that linked the hill dwellings with the valley, and she saw footbridges spanning a creek below them in the hollow.

A short thick man rushed down the hill and across a bridge, waving frantically at them. "Hello! Hello!" he shouted.

"That would be the prefect," explained Hanua. "We don't have many governmental bodies, just local prefects and the Assembly, which meets twice a year."

The little man ran toward them as quickly as he

could. Like the other Rigelians, he was dressed entirely in black, although his outfit included a stained white apron. Teska shied away from him as he rushed up to Kirk and Spock.

"I am Oblek, the prefect of Ancient Grace. Welcome to our fair city!" He stopped to wipe his hand on his apron, then realized he was *wearing* an apron. He ripped it off and handed it to one of the children. Then he extended a hand, which Kirk shook and Spock ignored.

Kirk performed the introductions on their end, then said, "This area seems a little . . . pastoral, for a city."

Oblek grinned proudly. "We are spread out. Twelve hundred years ago, this was a very great city, of the type you are familiar with. On these hills stood great buildings many stories high, with massive white columns and porticos. We were a different people then—very competitive, distrustful, possessive, always seeking an edge. The numerologists warned us to change our ways."

"Please," said Denker, cutting in, "don't bore him with the long version of the story. The short version, Captain, is that a plague decimated our population. Our cities went to ruin, but the plant life flourished, as you see here. Once the plague had burned itself out, the survivors formed a vastly different culture, one that was rural and decentralized. To avoid having our families decimated again, we formed a different kind of family, with scores of members. We began to live more for today and less for tomorrow, or the past."

"But we remain poor," said Vitra, "compared to

other Federation planets. Our blessed forests give us some biomedical products, which we sell, but we have no fleets, no trade agreements."

She leveled a fiery gaze at Ambassador Denker. "This is not the way we can approach the next millennium. We need open trade; we need Federation credits and markets for the wares produced by our craft guilds. This low-technology lifestyle comes with a price, and you know it, Denker."

"Bah!" snapped the ambassador. *"I am not the one who is holding up progress; it is you."* He stomped off toward the creek.

"Oh, dear," said Prefect Oblek. "Should I take it that the trade negotiations did not go well?"

"It's not over yet," muttered Vitra, charging after Denker, with Mondral right behind her. Hemopar glanced at Hanua; at her nod, he dashed after the departing delegates.

Hanua turned to Spock. "We must be going, too. The solar transporters stop running shortly after dark. It's been a pleasure meeting you, Captain Spock. You, too, Captain Kirk, and especially Teska."

She bent down to pinch Teska's chin, an act to which a Vulcan should have objected, but affection seemed natural coming from the kind Rigelian. "Good fortune on your big day, Little One. Visit us if you ever have the chance."

Teska clutched the locket given her by Falona. "Thank you." She looked for her friend and found her standing in the clutch of Rigelians, many of whom were gazing worriedly at the setting sun. "Falona," she said softly.

"Teska!" shouted the young Rigelian. She ran over and grabbed the girl's hands. "It's goodbye for only a short time, isn't it? You will come and visit us, won't you?"

Teska glanced at Spock, whose expression gave her little encouragement. "It may be a long time," she answered, "but someday I will."

Waving, Falona ran to join her family. Like mourners headed for a sunset funeral, the black-suited Rigelians walked slowly into the shadows of the forest, away from the city on the hillside. Teska wondered how long the journey was to the lodge of the Heart Clan.

McCoy sidled up to Spock and smiled. "How about that drink you promised me?"

Spock produced some copper-colored, triangular-shaped coins. "I am prepared, Doctor."

"Why, Spock," said Kirk with a smile, "you're buying?"

"It would appear so. But our schedule only allows forty-six minutes for this stop."

The prefect eyed the coins with interest. "Gentlemen, near my home is a visitors' lodge, which accepts donations to its endowment. They have ale, mead, and other refreshments."

"Lead on," said McCoy.

With a wave, Oblek headed toward the gurgling creek with its picturesque footbridges. They passed scattered ruins, including the vine-covered foundation of an ancient building, which now seemed like a fanciful wall stuck in the middle of nowhere. All of the ruins had a sort of otherworldly appearance in this lush glade, like glimpses of another dimension phasing in and out of reality. The peaceful calm and gentle breeze had a lulling effect as they walked, and soft lights twinkled on across the hillside. Teska began to think that she had never seen any place as grand as this one.

"Beautiful, isn't it?" said McCoy. "I hear Romulus is a paradise, too. You know, Spock, when they were handing out planets to your genus of humanoids, it looks like the Vulcans got the short end of the stick."

Spock nodded thoughtfully. "That thought had occurred to me, Doctor. By all accounts, my ancestors were much more violent than either Rigelians or Romulans. Perhaps Vulcan was originally a prison colony, much like Georgia in the United States."

McCoy blinked at him, aghast. "Are you speaking ill of Georgia, sir?"

"Merely a statement of fact."

"Well, it may be true," said McCoy, "but those convicts built a very genteel society."

"As did the Vulcans." Spock glanced at Teska, and she fell back a step. The girl was walking close on their heels, so as not to miss a word of their conversation.

"But, Bones," said Captain Kirk, "that genteel society kept slaves."

"Yes," conceded McCoy. "Underneath the most genteel societies there's often a rotten core."

Teska thought about the *pon farr,* the *kal-if-fee,* and the other violent Vulcan rituals. The fact that these moments of madness were rare didn't make them any less unsettling, and they were indeed at the core of the Vulcan being. She tried to forget about the ordeal ahead of her as she followed the men across one of the bridges.

Teska stopped on the bridge to look down into the creek, and she could see dark shapes gliding under the water. With the failing light, it was hard to tell if the shapes were fish or plants, but the sound of the running water was oddly soothing.

She felt a presence beside her, and she looked up to see Spock. Captain Kirk and Dr. McCoy were striding ahead of them, keeping pace with their friendly host.

"I am sorry to delay you," said Teska, jerking to attention.

"It would be illogical to hurry," answered Spock, leaning on the handrail. "I brought you down to the planet so that you might relax and feel refreshed, before we journey to Vulcan."

"Spock!" called a voice. They looked up to see Captain Kirk, Dr. McCoy, and the prefect waving to them from the base of a narrow staircase. "Come on! We don't want you to get lost!"

"Come," said Spock, lightly touching her shoulder.

As the Vulcans approached the staircase, more lights blinked on across the sprawling city of Ancient Grace, giving the dark hill the appearance of a giant Christmas tree. Staircases zigzagged crazily up the hill, intersecting lodges, dilapidated ruins, and other staircases. Lights hung in many of the bleached ruins, glowing like giant lanterns to light the way. Spock and Teska joined the others, and they began their meandering ascent, their boots scraping the rough stone.

After several minutes Teska saw a large gathering of people on a staircase twenty meters away. They were laughing, talking, and hugging one another, as various groups came and went.

She wasn't the only one who noticed the crowd. "What's going on over there?" asked McCoy.

"Oh," said Prefect Oblek, pausing to catch his breath. "Do you see the amber light above the alcove? That's a solar transporter. It appears to have shut down for the night. People are meeting their families, pausing to chat on their way home, that sort of thing."

"How far can you go on one of those solar transporters?" asked Kirk.

"Not far, about eight of your kilometers. They are programmed for each direction—this one goes north, for example, and the Heart Clan took another one east. You have no choice in your destination; it takes you to the next transporter station, where you can transport again, if you wish, or walk. We keep the power requirements low that way. To make a journey of any distance, you have to transport many times."

"Charming," grumbled McCoy.

"Don't mind the doctor," said Kirk with a smile. "He hates transporters."

They were about to resume their ascent when Teska heard a strange shuffling sound. She turned to see an old woman climbing laboriously toward them. She was dressed shockingly in brown, not the usual Rigelian black. The prefect noticed her, too, and he hustled down to help her. She appeared to be as ancient as these ruins, as old as T'Lar, T'Pau, or any of the renowned Vulcan high priestesses.

The prefect conducted the old woman into their midst, and Teska saw that her brown dress had hand-stitched numbers, symbols, and figures all over it, many of them faded and unrecognizable. More than a few of the stitches were unraveling, and the woman's hair was a bramble of gray with twigs and leaves shot through it.

"Mother Ganspul, come this way!" said Oblek with great pride. "Come meet our guests, from the *Enterprise!* Captain Kirk, Dr. McCoy, Captain Spock, and the little girl—"

"Teska," she informed him.

Oblek steered the woman toward Spock. "Can you enlighten them, Mother, with your wisdom?"

Mother Ganspul eyed Spock appraisingly, and Teska wondered if he had been selected for scrutiny because he held the coins. Ganspul snorted in disdain. "Three men and a child? They don't think much of our customs, do they?"

The prefect looked embarrassed. "They don't know our customs, Mother."

She looked earnestly at Spock, as if recognizing him from some incident in the foggy past. The Vulcan didn't change his expression or reveal what he thought about numerology—he simply returned her gaze and waited.

"How many letters in your primary name?" asked Ganspul.

"Five."

"How many in your entire ship's complement?"

Spock had to pause to compute the number, then he glanced at Teska. "Counting our single passenger, forty-nine."

The old woman clucked her tongue, as if that wasn't very good. "How many wives do you have?"

"Yes," remarked Kirk with a smile, "how many wives do you have, Spock?"

"Zero."

Mother Ganspul nodded, as if that only confirmed her unfavorable impression of him. "You have come here out of balance, and you will not leave until you add or subtract from your number."

"That is out of the question," answered Spock.

Nevertheless, Mother Ganspul held out her withered hand as if expecting payment. Prefect Oblek laughed nervously and tried to escort the soothsayer down the stairs. "Come along, Mother, they don't understand our customs."

"On the contrary," said Spock, "I understand your customs quite well." He took a coin from his jacket pocket and placed it in the old woman's hand. She studied the coin suspiciously, nodded, and shuffled off.

Oblek looked pained. "You never know what they'll say! But three men traveling with a child is a known omen of ill-fortune. I think we can ignore her warning because you came down here with so many people. In reality, you have *already* changed your number!" This numerical rationalization seemed to please the prefect, who led them at a brisk pace up the stairs.

Captain Kirk tried to put the best light on the

subject. "On Earth, we have our share of numerical omens. I can remember one I used to hear around the corn fields in Iowa. It involves crows."

"Crows?" asked Spock doubtfully.

"Yes," said Kirk, "it depends on how many crows you see together. It goes like this: 'One crow sorrow, two crows mirth, three crows a wedding, four crows a birth. Five crows silver, six crows gold, seven crows a secret which must never be told.'"

"Oh, I like that one!" said Oblek. "But what's a 'crow?'"

"A large black bird," answered Teska. "Often a scavenger."

"Ah," said the prefect, "we don't have many birds. Maybe I could adapt it to dung beetles. How does it go again?"

They passed the rest of the climb teaching the nursery rhyme to the prefect, and Teska began to have more respect for Vulcan logic. Vulcans had their lapses, but not on a daily basis.

All but the two Vulcans were out of breath by the time they reached a landing two-thirds of the way up the hill. An adjoining staircase led down to a small lodge nestled among overhanging trees. There were a few colorful lamps twinkling in the doorway, and Oblek charged ahead with great relish. "Refreshments are at hand!" he promised.

"And not a moment too soon," replied McCoy.

The humans picked up the pace, and Teska and Spock followed them into the visitors' lodge. The communal home, which appeared warm and friendly from outside, was surprisingly tawdry inside. There were dingy furnishings in the outer room—little more than wooden frames with animal skins covering them. The walls looked as if they were made of splintered bamboo, and nothing but a curtain of beads separated the common room from a hallway that led to rows of sleeping quarters. Teska could hear voices from beyond the curtain, some of them laughing, arguing, or cooing romantically.

Two black-suited residents apparently heard their voices and scuttled through the curtains, sending the beads clattering into one another. One was an older man, and the other was a young woman, who kept her eyes lowered.

"Hello! Welcome to the Sundial Visitors' Lodge," said the man with a smile. He cast a disapproving glance at Oblek. "Prefect, you didn't warn us we were having off-world visitors."

The prefect shrugged. "I didn't know. After the crew from the *Enterprise* paid their respects, they said they wanted some refreshments."

The lodgekeeper looked doubtfully at Teska. "We have far too many adults in the lodge to accept a child—it is out of balance. For the child to pass some time, I would suggest the cooperative school by the old library. They have a playground, and children are always playing there."

"Come," said Oblek to the girl, "I'll show you the way."

Spock started after them. "I will come, too."

"There is no need, Uncle," said Teska, anxious to get out of the seedy lodge. "You should stay with your companions."

"We won't be here long," said Kirk, checking the

time on his wrist device. "It's just another twenty minutes before we have to leave."

"Besides, Spock can't leave yet," said McCoy. "He's buying."

"Very well." Spock looked at Teska. "Do not go far away."

"I won't," promised the girl. "I'll probably sit and watch the people go by."

She was relieved to step outside into the cool scented air, away from the animal skins and unhealthy atmosphere of the visitors' lodge. Teska couldn't explain her adverse reaction to the lodge, except that she wanted all of Rigel V to be beautiful and unspoiled, when this was clearly impractical. She reminded herself that travel on Rigel V was time-consuming with a solar transporter range of only eight kilometers, so weary travelers probably weren't too selective when it came to choosing a place to sleep.

Oblek pointed her toward the staircase they had already ascended. "Go back the way we came and climb to the next landing; go to the right and keep bearing that direction until you see a large ruin with many lights. You'll probably hear the children's voices before you see the place. It's close."

"Thank you," said Teska with a polite bow.

Oblek nodded and headed toward the lodge, and Teska could see Spock standing in the doorway. For a moment she thought he would come after her, but the prefect shepherded the Vulcan back into the lodge.

Suddenly the girl was struck by the novelty of being alone in a strange place. During so much of her young life she had been shunted here and shunted there, at the whim of adults. For once, they were giving her a small taste of autonomy.

Teska nearly skipped along as she hurried to the staircase. Three Rigelians walked by and nodded pleasantly at her, and she fought the temptation to smile back. The girl followed the Rigelians to the next landing and turned to the right, as instructed. She saw many ruins with lights dotting the hillside, but one was substantially bigger than the others. Sure enough, she heard the laughter and shouts of children wafting on the evening breeze.

But Teska was in no hurry to join another throng of strangers. She was enjoying this brief respite on her own, and she knew it would be her last solitary moment for many days to come. She was quite content to stand in the darkness, listening to voices and watching the lights twinkle on the hills of Ancient Grace. She wandered a few more meters along the maze of steps, always remembering how to get back to the lodge. In fact, she kept the lodge in sight, so that she could see Spock and the others when they came looking for her.

The girl finally found a place to sit on a deserted stretch of stairs, and she decided to wait there until it was time to leave Rigel V. She clutched her locket, wondering how old she would be before she could return to this planet to visit the Heart Clan. It was definitely something she intended to do. If she were a human planning to get married, she could come here on her honeymoon. But she wasn't a human, and Vulcans didn't have honeymoons.

Suddenly she heard the rustling of bushes and a

muffled shout, followed by footsteps running. Teska jumped to her feet and turned in the direction of the sound, but all she saw was a man walking slowly toward her down the staircase. As he drew closer, she saw that something was wrong with him. He was staggering and not looking where he was putting his feet. When he saw her, he waved frantically, clutched his throat, and made horrible rasping sounds. She watched, dumbfounded, as the man collapsed and tumbled down the stairs.

He looked like a wounded bird as he flopped down the stairs and came to rest at her feet. The young Vulcan stared in shock at the lifeless body, trying to remember the training she needed to stay calm and unemotional. But it didn't help when she saw who it was—Ambassador Denker—with a crude dagger sticking from his throat!

"Help!" she called. "Help!"

But the two of them seemed alone in a vast necropolis of ruined buildings. Even the sound of the children's laughter was gone.

Teska was about to run to the lodge for help, when Denker reached a bloody hand into the air and tried to grab her. Teska stumbled backward. Denker gurgled and croaked in desperation, but his vocal chords had been severed by the dagger—he had no way to speak. Overcoming her shock, Teska gripped his hand and knelt beside him, to do what she could for the man in his final moments of life.

If he were a Vulcan, she knew exactly what she would do—she would mind-meld with him, so that he could pass his *katra* on to her. Then his memories, experience, and knowledge would not be lost but

91

would be retained and passed on to his family. His soul would live in their collective consciousness.

But Denker was not a Vulcan.

"Help!" she shrieked again, sounding as desperate as the dying man.

Now he gripped her tunic, spreading blood across her chest as he tried valiantly to speak. Nothing came from his mouth but frothing green liquid, and his body rattled in its death throes. Still, he gasped, trying to tell her something.

So urgent was his need to communicate that Teska forgot her usual caution. She spread the fingers of her right hand and laid them upon the dying man's cheekbones. His spasms instantly subsided, and a peaceful expression spread across his face.

But Teska's face twisted in agony, and she screamed.

Chapter Six

IN THE SUNDIAL VISITORS' LODGE, Spock rose to his feet, walked to the doorway, and peered into the darkness. If he were a human, he might be accused of pacing nervously, so he tried to think of a logical reason to leave the bridge and check on Teska. He had heard some childlike shouts, but he wasn't sure if they came from outside or from one of the back rooms. Suddenly the forty-six minutes they had to spend on Rigel V seemed like a very long time.

Behind him, McCoy laughed at the antics of Oblek, who had proven to be an adroit juggler as well as a jovial host. Kirk and Spock were nursing their first glasses of ale, and Kirk glanced at him sympathetically. Spock remembered that his friend had been a parent, even if he had never watched his son grow up. If unwarranted concern was part of being a parent, he was glad that he had been spared such unpleasantness.

Oblek noticed that he was losing his audience, and he dropped the four sacks of seed he had been juggling. They hit the floor and spilled open.

"Hey!" the proprietor cried. "We don't pay you to make a mess around here, Oblek."

"Sorry," said the prefect, looking crestfallen.

Kirk slapped his hands on his thighs and stood up. "I think it is time to be going. We can beam up from here. Spock, you *are* the only one with any money."

"This is all I have," said Spock, handing a stack of coins to the proprietor. "Will that be sufficient?"

"Oh, my, yes!" said the man with a big grin on his face. "Half of that would be enough."

As he returned a few coins to the Vulcan, the man's face dissolved into shock, and he stared past Spock. The Vulcan whirled around at the same time the others did, to see the cause of his alarm.

Standing in the doorway was little Teska with a vacant look on her face, and covered in blood.

Kirk rushed to the girl's side. "What happened to you?"

McCoy was right behind Kirk, and he opened a small medical pouch on his belt and took out a diagnostic instrument. Despite the blood all over her clothes, she didn't appear injured.

"She's suffered some kind of trauma," said McCoy. "Alert Sickbay, Jim, and tell them we're on our way."

"No!" said Teska forcefully, as if snapping out of a trance. "I am not hurt. But Ambassador Denker is dead."

Prefect Oblek gasped and sunk down into one of the seedy chairs. "Denker is dead?"

"Murdered." The girl looked up at Spock. "I did not intend to do it, but he was dying."

"Do what?" asked Kirk. "What did you do?"

Spock's jaw tightened. "You performed a mind-meld."

The girl nodded. "I saw it all. They argued, and Denker walked off. Vitra sent Mondral after him, and they fought. Mondral stuck a knife in his throat."

"You *saw* this?" asked Oblek, amazed.

"Yes."

"No," said Spock. "She did not actually witness the murder. But she did a mind-meld with Denker, and she shared *his* vision of it. Is that right, Teska?"

The girl nodded vacantly.

Oblek shook his head, confused. "What is a *mind-meld?*"

Kirk looked at Spock and sighed. If anybody was going to have to explain the Vulcan mind-meld, it would be Spock.

"Wait a minute," said McCoy, "maybe Teska is mistaken. Maybe the man is still alive." He was headed out the door when they heard shouts and running footsteps coming closer.

The girl suddenly jerked her head and looked outside, as if reminded of something. "I know *why* he did it, too. So Denker could not tell the Assembly about Vitra's illegal activities. Denker refused to falsify his report."

"Let me note the time," said Oblek, fumbling in his pocket for a timepiece.

"I want to see the body," insisted McCoy. Before he could get out the door, two Rigelians ran up to the doorway, shouting, "Prefect! Prefect! There's been a murder!"

"Yes, I know," grumbled the pudgy bureaucrat. "Ambassador Denker."

The Rigelians looked at each other in amazement. "That's right. But we just found his body."

"Are you sure he's dead?" asked McCoy.

"I think so," said one of them. Then his eyes trailed down to the blood-covered girl, and he gasped. "Was it *her?*"

The prefect muscled past Spock and Kirk and headed for the door, with McCoy in pursuit. "Don't anybody jump to conclusions. We have a witness, I think. I'm not really sure," Oblek said.

"Prefect, we can appreciate your difficulty, but we must return . . ."

"She cannot leave!" growled the prefect. "Not until there's an inquest." He turned to the proprietor. "Give them all beds for the night, at city expense. And don't let that little girl out of your sight."

As Oblek and McCoy rushed off with the others to examine the body, the proprietor crossed his arms and stared at his unexpected guests. He didn't look very happy, and neither did Captain Kirk.

Spock picked up a cloth napkin and began to dab the blood from Teska's face. "Do you have some clean clothes that would fit her?"

"Yes," admitted the man. He turned to the woman standing motionless in the curtained doorway.

"Clothes for the child," he ordered. She rushed off, sending the beads clattering.

Kirk bent down and whispered to Spock, "We can't stay here. We'll miss our rendezvous on Vulcan."

"I know," replied Spock, still cleaning Teska. "But we cannot ignore the laws of a member world of the Federation."

The proprietor moved closer to them. "What are you two talking about?"

"We understand the need for Teska to testify," said Kirk, "but the *Enterprise* is on a mission. How soon will the inquest be?"

"Can't be until tomorrow at the earliest," answered the man. "We need a balance of twenty-six men and twenty-six women to hear her testimony. And we have to have numerologists examine the body."

Spock said nothing. It was important to bring a murderer to justice, but his main concern was Teska. Frowning, he gazed into her eyes. "Are you in any discomfort?"

She paused as if taking inventory, then shook her head. "I am well. I was taken aback at first—there was a knife in his throat. I called for help, but no one came. He was dying, and he wanted so badly to speak to me. Did I do wrong, Uncle?"

"No, you behaved logically. However, if we are delayed, your *koon-ut-la* will be delayed. The ramifications of that are unknown."

Teska swallowed hard and looked down at the floor. "I was not thinking clearly."

The Rigelian woman returned from the back of

the lodge with a stack of black clothes. She handed them to Teska and gave her a sympathetic smile. "Come with me. I'll take you to a room where you can change."

"Don't let her out of your sight," warned the proprietor.

As the two females filed out of the room, Kirk slumped into a chair and drained his glass of ale. "What are we going to do, Spock?"

The Vulcan cocked his head. "It would appear that we will spend the night on Rigel V."

A moment later McCoy shuffled back into the lodge, shaking his head. "He's dead, Jim."

"Any evidence that would help to back up Teska's story?" asked Kirk.

"Well, the knife is very crude—homemade with a wooden handle—but it did the job. The only way Denker was going to communicate with anyone was through a mind-meld. I can't speak for the Rigelians, but Teska's story certainly sounds plausible to me."

"Several times he mentioned a report he was working on," said Spock. "Has anyone found those documents?"

"The prefect is looking for his luggage now, and he's also trying to round up Vitra and Mondral. Apparently, the three of them were staying at a different visitors' lodge, farther up the hill. No other witnesses have come forward, other than Teska."

"Who is not really a witness," muttered Kirk. He jumped to his feet, looking anxious to take some sort of action. "I've got to report this to Sarek. Bones, let's go back to the ship."

"Oh, no," said the anxious proprietor, "you're not allowed to leave!"

"No, the girl is not allowed to leave. I have a job to do." The captain activated his wrist communicator. "Kirk to *Enterprise*. Two to beam up."

The Rigelian proprietor was still sputtering in anger as McCoy and Kirk disappeared. He put his hands on his hips. "Does he always do exactly what he wants to do?"

"Under most circumstances," answered Spock.

The Rigelian woman entered through the curtain and approached Spock. "After she put on the clothes, she lay down on the bed and went to sleep instantly."

"That is to be expected," said Spock. "Do not wake her."

"And you?" asked the proprietor. "Do you want a room?"

"No," said the Vulcan, sitting in one of the decrepit chairs. "This will be sufficient."

"Suit yourself. It's going to be a long night."

Of that, Spock had no doubt.

Spock was awakened from a light sleep by a chirp on his wrist communicator. He sat up, feeling twinges of stiffness in his back, and activated the device. "Spock here."

"Kirk here," came the captain's voice. "Any new developments?"

Spock looked around the dreary foyer, which was even drearier now that several lights in the doorway had been extinguished. From the silence, darkness, and the coolness of the breeze that wafted through the open door, he judged it to be the middle of the night on Rigel V.

"No developments," he answered. "But then, I haven't spoken to anyone recently."

"Well," said the captain, "we may have gotten a break, along with a tragedy. Can I speak freely?"

"I am alone."

Kirk went on, "I've spoken to Sarek, and the Romulans have had their share of problems, too. The boy's father was killed when his shuttlecraft was destroyed by a Romulan border patrol."

"Is the boy safe?" asked Spock.

"Yes. This apparently happened *after* the boy's father turned him over to Pardek. The boy doesn't even know his father is dead. And now Pardek is afraid to venture very far into Federation space in a Romulan scout ship, and I can't say I blame him. They're hiding out in the Duperre Asteroid Belt, and they've requested that we escort them to Vulcan."

Spock lifted an eyebrow. "I see. Then a delay of a few days will not be fatal to our mission."

"No," said Kirk. "In fact, I can probably go get them and be back for you by the time the inquest is over. I have a feeling the Rigelians are not very efficient about such things."

"Are you leaving now?" asked Spock.

"I hate to leave you and Teska down there all alone, but we don't have much choice."

"The needs of the many outweigh the needs of the few."

"I figured you would say that," answered Kirk.

"Keep your communicator on you, and I'll see you in a few days. Kirk out."

Spock stood up and stretched, trying to get the stiffness out of his back. Not even a Vulcan could sleep in these chairs, he decided, perhaps not even a Klingon. Before falling asleep, he had checked on Teska and found her to be sleeping peacefully and breathing regularly. Often a mind-meld with a non-Vulcan could be dangerous to one or both parties. But young Vulcans were very resilient, and Teska had abilities and control beyond her years. Still Spock regretted that his young charge had to grow up so quickly.

Ignoring the cold, Spock stepped out of the doorway into the night. Most of the lights on the hillside had been extinguished, except for a few on the main staircases. With no moons or conventional city lights, with nothing to obscure the stars, they spilled across the sky like spun sugar on black velvet. He breathed in the cool air, still filled with floral scents, and gazed at the starscape. One of them suddenly vanished, and he wondered if that was the *Enterprise* leaving orbit, or if it was a meteorite burning up in the atmosphere.

From the darkness came a cackling laugh, and Spock whirled around to see a hunched figure shuffling toward him. He didn't move until the figure came close enough for him to catch a glimpse of brown robes with numbers and symbols stitched through the cloth.

"Here you are," wheezed the old numerologist, Mother Ganspul. "I heard what happened."

101

"To Ambassador Denker," replied Spock.

"Not him," she said with a dismissive wave. "*You.* As soon as I saw your party—three men and a child—I knew that somebody would die. Denker had the look about him of a tormented man, didn't he? But your number—now that some of your comrades have left, how many are you?"

"Myself and the girl."

She nodded with satisfaction. "One man, one child—much better. You are *almost* in balance."

He turned away.

"You don't believe what I say, do you?" she asked.

Spock shook his head. "I am not a believer in numerology, astrology, phrenology, and other pseudo-sciences and superstitions."

"Then what *do* you believe in?"

"Logic."

The old woman hooted with laughter until spittle ran down her chin. "Logic may work some places, but not on Rigel V—and you seek balance, no matter what you say."

"That is possible," the Vulcan conceded. He reached into his pocket for one of his few remaining coins.

"No," said Mother Ganspul, touching his wrist with a hand that was withered and cool. "You cannot afford to give up anything. Hold on to what you have, and *add* to it."

She reached into a dirty cloth pouch that hung from a rope on her waist and took out a miniature dog-eared book with a cover of brown parchment. She thrust it into Spock's hand.

"It is the *Doctrine of Lollo*," she said solemnly. "Abridged. As you are new here, you will need to read it. Even if you do not believe as we do, you will understand us better. There is great wisdom in this book."

Once again, Spock was polite and said nothing to refute her illogical assertions. He held the tiny book hesitantly, wondering if he should refuse the gift. However, the concerned look in her rheumy eyes convinced him she would interpret a rejection of the present as an insult.

"Thank you," he said, slipping the book into his jacket pocket.

She winked at him. "And watch out for women. They will try to fill your void. Good combinations to you, Vulcan!" With that, the aged numerologist shuffled off into the darkness.

Spock was suddenly curious about the miniature book in his pocket. There was always value in reading a text that the locals held in high regard. Besides, he had little else to do, and this was the only reading material at hand. The Vulcan reached into his pocket and withdrew the book, wondering if he would even be able to decipher it. The type was so small that he was thankful for his Vulcan eyesight, but it was written in Federation Standard, evidently intended for export.

He turned at random to various pages in the book and read. There were complex equations for determining a person's balance in love, career, family, gambling, athletics, and other endeavors, mixed in with aphorisms and admonitions. According to

Lollo, it was a terrible risk to wear a shirt with nine buttons on it, unless you had one hidden under your cuff. It was desirable to have nineteen spouses—men or women allowed—and a union of ten women and ten men offered the most balance. Marrying beyond this number was discouraged, however, as that began to throw the marriage out of balance.

He saw some rules he already knew, such as the wisdom of making important journeys with four men, four women, and four children, the exact complement of the Rigelian delegation to Earth. Three men and one child traveling together was, indeed, an omen of ill fortune. With Denker's murder, many Rigelians were probably equating the two right now, thought Spock.

The book contained several gruesome bits of wisdom as well, such as the advice that the ideal number in an assassination party was three women and two men. There was a suggestion that children be given away to attain certain combinations, which disquieted Spock. He turned to the back and found food recipes which depended upon strict numerical combinations of ingredients. Strictly dictated by Lollo were the numbers and types of animals to keep, plus the dates and times when they should be slaughtered, neutered, and bred.

In rules pertaining to clothing, he discovered that Rigelian clothing was communally owned, and the correct number of sets had to be kept in a household. He even learned why almost all Rigelians wore black: Primary colors were assigned numbers, and black was number one, the most in balance. Numerologists and some other privileged classes could wear

brown, as such a humble color balanced their impor-
tance. He saw several references to the "void" and
recalled that Mother Ganspul had used the term to
describe his circumstances—one with a void was
seeking to add to his life.

His thoughts turned to their predicament, and
Spock closed the tiny book and put it in his pocket.
The *Enterprise* was gone, and he and Teska were
alone here, about to enmesh themselves in the
Rigelian legal system. As members of the Federation
went, the Rigelians were somewhat reclusive, sending few youngsters to Starfleet Academy, seldom
going to conferences and trade talks. As Vitra had
said, only in the field of medicine did they contribute much to the Federation.

There was no sense belaboring the unknown,
thought Spock. He should try to sleep; he would
need to be alert in the morning to shepherd Teska
through the legal procedures.

Spock returned to the visitors' lodge, slipped
through the beaded curtain, and walked quietly
down a foul-smelling hall to the room where Teska
was sleeping. The girl had turned upon her side, and
her face was gently lit by the light from the hallway.
Without the intellect of her dark eyes peering outward, Teska finally looked her age.

The thought of returning to the barren common
room with its uncomfortable furniture had little
appeal, so Spock glanced around the tiny bedroom.
He spotted an animal skin in the corner, and he
picked it up and smelled it. The skin had only a
slight odor, which meant that it had been well-cured.
In most of the Federation, trade in animal skins had

been outlawed, but it was still acceptable on home-worlds where the use of skins was traditional.

Spock spread the skin on the earthen floor and lay down with his arms crossed. He went to sleep between Teska's bed and the door, guarding her like an old watchdog.

Chapter Seven

SHOUTS AND FOOTSTEPS woke Spock, and he bolted upright on the floor. The first thing he saw was Teska sitting on the edge of her bed, alert and calm; the second thing he saw were slices of gray sunlight seeping through uneven slats in the wall. The two Vulcans had no opportunity to exchange greetings before the prefect and two other Rigelians burst into the room.

"We are ready now," declared Oblek. "My marshals have assembled the twenty-six men and twenty-six women for the inquest, and it has not been easy. But we know you must be in a hurry to leave with your comrades."

Spock picked his lanky body off the floor. "Our need for haste has been reduced, as the *Enterprise* has left to attend to other business. She should return in a few days."

The prefect nodded with satisfaction. "Then you are alone, just the two of you. That is good—more in balance."

The Vulcan resisted the temptation to debate this conclusion. "Permit us a moment to speak and wash ourselves, and we will go with you."

"All right, but don't be long." The stout prefect herded his marshals down the corridor toward the outer room.

Spock sat beside Teska on the bed and asked, "How did you sleep?"

"I am rested," she answered. "I am still troubled by what I saw in the ambassador's mind."

"They may seem like your own thoughts and experiences, but they are not yours," said Spock. "You must separate these shared thoughts from your own."

The girl nodded slowly. "I have. I believe I can talk logically about what happened, without emotion."

"Good." Spock gave her an encouraging pat on the back. It was a human gesture, to be sure, but it somehow seemed appropriate under the circumstances. If Teska had been human, he would have reminded her to tell the truth—to avoid embellishing her story. As a Vulcan, she would automatically tell the truth; to do otherwise would not occur to her.

They took turns using a small washroom, then uncle and niece took a long walk down the center hallway of the lodge. Other guests peered at them through slits in their doors as they passed, and both Vulcans did their best to ignore the scrutiny.

Spock glanced at Teska walking beside him. In her black tunic and black pants, she should have looked more like a Rigelian than a Vulcan, but her somber expression left little doubt about her background. He was gratified to see her coming through this experience with such determination.

After they met Oblek and his marshals, they stepped outside, and Spock was surprised by the density of a fog that had crept into the valley during the early morning. It chilled him despite his Starfleet jacket, and he put his arm around Teska's shoulder to afford her a bit more warmth. The fog was so thick that he had to concentrate on where to walk on the uneven landings and steps. Even so, he saw curious Rigelians staring at him and the girl from doorways as they made their way toward the top of the highest hill in the City of Ancient Grace.

The fog bank ended just as they reached the summit, and Spock turned to view the shrouded valley below. A layer of billowy gray clouds stretched endlessly in every direction, broken only by distant peaks, which poked from the clouds like shimmering green islands.

Teska tugged at his sleeve, and he turned to see what she had been looking at—a gigantic bunker dug into the solid rock. The metal pillbox had gunnery slits on its sides and a forest of advanced weaponry and electronic equipment on its roof, all of which looked out of place in this pristine forest.

Other than the solar transporter, the bunker was the first overt sign of modern technology that Spock had seen on Rigel V.

"That is our hospital," explained Oblek, "and a meeting place and shelter for a thousand people in case of emergency. It's also the place of last stand in case of invasion—every populated hill has some reinforced structure at the top."

Spock made no comment. Under the umbrella of the Federation, an invasion of Rigel V was highly unlikely, but it was hard to argue with tradition. Besides, there was a certain logic in the idea of a fortified hospital.

He and Teska followed the prefect down cement steps into a sunken entrance, around which a clutch of black-suited Rigelians were gathered. They parted for the Vulcans, but not without giving them hostile and suspicious looks. Spock tried to ignore the hostility, but he was troubled because he couldn't understand the basis for it. He and Teska were only trying to help them apprehend a murderer.

Then again, thought Spock, perhaps these people were loyal to Madame Vitra. She was a wealthy individual by Rigelian standards, and she was bound to have her share of followers, such as Mondral. Or perhaps the Rigelians still harbored ill feelings over the omen of the three men and the child, a simple mistake that Spock wished he hadn't made.

He glanced at Teska, knowing the girl would relay the story with as much accuracy as she could. The rest was up to the Rigelian authorities.

Spock had to duck as he descended hollow-sounding stairs into the bunker. For several meters all he could see were metal walls on both sides of him, but the staircase widened out on the lower level into a large receiving area with information desks and corridors leading off at odd angles. Spock realized that the bunker was much larger underground than above ground, and he had no idea how far it extended into the mountainside. This was a formidable complex, indeed, and one could easily mistake it for a prison instead of a hospital and sanctuary.

He and Teska were ushered past a desk and down a drab corridor into a gigantic room with a low ceiling. It appeared to be the main shelter, where at least a thousand refugees could be housed during an emergency. At the moment about a hundred Rigelians were gathered there—with an equal number of chairs—and their animated conversation stopped when they caught sight of the Vulcans.

Little Teska stiffened beside him, and Spock followed her gaze to the far wall, where Madame Vitra, Mondral, and several other tough-looking Rigelians had gathered. Vitra looked somewhat saddened, which might have been an act, but Mondral glared at the girl. Spock stepped in front of her, breaking their eye contact. He could sense Teska's fear beneath her calm exterior. Most of it was due to Denker's terrified memories, seared inside her mind.

He was about to warn Teska to remain calm and ignore the guilty parties, when a young woman dressed in a tailored black suit came striding toward them. She held out her hand in the human fashion, and Spock took it, sensing from her warm smile that she was an ally.

"I am Jeshul," said the young woman. "Officially, I'm your interpreter, but you can empower me to speak for you. Look upon me as an advisor."

"I see the accused is here," said Spock. "Is there a prosecutor?"

Jeshul scratched her spiked black hair. "No, inquests on Rigel V are not conducted the way they are on Earth—I studied Federation law there for two years. On this planet we have a panel of twenty-six men and twenty-six women, and essentially all of them are prosecutors, entitled to ask questions."

Spock looked around and saw most of the assembled crowd starting to take their seats. Many of them kept stealing glances between Madame Vitra and the Vulcans, as if expecting them to go for each other's throats. This crowd seemed more curious than hostile, and Spock reminded himself of a human aphorism:

The truth will out.

"We are almost ready to begin," said Jeshul. "They've saved us seats over here next to the microphone."

The microphone was on a stand that rose from a hole in the floor and was adjustable. There was no place for a witness to sit. Spectators in the front row of chairs begrudgingly gave up their seats and made room for the interpreter and the two Vulcans. Despite what Oblek had said, finding a panel of fifty-two could not have been all that difficult, as there seemed to be twice that many in the spacious but dreary shelter. Surely, they couldn't all be witnesses.

"Attention! Attention!" shouted Prefect Oblek for

no logical reason, as no one was speaking. The only sounds were chairs scraping across the floor.

"Shut the doors." Oblek motioned to his marshals, who clanged the metal doors shut at the far end of the shelter. "We have the fifty-two in balance—how many more?"

His assistants were scurrying around making a head count, and Jeshul, their interpreter, gave them an encouraging smile. Spock glanced at Teska to see if she would smile back, but the girl stared ahead with eerie self-possession.

"One hundred eleven in total!" announced the prefect, to murmured agreement that this was a good number with which to begin the inquest. "A balance has been achieved! We begin the inquest into the death of Ferlindo Omayo Denker of the Forgiveness Clan, ambassador from Rigel V to Earth and a member of the Assembly."

Someone behind Spock began to sob, and he glanced back to see a lone woman dressed in brown, crying. Oblek strode in front of him, and Spock had to turn his attention to the prefect, who was consulting his notes on a computer padd.

"At fourteen past the hour of nineteen last night, I was in the Sundial Visitors' Lodge with our esteemed guests from the *Enterprise*—Captain Spock, Captain Kirk, and Dr. McCoy. They were so kind as to bring back our trade delegation from Earth, of which Ambassador Denker was a member. Captain Spock's niece, Teska, was also a passenger on the *Enterprise,* so she knew the murdered man.

"She had been playing outside, or so we thought.

At nineteen-fourteen, she entered the lodge covered with blood, saying that Ambassador Denker was dead, stabbed to death in the throat. Further investigation proved this to be true. There were no fingerprints on the weapon, except for his, so we assume the murderer wore gloves."

The prefect looked troubled as he regarded his star witness. "Teska made certain accusations at the time that would give the impression that she was a witness to the murder, and that she heard Denker's final words. I suggest to the panel that you question Teska of Vulcan. Does anyone on the panel move and second?"

An older woman raised her hand. "I move we question the Vulcan."

"I second," said another woman, without much enthusiasm.

Oblek went to the microphone and adjusted the height, as Jeshul whispered to Teska, "Just take your time and tell them what happened. When you're finished, they may ask you questions."

Spock gave Teska a nod, and the girl rose from her chair and walked slowly to the microphone. In her black outfit, she looked tiny and insignificant, and her childish voice sounded disconnected as it spilled from a loudspeaker overhead:

"While the adults stayed in the lodge, they sent me out to find a playground. Near the old library, they said. But I did not get all the way there—I stopped and sat down on some steps, and just looked around. I heard a scuffle, like a struggle, then some footsteps running off."

Teska's dark eyes grew large. "I turned around and

saw him coming down the stairs. I didn't know who he was at first, and I didn't know he was hurt until he tried to say something, but couldn't. Then he fell down a lot of steps and came to rest near me. That's when I saw who it was. I shouted for help, but there was no one around. No one came."

She lifted a small hand to her throat. "He had a dagger in his throat, like this. He couldn't talk, but he wanted to tell me something. He grabbed me with his hand, and that's when he got blood on me."

She swallowed hard. "He kept trying to talk to me, and I knew he wanted to communicate before he died. So I used the Vulcan mind-meld to link with him—to see into his mind."

This final admission was accompanied by puzzled expressions and whispered commentary among the panel and spectators. Jeshul stood up and addressed the crowd: "As interpreter, I would like to define this term 'Vulcan mind-meld' for the panel. Specifically, I would ask Captain Spock to do so."

"I move we hear from Captain Spock," grumbled an older man.

"I second," said a younger man.

Oblek adjusted the microphone one more time for the height of Captain Spock, as Teska took two steps back. Someone gave her a chair, and she gratefully took it.

Spock folded his hands in front of him and patiently explained the Vulcan mind-meld, in both its ritual and practical uses. He concluded by saying, "Even though Teska is young, she is very adept at the technique. I will take questions now."

Hands shot up all over, and Spock spent half an

hour explaining the finer points of the Vulcan mind-meld. The mind-meld had served him well in a variety of emergency situations, and he hoped that his faith in the technique would be impressed upon the audience. If this terrible crime had occurred on Vulcan, thought Spock, the inquest would be all but over.

Oblek nodded, still looking confused by the lengthy explanation. "Thank you, Captain Spock. That's an amazing ritual you have. Let me adjust the microphone for the young lady." Spock relinquished the witness stand to his niece, who once again set her jaw determinedly. "Continue with your testimony," ordered the prefect.

"Perhaps I should not have melded with him," said Teska. "If he had not been dying—and so anxious to speak—I would not have done it. But it seemed logical at the time."

The girl swallowed hard, then she seemed to become another person, a figure of authority and sadness. "The moment I touched him, his pain, his terror, and all his memories flowed into me. I could tell you details about his life—his wives, the deafness in his left ear—but they are not important.

"What is important is that he went to Earth with Madame Vitra and the others to negotiate a trade agreement. But the Federation is still insisting upon an official finding from the Rigelian Assembly, *proving* that Rigelians are no longer practicing illegal activities, such as children marrying adults and animal-skin trade."

There was a concerned murmuring in the crowd

over this news, delivered in such a straightforward manner by a child. Spock gazed toward the back of the room, where Vitra was fidgeting angrily. He was certain that she was only waiting for her name to be mentioned again to explode in anger.

Then the clear youthful voice rang out, silencing the crowd. "Ambassador Denker was going to be honest when he talked to the Assembly—he was not going to suggest that they concoct a false document to give to the Federation. He knew firsthand of illegal activities within his own trade delegation, and he was going to make them public, to show everyone how serious the problem was."

Teska pointed to Mondral, and a hundred necks swiveled in unison. "Mondral killed him, on orders from his patron, Madame Vitra. She is involved in various illegal activities."

"Slander!" shouted Vitra, shaking her fists at the girl. *"Lies!* All lies!"

There were a variety of reactions in the room, ranging from outrage to confusion, and pandemonium ruled for a few minutes as everybody had their say. Teska stood her ground, even as people shouted questions at her, even as Vitra stalked down the aisle toward her. Spock rose to his feet to protect the girl, but the prefect headed off Vitra and took the brunt of her anger. At least Mondral had the good sense to stay in the back of the room, leaning against the wall with his head bowed low.

The prefect bumped Teska out of the way and commandeered the microphone. "Quiet! Will this inquest come to order!"

With Oblek's frantic waving, the room finally settled down, and so did Vitra, who continued to stand near Teska, looking injured and outraged.

"Before we go into a lot of questions about the mind-meld and what this child really knows, we have some legal matters to consider. I believe one of the panel members made a motion to disregard the charges against Mondral."

"I did!" shouted one of Vitra's surly supporters at the back of the room. "The girl didn't actually *see* or *hear* anything! Our laws call for *eyewitness* testimony—we don't recognize telepathy, mind-reading, channeling, and other such claptrap!"

"The Vulcan mind-meld is a recognized procedure throughout the Federation," declared Spock. "There are thousands of incidents of clinical use of the mind-meld. As Rigelians practice no forms of telepathy, perhaps you lack a frame of reference."

"*Famous* claptrap is still claptrap!" snapped Vitra. "In a local case, local laws overrule the laws of the Federation. At best, you would have to call this girl's testimony hearsay. So she found the body, and he wasn't quite dead yet. That doesn't give her the right to accuse innocent people of murder! Doesn't anyone second the motion to disregard these lies?"

To their credit, no one else in the panel seconded the motion. Perhaps they wanted to hear more accusations and innuendo.

"It doesn't matter," said Vitra, glaring at the little girl. "Other witnesses will impugn her." This seemed an empty threat to Spock, for what possible witness could impugn a mind-meld? Having seen the panel reject Vitra's self-serving motion, he felt more confident that justice would be served.

The prefect cleared his throat and spoke into the microphone. "It would be wise to remember that this is only an *inquest*. We haven't voted to charge anyone with a crime, and we *do* have more witnesses to hear from. Can we excuse the witness Teska for the moment, reserving the right to recall her?"

The motion was made and seconded, and Teska slumped wearily to the seat beside Spock and closed her eyes. The last time they had eaten had been aboard the *Enterprise* the day before, and Spock wondered if he should demand food for the girl.

"We have the numerologist who examined the body," announced Oblek. "Would someone motion to call Mother Fergolin?"

After that formality, the brown-robed woman who had been weeping behind Spock rose to her feet and padded to the microphone. A moment later Spock joined Teska in closing his eyes, and he wished that he could close his ears, too, as he listened to a rambling discourse on the numerical clues associated with Denker's corpse. The pertinent facts included the number of blood droplets on the ground, the buttons that had popped off his shirt, the number of stab wounds, and the time of death. From this, the numerologist deduced that it had been a murder, a violent killing, by someone who knew the man.

"That was helpful," whispered Jeshul, their interpreter.

Spock nodded. As none of the woman's ramblings

contradicted Teska's testimony, he kept his opinions to himself.

After the numerologist spoke, the prefect declared a short and welcome recess, during which Spock and Teska were given cups of bitter tea and some sweet cakes. They ate hungrily and silently, saving their energy for the ordeal to come.

As the day progressed, the panel heard from a medical examiner, who gave an erudite and concise report on the time and cause of Denker's death. Once again, Spock was convinced that reason and logic would prevail.

Then the panel made and seconded a motion to hear from the accused, Mondral. The stone-faced Rigelian took the stand and scrupulously avoided looking at Spock and Teska. The prefect began the questioning: "When you transported down from the *Enterprise,* I personally witnessed you and Madame Vitra arguing with Ambassador Denker."

"So what?" asked Mondral. "We'd been arguing with Denker for two weeks, but that doesn't mean we killed him."

Oblek continued, unfazed: "You and Madame Vitra were also seen arguing with Denker at the Summit Visitors' Lodge shortly before his murder. We know the time of death was a few minutes before nineteen-fourteen, when Teska reported finding the body. Where were *you* between the hours of nineteen and nineteen-fourteen?"

Mondral scowled as if the question was beneath him. "I was with my patron in the common room of the Summit Lodge. We were not alone—others came in and out, including Ambassador Denker. I remember him stomping out of the room at about nineteen hours, but I had no idea where he went. I *didn't* follow him outside."

Oblek nodded, as if he had been expecting that. "Can anybody verify your whereabouts at the time in question? Someone other than your patron, Madame Vitra."

Mondral finally smiled, in triumph. "Yes, they can. There was another person in the room with us during that period—Hemopar of the Heart Clan."

Spock raised his eyebrow at this news, and he glanced at Teska, who was frowning darkly. He remembered that Hemopar had followed Denker, Vitra, and Mondral up the hill at Hanua's request, rather than leaving with the rest of the Heart Clan. So much else had happened that he had forgotten this small fact.

Oblek was taken aback by the revelation, too, and he was slow to react. Someone in the audience shouted, "I motion we excuse this witness and question Hemopar."

"I second!" shouted several people at once.

Spock gazed around the room with the rest of them, wondering if Hemopar was even present. Finally a slim Rigelian rose to his feet at the back of the room and walked slowly toward the witness stand. Hemopar was even more careful not to look at Spock and Teska than Mondral had been, and Vitra's thug gave him a knowing smile as he stepped back from the microphone.

The prefect cleared his throat importantly and turned to the member of the Heart Clan. "You were on the trade delegation to Earth?"

"That is correct." Hemopar spoke so softly that no one would have heard him were it not for the microphone amplifying his voice.

"Please explain what you saw on the evening in question."

"I saw nothing, really," answered Hemopar. "As Mondral said, the four of us were in the common room of the lodge, discussing our trip to Earth. Our major disagreement was over what kind of recommendation we should make to the Assembly. Most of us wanted to get to work on the document required by the Federation, but Denker wanted to first investigate the charges of illegal activities."

The Rigelian took a deep breath and twisted his hands in front of him. "Denker left the lodge at about nineteen hours, but no one left with him. I was with Madame Vitra and Mondral at the time in question—they never left."

"He was not there," whispered Teska. "He was not in Denker's memories of those final minutes."

"I know," answered Spock. However, they were the only ones who shared this certainty as the room erupted with people making motions.

"I move to disregard the slander against Madame Vitra!" shouted one.

"I second!" shouted another.

"I move to bring a finding of murder by assailants unknown," motioned someone else.

"I second!"

It was bedlam for several moments, but the prefect took over the microphone and finally restored order.

"Order! Order!" called Oblek. "In the death of

Ambassador Denker, it has been moved and seconded to bring a finding of murder by assailants unknown. How say the twenty-six and twenty-six? All in favor of the motion, say 'Yay.'"

"Yay!" echoed voices throughout the dreary underground shelter. Spock looked down at the floor.

"Well," said Jeshul sympathetically, "perhaps the girl was mistaken."

"A man does not mistake his own murderer," said Teska with an eerie maturity.

Hemopar was trying to slip away into the excited crowd, and Spock jumped to his feet and pursued him. He caught him just before he reached the door, grabbed his arm, and spun him around. Sensing some excitement, people near them fell back while others crowded closer to see.

"Why did you lie?" asked Spock.

"Uh, lie?" Hemopar stared down at his feet and tried to get away, but Spock held him firmly.

"Let me go!" begged the Rigelian.

Spock clamped his arm tighter. "I wish to know why you lied."

Suddenly Spock felt a grip on his upper arm, and he was spun around to find himself facing Mondral, who was considerably younger, taller, and more muscular. "Let go of him, Vulcan."

As he surveyed the hostile crowd of over a hundred people, Spock saw the wisdom of such a course. He released Hemopar, who bolted out the metal doors and dashed up the stairs, but Mondral still held firmly to his arm. "I know you're a VIP in Starfleet, but you're a long way from home."

"Release me," said Spock.

"What if I don't want to?" Mondral sneered. He brought up his other hand in a fist, and Spock was beginning to duck when the thug's expression twisted into a look of pain and surprise. He bent over and gripped his leg.

Spock looked down and saw Teska draw back her booted foot and kick him in the other shin. "Aaaggh!" cried the big Rigelian as he dropped to his knees.

With the crowd surging around them, Spock grabbed Teska and ran for the door.

Chapter Eight

ONLY A HANDFUL of the 111 Rigelians in the underground shelter appeared hostile, but they were enough to alarm Spock, especially with Mondral leading them. He pulled Teska toward the closest exit and slammed the metal doors open, as curious and excited people pressed all around them. Teska had wounded Mondral's pride as much as his shins, and the big Rigelian was hobbling after the two Vulcans with revenge in his eyes.

He heard Oblek yell for calm, but Spock couldn't rely on the prefect to save them from Vitra's thugs. His intent was to put as much distance as possible between them and Mondral, and he would worry about the rest later. So Spock struggled up the stairwell, pushing people out of his way and dragging the girl after him, as Mondral stomped up the stairs behind them. Maybe he could seek refuge in the hospital, thought Spock, until order could be restored.

Out of nowhere, a shrieking sound rent the enclosed stairwell, and Spock and Teska gripped their ears and sunk against the walls. Mondral and the crowd of Rigelians fared no better as they collapsed along the lower flight of stairs. The door opened at the top of the stairs, and a uniformed man wearing a helmet, dressed shockingly all in gray, stood there with his hands on his hips. The horrid siren stopped, and was replaced by the man's hollow voice, amplified from inside his helmet.

"Order will be resumed inside this facility," said the guard. "Please file out in an orderly fashion."

"We need sanctuary from this mob!" insisted Spock.

"Oh, no, you don't!" declared a brash voice. Spock turned to see Madame Vitra squeezing past the others and flashing him a gleaming smile. "Captain Spock is in no danger."

She stared at Mondral as she passed him. "Now go back and sit down. *You* will be the last one out."

The Rigelian scowled at his patron, then at Teska. He slammed his fist into his palm and stalked down the stairs.

Vitra turned to Spock with a mixture of charm and outrage. "I'm sorry you were treated so badly, but murder is very rare on Rigel V. It inflames all sorts of passions. Can we go somewhere and talk? I assure you, I can handle Mondral." She smiled pleasantly at Teska. "He doesn't like to be accused of things."

"He killed Ambassador Denker," said the girl.

"You're welcome to your opinion. Can we talk?" Spock nodded slowly. "Very well."

Madame Vitra ushered them toward the stairs, and Spock looked down at his niece. She was calm, if slightly out of breath. Although her attack on Mondral was opportune, it was also ill-considered, and Spock would have to talk to her about such rashness.

At the top of the stairs, Vitra spoke to the guard. "Captain Spock and I need to talk. And get away from that crowd. Do you have a small meeting room? An examination room?"

The gray-uniformed guard motioned for them to follow him, and he led Madame Vitra, Spock, and Teska down a corridor into the hospital wing, which was as dreary and utilitarian a place as Spock had ever seen. Buildings on Vulcan were more interesting.

As he watched black-suited Rigelians hurrying about their business in the hospital, he thought about what a dichotomy they were. The Rigelians were advanced technologically, yet many of them had turned against technology in favor of an agrarian communal society. Spock had yet to see weapons on Rigel V, other than knives and sickles, but he had seen an armored guard stop a near-riot by unleashing a powerful aural disrupter. Spock was grateful for the intervention of the hospital guard, but the mysterious figure seemed just one more oddity on Rigel V.

Vitra kept smiling apologetically at him. Or was she flirting? Spock found the romantic proclivities of the Rigelians to be rather disconcerting. They should realize that a Vulcan would not be swayed by such attention. Then again, Spock had to remind himself that he *looked* like one of their own race—he only acted alien.

The guard stopped, pushed a wall panel, and opened a door. "This is an empty office, I believe." He motioned them into a small room with two empty desks and two chairs.

Vitra instantly made for one of the chairs and planted herself in it. She shook her head, and waves of gleaming black hair cascaded over the back of her chair. With an innocent smile, she brushed the hair behind her pointed ears. Teska stiffened at the sight of this, and Spock had to push the girl into the room. The door shut behind them.

Cocking an eyebrow at Spock, Vitra said, "So what are you going to do next?"

"We are going to leave," answered Spock. "Our efforts to aid you in bringing a killer to justice were unwelcome."

Vitra gave him a pained expression. "Captain Spock, it's not like that at all. The young lady simply wasn't a witness to what actually happened. Despite the well-deserved reputation of the Vulcan mind-meld, it's not exactly the same as firsthand eyewitness testimony. That's what our laws demand. Did you enjoy watching the Citizen's Court in action?"

Spock felt Teska stiffen beside him. "Acting as an inquest," he said, "they reached the correct conclusion—Ambassador Denker *was* brutally murdered. However, the guilty parties will not be held accountable."

"By guilty parties, I suppose you mean *me.*" Vitra shook her head glumly. "May I suggest that you forget about Ambassador Denker, who can't use your help anymore, and think about yourselves. I can send Mondral away, so he's no problem. So why can't you just let this matter rest?"

Now, thought Spock, they came to the heart of the matter. Vitra wanted to know if they were going to make a report once they got back to the *Enterprise.*

"I will tell Captain Kirk," answered Teska. "He will come and put you in the brig."

Spock tightened his grip on the girl's shoulder in order to warn her not to speak so freely. She stared at him, misinterpreting his action. "Why should we hide the truth?"

Vitra rose slowly from her chair. "Our relationship with the Federation is at an impasse—we can't continue to remain members and receive no trade benefits. Denker tried to derail the trade negotiations, even though he *knew* how many people needed these agreements. People like the Heart Clan and rural families have to have a better chance to be self-sufficient. We must progress, we cannot stagnate."

"Have you stamped out the illegal activities?" asked Spock.

Vitra laughed and rolled her eyes. "Do you know how many children some of these clans have? Scores of them! They can't feed them all. If you want to stamp out our tradition of children marrying adults, then you do everything you can to get us these trade agreements."

"Do you have Denker's documents?" asked Teska, surprising both Spock and Vitra.

"Persistent little thing, isn't she?" Vitra cocked a suspicious eyebrow at the child. "Get it through your head—he's dead!"

"Not while I hold his memories," answered Teska.

For a microsecond, Vitra looked genuinely frightened by the eerie certainty in the little girl's voice, then she regained her composure and gave the girl a snide smile. "I was like you at that age—a tough little brat."

Spock stepped between them. "Is our business completed?"

"No," said Vitra, "because I haven't made my suggestion yet. I know you've got to wait until the *Enterprise* comes back, and I was going to suggest that you go to one of our rural retreats. There your needs would be taken care of, and you could wait for your ship in peace. If you still fear Mondral or myself, then don't tell us where you've gone. There's a transporter right here in the hospital."

"Thank you," said Spock, wondering if Vitra's concern was at all genuine. She must know that they would report Denker's murder to the Federation, and there would be further investigations, whether the Rigelians wanted them or not. On the other hand, there was some truth to her assertion that a trade agreement would benefit the poorest Rigelians, making it easier for them to end their more onerous practices. He didn't want to harm average Rigelians, but people like Vitra had to be curbed.

Madame Vitra sauntered to the door and glanced back over her shoulder. "It's only a suggestion, Captain Spock. If I see the prefect, I'll tell him you're here. Maybe he can make arrangements for you. I sincerely hope that our next meeting is more pleasant."

"As do I," said Spock.

The door whooshed open, and the Rigelian ambled into the corridor. The gray-uniformed security officer was also on duty, and he glanced into the room, as if expecting Spock and Teska to leave.

"I wish to speak to the hospital administrator," said Spock.

The officer motioned for them to remain in the room, then he pressed a panel, shutting the door.

"I do not trust her," said Teska.

"Nor do I," said Spock. "In fact, I am uncertain exactly whom we can trust."

Teska's hand went for the heart locket around her throat. "The Heart Clan," she breathed. "We know we can trust them, and I have their address."

"I gather they are some distance away, perhaps more than a day's journey. We would be all alone, and conspicuous."

Teska smiled slightly and picked at her black tunic. "I am inconspicuous in these clothes, and you would be, too, in black."

"I am on official Starfleet business," said Spock. "It would be inappropriate to disguise myself under these circumstances."

"But the Heart Clan would protect us," said Teska with certainty. "I know they are our friends."

"The captain will expect to find us in this city," answered Spock, gazing doubtfully at the vacant office. What had started as a simple attempt to relax Teska and take her mind off her *koon-ut-la* had turned into a fiasco.

The door opened and the gray-uniformed guard with the helmet stood outside their room. He motioned for them to follow him, and the two Vulcans dutifully filed out of the vacant office. Spock glanced around the corridors but saw no trace of Madame Vitra, Prefect Oblek, or the jurors of the Citizen's Court. There were only black-suited orderlies and nurses going about their tasks in the hospital, and they paid little enough attention to the Vulcans.

They followed the guard through the hospital wing back to the main entrance and its information desks. To Spock's surprise, the uniformed guard proceeded straight through the doors and up the stairs leading outside the massive bunker. Spock and Teska exchanged wary glances, but Spock knew how disjointed authority was on Rigel V. Perhaps they would find the hospital administrator in the back, weeding a garden. He nodded, and they followed the guard into the sun-splashed forest at the top of the hill.

The fog was gone, and the blue giant sun was high in the sky but already beginning its descent toward the peaks behind them. Spock judged it to be late midday. As they followed the hospital guard across a field of tiny blue wildflowers, Teska looked up at him questioningly.

"Where are we going?" she asked.

The gray-uniformed guard turned and gazed at them, and Spock wished that he could see his face through the tinted helmet. The man reached down to his boot and pulled out a small instrument, which Spock feared was a weapon. As he grabbed Teska to shield her, a rotund figure ran up behind the guard and shouted, "They're mine!"

The guard whirled around to see Oblek, who had apparently been lying in wait for them. "I'll help them get where they're going!" he insisted. The guard shrugged and handed the small device to the prefect, then he walked back toward the hospital.

"Oh, that's nice," said Oblek, studying the instrument. "He wanted to give you this portable diagnostic device. It takes your blood pressure and such. The hospital has been trying to distribute them, without much success."

"I see, another gift." Spock took the proferred device, recognizing his misjudgment in thinking they were about to be attacked. Despite the murder and the bungled inquest, Rigel V was still a civilized planet, as old as Vulcan. He couldn't distrust everyone on the planet, or their stay would be extremely unpleasant.

"Are there hand weapons on this planet?" asked Spock.

"No," answered Oblek. "The penalties for possessing any sort of hand weapon are extremely high. Of course, people come and go from the planet all the time, and who knows exactly what they bring with them. But weapons are discouraged."

Teska nodded gravely. "Vitra has them."

Oblek laughed nervously. "Well, Vitra often journeys off-world, so she has her resources. Listen, I would suggest that you two lay low and stop making accusations for the rest of your stay. I'm sorry the girl's testimony wasn't accepted, but you have to be realistic. This isn't Vulcan—it's Rigel V."

"We are aware of that," admitted Spock. "And I am quite willing not to arouse any more enmity. Where can we stay in privacy for the rest of our time here?"

"You've seen our guest lodges," said Oblek, scratching his chin. "They don't offer much in the way of privacy. We have retreats in the country that are more private."

"Vitra mentioned them. Are they safe?"

"Certainly," said Oblek, heading down a path toward a staircase. "Let's go back to my office, and I can give you a letter of recommendation. A favorite retreat of mine is up north in the Windmill Township."

"We want to go east," said Teska, "where the Heart Clan lives."

Oblek smiled obligingly. "Wherever you want to go is fine with me. I just want to make your stay pleasant—more pleasant than it has been."

In a copse of trees a hundred meters away, the prefect's voice sounded clearly over a tiny receiver, gripped by a hand with lacquered black fingernails.

"This has worked out even better than I expected," said Vitra with satisfaction. "That fool of a prefect will send them to some backwater, I'm sure."

Beside her stood Mondral in the gray guard's uniform, his helmet under his arm. "I was alone with them—it was the perfect time."

"No," said Vitra, listening for more voices. But all she heard were footsteps. "You gave them the listening device, now let it work. A killing in front of the hospital would only bring more problems. They must *disappear* altogether, so the *Enterprise* will find nothing when she returns."

Her dark eyes narrowed. "I don't know what that little girl has inside her mind, but she's not leaving Rigel V. This time we won't take any chances."

At warp five, the stars on the viewscreen were little more than streaking blurred lights, yet Captain Kirk found the view oddly soothing as he sat in the command chair of the *Enterprise*. Movement— that's what he liked—anything but standing still. Desks stood still, which is why he didn't like them. Many friends in Starfleet had suggested to him that he could have his admiralty back. The only trouble was, Kirk had never *liked* admirals; he hadn't liked himself when he was one. He liked bending the rules, not making them.

"Spock, what's our ETA?" he asked, turning around.

Only Spock wasn't at the science station. Instead an impossibly young woman with blond hair piled atop her head jumped to attention and punched buttons at the console until she came up with the requested figures. "Um, fourteen and a half hours, sir!"

He laughed. "I'm sorry, you're not Spock. I mean, I'm not sorry you're not Spock—I'm sorry I *called* you Spock."

"Understood, sir," she said nervously.

"What is your name, Ensign?"

"Patricia Donnelly," she answered.

Kirk stroked his chin. "You remind me of someone, with your hair up like that."

"If it's not according to regulation—"

"No," he said with a smile. "It's fine. When you reach a certain age, *everything* reminds you of *something.*"

"Yes, sir," she said brightly, not having a clue what he was talking about.

There was a time when he would have chatted with the young lady, but he could tell that he was making her nervous. Once upon a time, he had been an equal with his crew—the captain, yes, but a peer. Now he was an icon, a legend, and younger officers treated him as if he were not a real person, which is why he preferred the company of his old shipmates.

To those who held him in awe, he wanted to say that he was still just feeling his way, still luckier than good. Someday his luck would run out—Bones had always told him that—and he hoped he would be alone when it happened, not with a shipful of lives riding on a rash decision.

"Captain?" asked the young ensign. "Are you all right, sir?"

"Oh, fine. I was just thinking."

"Yes, sir," she said doubtfully.

Kirk tapped his finger to his lips, coming to a

conclusion. "Ensign, if you could be anyplace in the entire universe, where would it be?"

"Why, here, sir. I've dreamed about this my entire life."

He pointed a finger at her. "Don't ever lose that dream. I envy you when I think of the star systems you will map, the worlds you will explore. When you go, you want to know you've been here, right?"

Ensign Donnelly nodded excitedly. "Yes, sir. What's the most amazing world you've explored?"

"Well," answered Kirk, gesturing in the air, "there have been so many. . . . I'll have to sit down sometime and tell you about them all."

"I would like that," said the young lady with a shy smile. She checked her console. "We are due to be relieved in forty-six minutes. Perhaps you would have a few minutes to chat—" she continued uncertainly.

Captain Kirk scratched his chin thoughtfully and suppressed a smile. "I'll have to break a date with Dr. McCoy, but I've heard all of his stories before. Certainly, Ensign, thank you for the invitation."

In front of him at the helm, Chekov did not do so well suppressing a smile. "Keptin, all systems operational. Nothing unusual to report."

"Thank you, Mr. Chekov." James T. Kirk relaxed in his command chair. "Steady as she goes."

Midway down the largest hill in the City of Ancient Grace stood the prefect's thatched office. Spock had no difficulty picking it out from similar humble buildings, thanks to a clutch of people standing out front. As he, Teska, and Oblek descended the stairs, Spock realized that the clutch consisted of three people and one large tapered case—black, about two and a half meters high, standing on end. One of the citizens was the brown-robed numerologist who had testified at the inquest, but he didn't recognize the two men with her. Spock had an uneasy feeling about the large case and its contents.

"Oh," said the prefect with a crestfallen look, "it's time to send Ambassador Denker home." With a wave to the mourners, he quickened his step. "I'm coming, Mother Fergolin!"

The numerologist was still dabbing her eyes as they approached. "We've been waiting for you to release the body," she said in an accusatory tone. "If we can leave quickly, we can make it halfway to the Forgiveness Clan by nightfall."

"Absolutely," said the prefect, rushing into his office. "Let me get those documents."

While the prefect attended to official business, Spock and the woman exchanged glances, but her gaze settled on the little girl. "I, for one, was impressed with your testimony," she said. "I wish we had a ritual like the mind-meld."

"He loved you very much," said Teska.

The woman began to weep anew, and the two men crowded around and tried to comfort her.

The numerologist brushed off her retainers and took control of her own emotions. "I know he did, Little One. He would have married me had he been able, but I took a vow of solitude when I put on this color. If only he had been with *me* that night, instead of arguing with *them*—"

She shook her head at the injustice of it. "He should be alive—he only wanted what was best for Rigelians. But we are fiercely independent, and sometimes we refuse to be helped." She bent down in front of Teska and managed a smile. "Is there anything I can do for such a brave little girl?"

"Yes, there is." Teska glanced at Spock, who didn't dissuade her from asking for help. "We are looking for a place where we will be safe until the *Enterprise* returns. Might you know of such a place?"

The woman frowned in thought, then nodded. "We are going east, and there is a retreat in the village of Atwater. It's not a big place, but we should reach it by nightfall."

"Yes, east!" said Teska with a big smile on her face. Spock looked at her, and she resumed her usual impassive expression. He knew that the girl was suffering some aftereffects from her mind-meld with Denker, and he was willing to forgive sudden bursts of emotion, as long as she could control them.

The prefect emerged from his humble office a moment later, holding various transparency sheets with colorful markings on them. He handed several sheets to Mother Fergolin. "Here are your permits to transport the body, plus the death certificate and the inquest finding. If you need more than that, you'll have to send for it."

She rolled the documents up and stuck them into her belt. "Thank you, Prefect. I don't know if I will be coming back to Ancient Grace right away—I may take a sojourn in the country."

Oblek bowed politely. "We will miss your wisdom, and we will count the days until you return." With a grin, he turned to Spock. "Captain, I have an idea! Since Mother Fergolin is headed east, perhaps you could go with her. There is a retreat in Atwater—"

"Once again, Oblek, we are ahead of you," said Mother Fergolin with amusement. "We have already discussed this, and have agreed to it."

"Excellent!" The prefect handed a clear page to Spock. "This is a letter of introduction to the proprietor of the retreat. It says that they may request payment from me for your stay." He winked. "That doesn't mean I'll pay it, but there's nothing to stop them from requesting it."

"Starfleet will pay our bill when the *Enterprise* returns," said Spock, as he took the document.

The two pallbearers reached for the casket, and Spock stepped forward to help them. "May I be of assistance?"

"That's not necessary," said one of the men, opening a panel on the side of the coffin. "It has antigrav built in. All you have to do is to guide it. The child could do it."

As if to demonstrate, he pushed a button and shut the panel door. The casket tilted slowly onto the ground and then levitated half a meter into the air, just enough to clear the stairs, Spock judged. The other man gripped a handle on the rear of the casket and guided it down the landing toward the first flight of stairs. Despite the rakish angle of the coffin, it maneuvered easily down the steps.

"The child could do it," said Mother Fergolin, "but it is required that two men and a woman deliver the body." She gave Spock a smile. "Fear not, three men, one woman, and one child is a most opportune combination. It denotes the winter season, when the fields lie fallow, but there is still the promise of spring. With Denker dead, this is an appropriate symbol."

Spock nodded politely at the sentiment. There was no point in commenting on the Rigelians' belief system—if it brought some order to their chaotic lives, then he would not dispute it.

He and Teska followed the coffin, the pallbearers, and Mother Fergolin all the way down the hill and into the lush valley filled with pockets of ruins. They crossed the creek on one of the picturesque footbridges and passed close to the site where they had beamed down the evening before. Spock could scarcely believe that such a short time had elapsed. With the murder, his restless night, the inquest, and all the unpleasantness, it seemed as if he had spent weeks on Rigel V.

Walking on the same trail that Hanua and the Heart Clan had taken the day before, they soon reached the solar transporter. Nestled inside an alabaster alcove, it looked little different from similar ruins, except for an array of orange solar panels on the roof. The angle of the panels in relation to the sun suggested that they adjusted automatically as the sun drifted overhead. Spock glanced inside the

141

alcove and saw only two transporter pads, which further reduced power requirements. Lettering marked the left pad as *Out* and the right pad as *In*, and a larger sign bore the Rigelian symbol for *East*.

The pallbearers stopped the casket and made some adjustments which righted it upon one end. While they were doing that, two travelers arrived on the *In* pad, stepped off, and hurried past them.

"Step off quickly, as they did," advised Mother Fergolin. "Someone is likely to be right behind you."

"Understood," answered Spock. "How many jumps will we have to make to reach our destination?"

"Atwater? I think it's about fourteen."

Spock shook his head.

"What's wrong?"

"Nothing," replied the Vulcan. "I was merely thinking that a shipmate of mine would certainly not enjoy travel on Rigel V."

"We don't like the transporters either," said Fergolin, "but they are nonpolluting and still allow us the opportunity for considerable walking."

"We are ready," said one of the men, shutting the panel on the side of the casket. He then stepped upon the *Out* transporter and promptly disappeared in a blazing shaft of light. His partner maneuvered the upright casket upon the transporter pad, and it, too, was consumed in a shimmering glow and disappeared. After waiting a few seconds, presumably for his partner to remove the casket from the transporter eight kilometers away, the second man jumped on and was gone. He was quickly followed by Mother Fergolin.

Teska cocked her head gamely and jumped upon the transporter pad. She was gone before Spock could take a stride to follow her. With a heave of his shoulders, he stepped upon the transporter and began his journey deeper into the countryside of Rigel V.

Chapter Nine

SPOCK STOOD PATIENTLY in the gloom of twilight as another prefect in another village dutifully checked Mother Fergolin's documents. He had ceased counting how many stops they had made in their journey east from the City of Ancient Grace. This wooded glen looked like the last half-dozen stops, except for slightly flatter fields of grain surrounding it. As they had traveled east, dramatic hills had been replaced by more gentle terrain. Teska and the two pallbearers also stood patiently beside the solar transporter, but the same could not be said of the numerologist, Mother Fergolin.

"It's getting dark!" she snapped at the prefect, an older woman who steadfastly ignored her. "We're not going to make it to Atwater by nightfall."

"We have a nice visitors' lodge," said the prefect,

going over the documents again. "Is that really Ambassador Denker in the box?"

Fergolin threw up her hands and stomped away. "Somebody else deal with her!"

"It is, indeed, Ambassador Denker," said Spock.

The prefect gave him a fishy look. "Who are you. And why are you wearing that red—thing?"

"Captain Spock of Starfleet." He produced his own slim transparency, as this prefect obviously held such documents in high regard.

As the prefect studied the letter of introduction from Oblek, lights flashed in the nearby transporter alcove, and a young woman stepped off the *In* pad. She looked as if she was about to step immediately upon the *Out* pad when she saw the party gathered around the entrance. So she stepped politely off to the side and waited. Two more women and two men arrived on the transporter in quick succession, making quite a gathering around the alcove. Upon seeing the party ahead of them, they all stepped politely to the side.

"You can go ahead," said the prefect, motioning to the newcomers.

They looked at one another, then at the quickening darkness. "This is Kite, isn't it?" asked one of the men. "And you have a visitors' lodge here?"

"Yes!" said the old prefect exuberantly, smiling for the first time. "Finest one between Ancient Grace and Atwater."

"Which is only two stops away," muttered Mother Fergolin. As if hearing her complaint, the lights in the alcove suddenly blinked on and off several times.

"Unless you hurry, you'll all be staying here," warned the prefect.

"That's fine with me," answered one of the young women, glancing at her companions. "We're from the Truth Clan, and we still have a long way to get home."

With frustration, Mother Fergolin snatched the documents out of the prefect's hands. "All right, we're all staying here. Are you happy now? Where is the lodge?"

Now the old woman really smiled. "It just so happens that I'm the proprietor. Follow me, please."

The old woman hobbled off, followed slowly by a self-levitating casket, two pallbearers, one numerologist, two Vulcans, and the three women and two men of the Truth Clan. Spock shook his head at the fact that he had dutifully counted up this odd lot. Only one day on Rigel V and he was already acting like a numerologist.

As they strolled through the peaceful fields of the farming community, with the sky darkening into a rich purple, even Mother Fergolin began to relax. Insects in the fields serenaded them with a dense layer of sounds, and earthy aromas of loam, manure, and fresh-cut grain wafted on the breeze. Teska began to bob her head back and forth as she walked, as if listening to her own internal music. In this bucolic setting, Rigel V seemed anything but dangerous, and Spock couldn't blame the prefect for trying to fill her visitors' lodge. He hoped that he had enough coins left in his pocket to cover a night's stay for himself and Teska.

The sky was awash with stars by the time they

reached the ramshackle lodge on the edge of a vast freshly plowed field. The lodge was so small that Spock hoped there was room enough for all of them to sleep there, then he noticed a smaller bungalow and a latrine behind the lodge. The endless horizon of stars and fields left him with the illogical feeling that he was standing at the very edge of the universe.

The old prefect stopped at the door and turned on a light, illuminating a foyer that contained several wooden benches, plus gaily colored kites hanging on the walls.

She began to take a head count. "The price is one triangle per person. Uh, Ambassador Denker may stay outside for free. Let me see, I have six compartments altogether, separated by screens and curtains. The Truth Clan may take the two in the rear, which are the largest, Mother Fergolin the next, and the funeral party the one beside hers. To whom does the child belong?"

"Myself," answered Spock, thinking what an odd sensation it was to claim a child as one's own.

She eyed his uniform suspiciously. "Does the child sleep with you?"

"Yes. We are of the same clan." He glanced down at Teska, who looked back at him with her expressive eyes.

"Excellent! You take the compartment on the left. That will leave me one compartment in case somebody else shows up." The proprietress bowed respectfully to Mother Fergolin. "I am sorry to have delayed you, but we are honored by your presence. Do the arrangements I have made meet with your approval?"

"They might," said the numerologist, "if a hot meal is included."

"Normally, that is extra, but due to the rank of our esteemed guest, why not? Let me collect your coin, and then I will get myself to the kitchen."

The guests dutifully paid in advance, and Spock noted that he had two triangular coins left after paying for himself and Teska. He didn't really see the need to make small talk with his fellow travelers, but his options were limited, unless he wanted to retire early to a cot on the other side of a flimsy thatched wall. In fact, he was quite hungry, having eaten nothing since earlier that day at the inquest.

For the next two hours, people sat on the wooden benches and conversed, checked their accommodations, or strolled in the night air, listening to the insects. Teska was anxious to talk, and she regaled the Rigelians with descriptions of Earth and San Francisco, which she assured them was much like their great cities before the plague of a thousand years ago. Normally, Spock would have discouraged such a talkative reaction, but he was relieved that everything the girl said was pure Teska. For the time being, Denker's influence over her mind seemed to have faded with the tranquillity of the rural lodge.

The conversation drifted to the subject of the kites hanging on the walls. Spock was able to contribute some data on the aerodynamics of kites, and he correctly predicted which kite was the best flyer, as corroborated by the proprietress. Finally she served them bread and steaming bowls of hearty stew, and Spock suppressed the reflex to ask exactly what was in the dish, but it was vegetarian, so he nodded to Teska that it was acceptable to eat.

After dinner, conversation dwindled, and the old proprietress bid them good night. The sequential order in which the compartments were arranged made it simpler for Spock and Teska to remain in the outer room until the others had retired, although this wasn't soon enough for Teska, who fell asleep on one of the wooden benches.

Spock picked her up and carried her to her cot behind the thatched wall. He could hear snoring from the middle compartments, which were occupied by Mother Fergolin and the pallbearers. He looked at his own cot directly beside Teska's and decided that perhaps a full night's sleep would be advisable.

While taking off his jacket, Spock encountered his collection of Rigelian souvenirs. He took out the diagnostic device, thinking that it might be interesting to compare the tiny instrument to a Starfleet medical tricorder. He would present the device to Dr. McCoy for that purpose.

Next he took out the miniature book on numerology, *The Doctrine of Lollo,* thinking that it was hardly worth the effort to carry such a thing around. Spock started to set the book in the corner in order to leave it for the next guest, who would surely appreciate it more than him, when some of the arcane wisdom in the volume came unbidden to his mind. Prescribed numbers for planting, mating, gambling—even the prescribed number of people for an assassination party.

Spock frowned and opened the book. Despite the numerous thin pages, his fingers went directly to the page he wanted. There it was in clear ink and paper: *The ideal combination for an assassination party is three women and two men.*

He gazed in the direction of some hushed voices at the back of the lodge, but he could see nothing in the darkness but the screens separating him and Teska from the other guests. The three women and two men of the Truth Clan were strangers to both Mother Fergolin and the prefect, so there was no one around to vouch for their identities. Still, thought Spock, it had to be a coincidence that the Truth Clan had followed them to this rural outpost, only to find their journey interrupted by nightfall. As Spock himself was traveling in a party of five, he could hardly consider five to be an unusual number.

But it was the exact number from the book, in the prescribed ratio of men to women.

Spock realized that he would not get a restful night's sleep. At the very least, he would have to stay alert as Teska slept. But that was a defensive posture, one that wouldn't bring him much tactical advantage in case of an actual attack. How could he, unarmed, repel five assassins? With his Vulcan strength, perhaps he could handle five humans if they attacked with knives and crude weapons. In pure strength, however, Rigelians were the match of Vulcans, and they would be well armed if they were working for Madame Vitra.

Spock rubbed his eyes, wondering if he was letting his imagination get the better of him. With a hearty meal in his stomach and the tranquil humming of insects all around him, it was difficult to believe that he and Teska were in grave danger. Yet he couldn't underestimate Vitra and her fear of what Teska would do with Denker's knowledge. The ex-prostitute had much to protect: her manufacturing facilities, her position in the Rigelian assembly, and, most importantly, the trade agreement. She was determined to conclude that agreement no matter what means she had to use.

Spock looked at Teska, who was sleeping peacefully, as he considered his alternatives. Running for it was an option, but until the solar transporters started operating again, they would be limited to travel by foot in unfamiliar country. He and Teska could not outrun five young adults. He needed a plan of action that was defensive in nature but would afford him a tactical advantage if necessary.

He looked around their sparse surroundings. Behind him was a wall that separated their chamber from the outside. In an emergency he felt that he could break through the bamboolike material, but that would not be a quick escape. To his right was a screen that separated him from the sleeping pall-bearers, and to his left was the exit into the outer room. There was a screen across from him, and it hid the compartment that was kept empty in case another traveler happened along.

Perhaps it was time to fill that compartment.

Gently he picked Teska up and slipped through the curtain into the empty compartment. The girl was sleeping so soundly that he could transfer her to another cot without disturbing her slumber. As quietly as possible, he went into the outer room, which was barely illuminated by a single tiny light, and picked up one of the wooden benches. His actions made a scraping noise, and he could hear the conversation abruptly stop in the rear of the lodge.

Spock froze, holding the bench in the air. Perhaps they wouldn't attack until they were certain everyone was asleep; in which case, a little noise would delay them. As he continued his preparations, the Vulcan consoled himself with a human proverb often quoted by his mother: *An ounce of prevention is worth a pound of cure.*

He carried the bench back into their original compartment and laid it on his cot. Then he covered it with a blanket to make it look like a sleeping figure. Spock fetched a second smaller bench and laid it upon Teska's old cot, also dressing it to look like a sleeping figure.

Satisfied with his preparations, Spock slipped into the supposedly vacant compartment and crouched in the darkness, waiting and listening.

Only the self-discipline of a Vulcan and the eclectic songs of the insects kept him awake those long hours. Spock heard various sounds throughout the night as the guests shifted on their rickety cots or exchanged mumbled words. When Spock saw the first rays of dawn through the slits in the outer wall, he decided that he had wasted a perfectly good night's sleep over the Rigelians' numerology. Then he heard the first suspicious sound of the entire night.

It was a modulated electronic burst that lasted no more than a second—and it could have been an insect at that. He remained perfectly still, wondering if he would hear it again; and he did, a moment later. The third time he heard the sound, he was certain that he recognized it.

Phaser fire!

As quietly as possible, Spock rose on stiff joints to his full height. Five armed assassins were creeping through the lodge, he warned himself, and they were so intent upon killing him and Teska that they had followed the numerical rules to the letter. Armed with phasers, they could vaporize the bodies and leave no trace.

Spock's immediate reaction was to wake the girl and tell her to run. But she couldn't outrun a phaser or five determined adults. If he didn't subdue the assassins here and now, there would be no chance of escape.

With many hours to acclimate his eyes to the darkness, Spock could see two shadows slip through a curtain and pass on the other side of the screen into the compartment where he and Teska were supposed to be sleeping. He also heard running footsteps behind him, outside, which meant that someone was headed to the prefect's bungalow, probably to stun the old woman. As it was already dawn, the transporter would be operating soon, and the others would wake up to find all of them gone. Spock steeled himself for the violence he would have to commit.

He stepped quietly through the curtain, hoping the slight rustle of beads would be interpreted as noise from their comrades. As he hoped, the two assassins were facing the cots in which two Vulcans were apparently asleep. One of them shot a phaser burst into Spock's bunk, giving him just the light he needed to make out the silhouette of the man's head.

Spock stepped forward and gripped him on the neck with the Vulcan nerve pinch. As the man slumped to the ground, his companion spun around with her weapon, but Spock gripped her wrist with all his strength, causing her to gasp and drop the weapon. Then he pinched her neck, and she crumbled to the floor, unconscious.

He dropped to his stomach as a phaser blast screeched through the dark, scorching a hole in the wall and setting it aflame. Spock scrambled on the floor, trying to find one of his enemy's dropped phasers.

"Teska!" he shouted, waking the child. "Drop to the floor!"

A phaser blast turned the unconscious Rigelian beside him into a smoldering fireball, but the additional light revealed the gleam of a phaser under the man's leg. Spock grabbed it, rolled onto his back, and fired in the direction of the shots. His blue beam raked across an assassin's face and dropped her to the ground. Spock hoped the setting was on stun, but there was no time to change it now.

"Pele-ut-la!" wailed Teska.

"Keep down!" shouted Spock, hoping his voice would draw fire away from the girl. He jumped to his feet and leaped through the burning hole in the wall. He hit the floor as a phaser beam sliced through the door, cutting a beam in two. A piece of flaming thatch dropped from the ceiling onto his leg, and

Spock kicked it off. The remaining two assailants had to be outside, thought the Vulcan.

Alarmed by the flames and the phaser blasts, Teska bolted from the back and ran out the front door. Spock had no choice but to stagger to his feet and follow her out. A protective blanket of fog swirled around the child, as two phaser beams crisscrossed over her head, causing an explosion that lit up the clearing like a nova. In the blinding light, the fog sizzled away like so much burning meat.

Shielding his eyes, Spock could barely see Teska as she stumbled along the uneven terrain. A phaser beam ripped up a chunk of ground at her feet, and she sprinted for cover. He dropped to a crouch and squeezed off a burst that knocked the fourth assailant off his feet, but the fifth one whirled and fired in his direction. The narrow beam tore into Spock's shoulder, spinning him around and causing him to hurl his weapon into the darkness. His right arm hung like an anchor from his useless shoulder, and he barely had time to groan before another beam slashed across his wrist and back.

Losing control of his body, the Vulcan pitched forward to the ground, and he was unconscious before he hit it.

Chapter Ten

TESKA KNEW INSTINCTIVELY that they weren't firing at her any longer, and she skidded to a stop. She turned to see Spock get hit by a phaser beam and spun around, his weapon flying through the air and landing a few meters away from her. She stared in horror as a second beam slashed across his back, and his slender body shuddered and plummeted to the ground.

The girl drew a sharp breath and seized control of her emotions. If she didn't, she would be dead, too. When the assassin knelt down for a moment to check on her fallen comrade, Teska lunged for the phaser on the ground. The woman looked up at the same instant that Teska's tiny fingers found the trigger mechanism. Their eyes locked, and there was more fear in the Rigelian's eyes than in the young Vulcan's.

Teska drilled the woman in the chest with the blue beam, and she slumped on top of her fallen comrade.

The seven-year-old ran to Spock, fighting back the emotions. The Starfleet officer was crisscrossed with burns. Calmly she reached for his wrist and saw that his communicator device had been fried into a lumpy bracelet, which had probably kept his hand from being severed. Her slender fingers encircled his wrist and, to her surprise, found a weak pulse. Despite his wounds, he was still alive!

Teska suppressed her initial excitement with the thought that they were still surrounded by enemies. With her phaser leveled in front of her, she moved warily toward the woman she had shot, who was slumped over a man that her uncle must have shot. They had no phaser burns on them and were breathing easily, so the girl reached the conclusion that her phaser was set on stun. She looked at the deadly instrument and thought about how everyone that she and Spock had shot would be waking up in an unknown length of time. Whatever she was going to do, she had to act fast!

She reluctantly came to the logical conclusion that she could simply *kill* all the assassins now while they lay unconscious. But Teska had been brought up to consider life as precious, and to kill defenseless people was beyond her capabilities. That certainly wouldn't keep her from stealing their weapons, though, and she shoved two more phasers into her bulging black clothing.

She heard a snapping sound, and she looked up to see the lodge burning fitfully and falling apart. Sparks shot upward into the night sky and looked like meteorites streaking in the wrong direction. She worried for Mother Fergolin and her friends, but maybe the numerologist was only stunned and would wake up any second. So might the assassins. Teska knew she had to do two things—escape and get Spock some help. Everything else was secondary. If he died without transferring his *katra,* it would be an incalculable loss.

Instinctively she touched the locket hanging around her neck and thought of the Heart Clan. They were the only ones she could trust. In the wavering light of the burning lodge, she opened the double hearts, looked at the engraving, and memorized it: *Heart Clan, Hermitage Township, Tanglewood Briar. Welcome!*

How could she move her uncle? The answer came at once, and she looked up at the flames and saw their reflection glimmering off the side of Denker's black coffin. Braving the heat, she ran to the coffin and tried to drag it away from the burning lodge, but it was too heavy. The girl crouched down behind the coffin and opened the small panel on the side; she tried to remember all the times she had seen the pallbearers activate the antigravity system.

As the intense heat singed her eyebrows, Teska entered what she hoped were the correct commands, and she shut the panel to activate them. The casket suddenly bolted upright and levitated a meter off the ground.

This wasn't exactly what Teska wanted, but it was

enough to maneuver the coffin away from the fire and closer to Spock. She pushed the casket like a butcher maneuvering a huge side of beef on an overhead track.

When Teska reached her uncle's fallen and scorched body, she began to experiment with the settings on the coffin, while stealing glances over her shoulder at the stunned Rigelians. The girl quickly figured out how to rotate the coffin to either the prone or upright position, and how to adjust the height of the levitation. She set the case upright, hovering a few centimeters off the ground, then punched buttons, trying to get the lid to open. This was something the pallbearers had never had to do, so she wasn't sure if it was even possible.

She heard a groan behind her, and she turned to see the man struggling under the woman's body, trying to push it off. Their eyes met, and both of them reacted swiftly, going for their weapons. Only Teska had a weapon, and he didn't—so she bathed his head with a blue phaser beam and sent him back to the void of unconsciousness.

Desperately the girl punched and pulled on the casket until she finally managed to spring the latch. The lid creaked open, centimeter by centimeter. Teska took a deep breath and tried to ignore Vulcan teachings against desecrating the dead. As far as she was concerned, the good of the living outweighed the good of the dead.

She threw the coffin lid open, only to reveal the ashen corpse of Ambassador Denker, resplendent in white with a black sash around his neck where his throat had been hacked open. With clammy hands, she reached up for his body, grabbed his trousers, and yanked him out. The girl jumped back as the stiff body tumbled from the coffin and hit the ground with a crunch.

There was no time to bemoan Denker's undeserved fate as she entered more commands on the side panel and brought the open coffin back to the prone position. Mustering all the Vulcan strength at her disposal, Teska pushed, pulled, and prodded Spock's body into the open coffin, and slammed the lid shut. She slumped against the black box, panting, and tried not to think that all her desperate action might be in vain. She had to try to save him, as he had saved her.

Teska felt warmth on her face, and it wasn't the fire—it was the sun. A layer of flame seemed to be rising over the flat horizon in the distance, and she knew that the transporters would be running soon. The girl set the coffin to hover half a meter off the ground, then she pushed it away from the visitors' lodge, which was still crackling with flames. If she could have helped Mother Fergolin and the others, she would have, but there was nothing to be done for them now.

As flames consumed the thatched building and sunlight flooded the fields, a small figure in black crept away, pushing a coffin in front of her.

Without incident and without seeing anyone else, Teska reached the solar transporter marked *East*. From the sunlight glinting off the solar panels and the amber lights aglow in the alcove, she assumed that the transporter must be working. The girl stole one last glance over her shoulder and could see a wisp of gray smoke in the distance. She put that out of her mind as she rotated the coffin into an upright position.

Because she had no one to help her on the other end, Teska pushed the upright coffin onto the transporter platform and stepped on with it. She gripped the black case like a drowning man grips a log, wondering if both she and the casket would be able to transport at once. Within seconds, the familiar tingle began to pulse along her spine, and the scene before her eyes shifted from wide-open fields to a more wooded terrain.

She steered the upright casket off the transporter pad and checked all of the available markings, looking for some sign of Hermitage Township or Tanglewood Briar. When she saw a sign that read *Flagstone,* she pushed the casket back onto the transporter and kept going—through Atwater, Gathering, Patio, Yellow Springs, and other stops she scarcely remembered.

Twice she passed fellow travelers who looked at her askance and kept on moving, as if it would be extremely bad luck to talk to a little girl transporting a coffin by herself. These encounters made her nervous, because she expected another assassination squad to be on her trail, materializing right behind her on the transporter pad.

Every two or three stops, she opened the casket to let in fresh air and check Spock's pulse. It was weak, but she consoled herself with the knowledge that

Vulcans did not die easily—they could reduce their rate of metabolism and brain activity to sustain life longer than most humanoids.

By midmorning, Teska was beginning to doubt whether she would ever reach the home of the Heart Clan, and her arms and shoulders throbbed with dull pain from pushing the casket, despite the anti-grav feature. But she dutifully heaved the coffin onto another transporter pad and made another jump.

When the scene in front of her eyes transformed into thickly wooded terrain with bleached ruins scattered among the trees, her heart began to beat with excitement. This stop reminded her of Ancient Grace, and she wondered if a township with the name of Hermitage might also denote a place of past glory, one of Rigel V's crumbling cities overgrown with trees.

With renewed energy, she maneuvered the casket off the transporter and searched for a sign. Then she saw the battered sign atop the alcove, reading *Hermitage*.

A quick search revealed no other signs, and no way of knowing how to get to her next destination, Tanglewood Briar. Remembering how spread out Rigelian communities could be, she decided to take the closest footpath and keep searching for other paths—one of them had to go there. She glanced over her shoulder at the solar transporter, relieved to finally be fleeing the rapid transit system. Death could materialize too quickly from that device.

Teska steered the black casket down a shadowy trail with green-barked trees towering all around her. Their willowy branches swayed in the morning breeze, and she could hear the chattering of insects and small animals in the dense foliage. Even though it was close to midday, it felt like night inside the forest, and the occasional ruins looked like the mausoleums she had seen in a San Francisco cemetery. She stopped twice to give Spock air and make sure he was still alive.

After traveling some distance, Teska came to a fork in the road. There was a low wooden signpost stuck in the ground, and she had to scrape off the mud to read it. Upon seeing the words *Tanglewood Briar* on the left arrow, she jumped to her feet and pushed the hovering casket down the rutted trail.

There was no sign of civilization until she came across a rather large cluster of ruins with a colorful awning stretched across the top of them. Under the awning stood a table covered with homemade crafts, jewelry, and other accessories, and behind the table sat a wizened old woman, apparently asleep. Despite the urgency of her mission, Teska took a few steps toward the table to peruse the beautiful baubles.

The old woman suddenly stirred and bolted awake, staring at the girl, and said, "Hello!"

Teska sunk back protectively toward the coffin, and the woman's eyes widened in horror. "The child and the dead!" she shrieked, grabbing her goods and shoveling them into a box.

The child shook her head vehemently. "No, he is *not* dead! He needs help from the Heart Clan." As if to clarify her statement, she gripped her locket and held it out to the woman.

The vendor raised a suspicious eyebrow. "You say there is a *live* person in that coffin?"

"Yes, yes! You must help him!" Teska fought the temptation to reveal Spock's name. "He is a friend of the Heart Clan. Do you know Hanua?"

The woman snorted. "Of course I know Hanua. Show me that he is alive."

Teska ran to the coffin and lowered it to the ground. Then she opened the lid. The old woman looked suspiciously at the burned and crumpled form, then she fumbled in her purse for a tiny vial. She opened it and waved it under Spock's nose, and the wounded Vulcan shuddered and began to cough weakly. The Vulcan grimaced in pain before lapsing back into unconsciousness.

"Yes, yes, hurry!" said the old woman, pointing down the trail. "The lodge is near! I will alert them. He needs air—leave the cover open."

Teska nodded and levitated the coffin again. She pushed it as fast as she could down the trail, straining her slender back and pumping her short legs. The girl had only gone a short distance when she heard a booming sound that shook the forest—an air horn. This brought shrieking from animals in the trees and shouts from somewhere ahead of her, but she tried to ignore them all and concentrate on her mission.

As she rounded a bend in the trail, she could see a pack of dark-clothed Rigelians charging toward her, probably thinking that the old vendor was under attack. To her immense relief, Hanua and other members of the Heart Clan were in the lead.

"Hanua!" she called, stumbling to the ground. With her last measure of strength, Teska rose and pushed the casket a few more meters.

Then a wave of black clothes surrounded her, and arms lifted her up and held her weary body. She saw Hanua bend over the coffin and peer inside, distress spreading across her kindly features. "Quick," she said, "the infirmary."

Several Rigelians took over Teska's duties and pushed the coffin away. The middle-aged man she remembered as Rassero held her tightly. "The child looks exhausted," he said.

"Bring her, too," ordered Hanua as she strode after the others.

Spock floated somewhere between a dark shimmering pool at his feet and a golden light overhead. The light looked like the Vulcan sun. He stretched his arms and reached for the sun, and the movement brought him closer; but he still felt a drag, like low-level gravity, pulling him toward the pool beneath. He could see the pool's soothing, concentric circles blossoming ever outward, and he had a strange notion that he had been here before, suspended in this netherworld between two extremes. He didn't remember having had a choice back then.

Now both choices were equally inviting, but a strange homesickness pulled him to the light, because it was so much like the barren reddish world of his youth. He vaguely remembered that he had to go there for some reason—some very important reason. So he clawed upward, like a man caught in a Jefferies tube on a starship with no gravity. He had no idea why he was so weak, his movements so ineffectual, or his thoughts so muddled—but he knew that he had to reach the sun before falling into

165

the pool. He had fallen into the pool once before, and it had covered him, drowned him in forgetfulness. Now he had a desire to remember.

As he drew nearer, the world above him opened into a panorama of dramatic plateaus, wispy spires, and jagged mountains, all bathed in the golden light. On a cliff, he saw the spare figure of High Priestess T'Lar, resplendent in red and yellow robes, beckoning him forward. He feared her stern expression and her disapproving eyes, because he was not supposed to be here—floating between the planes.

"You belong to this world," said her imperious voice, if only in his mind. "Do not slip backward. Come forward."

He tried to swim toward her, stretching out his hands, but the drag was ever present, and his feet seemed to hover constantly above the dark pool. Finally there were other voices, almost a chorus, and they, too, beckoned him to rise up to the light. He was reluctant to leave the peaceful pool, because it was familiar, but he couldn't shake the nagging certainty that he had a mission to accomplish. T'Lar confirmed it with a nod of her plumed headdress.

"Come home," she said.

Spock had no idea why he should believe a dream, but he did. His feet finally pulled away from the attraction of the pool, and he felt his entire body breaking free. But it was not a pleasant feeling, as itchy sensations surged along his body, reaching places he couldn't touch. When he tried to scratch them, the prickling turned to stabs of pain, bringing a gasp from his dry lips.

Spock's thoughts became terribly clear, and he could see his shoulder and leg being ripped by a phaser beam—then his mind went blank. He could feel and smell the scorching of his own flesh, and he could taste the metallic dirt in his mouth. At the moment, however, Spock had the sensation of floating—not in an airy place but in a place that was dark and salty. It felt as if he was in a coffin, sinking into the ocean, and a croak erupted from his swollen throat.

"Healer," came a calm voice. "He awakens."

Spock blinked his crust-covered eyes, trying to focus on the dim light of his surroundings. He realized with astonishment that he was no longer in a dream—that every prickle on his skin and every blurry face was real.

He seemed to be floating in a tank, immersed in a yellowish brine with wires attached to his extremities and a buoyant device holding his head above the liquid. Instruments beeped all around him, but those sounds were soon drowned out by voices, as more curious faces swirled before his eyes, chattering like a chorus gone mad. He closed his eyes, trying to block them out, but their hands and instruments probed his aching body.

Then he heard a voice, more soothing than the others and closer to his ear. "Captain Spock," came the voice, "this is Hanua of the Heart Clan. You are on Rigel V, in our commune, and you've been wounded. You were protecting your niece, Teska."

Spock groaned as he opened his eyes and stared into the hazy face in front of him. He tried to say something, but only pathetic grunts came from his raw throat. His arms and legs bobbed uselessly in the yellow brine.

"There is no need to talk or move," said Hanua. "Teska has told us what happened. She brought you here over a considerable distance. You are in our infirmary, and you are safe. The cerebral shock from the phaser was our biggest concern, but you responded well to treatment. Immersion therapy is working nicely on your burns, but I suspect you'll walk with a limp and a cane for a while."

Another face loomed in front of the kindly face, and they exchanged whispers. "You must rest now," said Hanua in no uncertain terms. "I will send for Teska."

Her kindly face moved away from his restricted field of view, and more black-garbed people swirled around the tank in which he floated. One of them adjusted the tubes poking into his wrist, and he could feel a rush of well-being and forgetfulness.

Then he slipped back into unconsciousness.

On the bridge of the *Enterprise*, Captain Kirk's face was set in a deep scowl as he surveyed the scattered debris of a planet destroyed before the dawn of history. Now it floated in the guise of a billion asteroids, ranging from fist-sized to moon-sized, spread in a ring across a hundred millions kilometers of space. If you wanted to play hide-and-seek, the Duperre Asteroid Belt was a good place to hide, but it was a lousy place to find somebody.

Kirk slammed his fist on the arm of his command

chair. "They *must* be here. These are the coordinates —they're *supposed* to be here."

"Aye, that they are," answered Scotty from the science station, "but that doesn't mean they're here."

"Keptin," said Chekov at the helm, "short-range scanners reveal nothing werry large—no scout ship—but I am picking up a reading. It may be a probe or a signal beacon."

Kirk glanced back at the communications station, where Uhura had taken over. He missed seeing all those fresh young faces on the bridge, but when things got touchy, he wanted his old crew at hand.

"I'm blocking out interference and searching for signals," said Uhura, pressing her headset tightly to her ear. Unlike most comm officers, who would have to run a detailed analysis through the computer, she could often identify a gizmo in space from its audio signal alone. Intermingled with those billions of asteroids, it wasn't going to be easy to find a ship, let alone a probe.

"Yes," said Uhura slowly, "there is a beacon of some sort, and it's putting out a modulated pulse. Until we get more data, I can't tell exactly what it is, but it's not Starfleet design."

"Is there a crew?" asked the captain.

Scotty shook his head. "Not by the looks of it, but there's a lot of interference. We need more data."

"How can we get more data?" grumbled Kirk.

The engineer frowned as though he didn't want to deliver bad news. "She's floating along about fifty thousand kilometers in, too far for a tractor beam or a transporter. I wouldna try either one with all those blasted rocks, and we can't get any closer in the *Enterprise*."

"So we have to fly a shuttlecraft into an asteroid belt," muttered Kirk.

"I wolunteer, Keptin," said Chekov with a game smile.

Kirk smiled appreciatively. "Thank you, Commander, I accept, but I can't let you have all the fun. I'll meet you in the shuttlebay in ten minutes, after you arrange for relief." Kirk sighed and then continued. "And I thought this betrothal was going to be an easy assignment."

The captain rose from his command chair. "Mr. Scott, you have the bridge. Get us readings on the speed and headings of all the large asteroids in our path."

When Spock opened his eyes again, he successfully fought down the confusion which had gripped him the first time. He was still floating in warm salty liquid, and it was even darker inside the infirmary, obviously night. He was weak and helpless, but alive.

Unlike the first time he had regained consciousness, Spock could now piece together what had happened to him. He had survived an attack and phaser burns, and Teska had somehow brought him to the Heart Clan in time. Despite their penchant for primitive living, the Rigelians were renowned for their medical techniques, and he was the fortunate beneficiary.

There were, however, some realities he had to

accept: for the immediate future, he would be considerably dependent upon the Rigelians, specifically the Heart Clan. Plus the assassins had not been stopped—they had only been thwarted temporarily. They would return. Despite his infirm condition, he would have to remain on constant vigil.

With that thought in mind, Spock surveyed his surroundings and found that he was the only patient in a drab room with mustard-colored walls and a ceiling of roughly finished plaster. From the corner of his eye, he saw a small black-clad figure sleeping on a wooden bench a few meters away.

He croaked her name: "Teska."

At once, the girl sat up and rushed to his side. A grin began to spread across her face before she realized what she was doing. She quickly replaced the happy expression with a somber look of concern, but she couldn't hide the pleasure in her voice.

"Pele-ut-la, you are recovered, almost! They have worked around the clock to care for you. You are out of danger."

"Am I?" rasped Spock, thinking of Madame Vitra, Mondral, and traveling parties of three women and two men.

The girl shook her head. "We have seen nothing of the assassins. There was a fire, and they may think we are dead. But do not concern yourself with that, Uncle, just get better."

"I am trying," he answered hoarsely. With considerable effort, Spock lifted his arm—the one he thought he would never use again. He actually raised his fingers above the yellowish brine in which his injured body floated. Teska immediately reached over the side of the tank and gripped his slippery fingers with her tiny ones.

"Any sign of the *Enterprise?*" he asked.

She shook her head. "No. But I am not sure they could find us, because your wrist communicator was destroyed by phaser fire. We would have to go back to Ancient Grace, and it will be some time before you can travel."

"Your *koon-ut-la—*"

She patted his hand as if their roles were reversed and she were the adult and he was the child. "I am alive, and you are alive—that is all that matters. There will be other boys."

Spock nodded. He supposed there would be other boys, although they would not be Romulans willing to begin the momentous journey that would result in reunification between two long-separated races.

As if sensing his disappointment, Teska squeezed his hand and said brightly, "The commune is a wonderful place. It is much more than just a lodge— they have this infirmary, and a school for the children, and a guild where they make very interesting crafts. I am learning to make jewelry and woven belts—Hanua says I am very good at it. They have a harmonious life here, Uncle."

"Do not grow too attached," he warned her.

Teska pulled her hand away from his, and he could tell that his warning was too late. "Hanua wanted me to tell them when you woke up, so they could transfer you to a bed. I will see you later, Uncle."

"Teska," he said hoarsely.

"Yes?" She was again an impassive Vulcan.

"How—how did you bring me here?"

"I stunned the assassin who shot you and took the phasers, three in all. Then I put you in Denker's coffin."

"Very inventive. You saved my life."

"We are family," said Teska. "I have learned that nothing is more important than that." With those words, the young Vulcan strode out the door.

Spock shifted, his back creaking with pain. He tried to relax, but it was difficult. It was, evidently, going to be a long recovery.

Chapter Eleven

A PANORAMA OF brown and black rocks filled the cockpit window of the shuttlecraft *Vespucci,* flowing in every direction as far as the eye, or short-range sensors, could see. The vast herd of boulders was moving slowly, or so it appeared, but Kirk knew that a single false move within this obstacle course would be disastrous, especially out of range of the *Enterprise*'s transporters.

"Keptin," said Chekov, seated in the pilot's seat, "we have downloaded the coordinates of the beacon, and the speed of the surrounding asteroids. To cut across the asteroids would be suicide. My suggestion is that we match their speed as closely as possible and work slowly toward the beacon. That is the only safe way to intercept it."

Kirk nodded. "Enter upstream and drift down to

the beacon. I approve your plan, as long as I don't have to watch."

Chekov smiled. "You can check the grappling hook, sir. Considering the speed of the asteroids and the distance we have to go, I will enter ten thousand kilometers upstream."

"Good luck," said Kirk, leaving the co-pilot's seat to go to the back of the tiny craft. He sure wished the shuttlecraft had a transporter on it—maybe someday they would, but not now—so they had chosen the *Vespucci* for this mission because she had a grappling hook and a small cargo bay. Kirk would be responsible for snatching the beacon with the grapple.

He felt a slight jolt as they changed course and decreased speed. He wondered if he should hurry to his seat and strap himself in. No, he finally decided, if they struck an asteroid, he'd be just as dead strapped to his seat as he would be floating around in the wreckage. Kirk might only have one chance with the hook, and he had better be certain there were no problems.

First he checked the control panel to make sure the outer hatch was closed and all readings were normal. Then he opened the inner hatch that gave him access to the grappling mechanism, which appeared deceptively fragile. Kirk climbed inside the small cargo bay and inspected the robotic clamps, servos, circuitry, cameras, and other crucial components, while trying not to look over his shoulder to see their shuttle floating insanely close to giant chunks of rock.

He could feel and hear small bursts of energy as Chekov fired thrusters to adjust their speed and cruise along beside the behemoths. Kirk went back to his inspection—the precision bearings looked clean. Suddenly several thuds hit the hull in swift succession, and Kirk felt as though he were inside a kettle drum with a two-year-old beating on it.

"What's that?"

"A few small meteorites," said Chekov, "about the size of grapefruit. I can't avoid *all* of them."

"Of course not," said Kirk. "I just hope you're right when you pick which ones to hit."

The shuttlecraft shifted dramatically, tossing Kirk onto his rear end, and he looked up to see a huge meteorite go drifting by the window at distressingly close range.

"A few are going in the wrong direction," explained Chekov.

"Right," muttered Kirk, thinking that *he* was going in the wrong direction. This was a job for a twenty-five-year-old ensign to command, not a busted admiral who should be collecting a pension. He was tempted to tell Chekov to turn back, but that would be even more dangerous than just floating along with the vast herd of asteroids.

Whenever there was a break in the flow of boulders, Chekov kept bearing to starboard, getting them closer to the beacon.

Kirk climbed out of the cargo bay, closed the hatch, and ran a diagnostic on the entire grappling system. Another staccato burst of small asteroids pounded the hull, and he tried to ignore them. Why, he wondered, was he risking his neck like this? Was there something inherent in his makeup that made him act like a damned idiot all the time?

The captain returned to the co-pilot's seat and looked at the dazzling array of asteroids fanning across the blackness of space. It looked like some giant's rock collection. "What's our distance?" he asked.

"Closing to a thousand kilometers." Chekov made another maneuver to starboard and passed another pack of asteroids.

"Let me see what I can pick up from the signal." Kirk sat in the co-pilot's seat tuned to the frequency pinpointed by Uhura, but there was nothing but the same monotonous pulse. It was probably some kind of low-level warning, like an SOS, but he hardly needed an alien beacon to tell him this place was dangerous.

Kirk did a life-form scan and discovered that the beacon, as expected, had no crew. A more detailed scan was possible at this range, and it picked up some markings on the beacon, which the computer promptly identified.

"It's Romulan," said Kirk with a trace of a relief in his voice. "They must have really been here at one time, but they had to vacate." As more tiny asteroids thudded against the hull, he couldn't blame anyone for not sticking around here indefinitely.

"Closing to two hundred kilometers," announced Chekov.

"I'll ready the grapple." Kirk brought up the screen for the grappling mechanism, complete with a small window for the video input from the camera. The video was blank at the moment, because he hadn't yet opened the outer hatch.

Chekov swerved the shuttlecraft around a floating mountain and had to decelerate to match a phalanx of large asteroids directly in front of them. Finally he found an opening in the line of boulders and slipped through, closing the gap with the beacon. Kirk enlarged the video from the nose of the shuttle-craft and got his first look at the object of their chase—the alien beacon. It was a tubelike device about a meter and a half long with a stalk of antennas at one end.

"In critical approach," said Chekov, "decelerating."

Kirk watched their speed and distance carefully, not wanting to open the outer hatch until the last moment, so as not to risk the grapple getting hit by tiny asteroids. What the hull could easily withstand would smash the delicate robot to bits, and he was only going to do this once.

At two hundred meters, he opened the outer hatch and activated the grapple. Now Kirk had grapple-view video, in addition to a constant array of other readings. The Romulans had done them one small favor, at least, by leaving the beacon in an area that was relatively clear of debris. Chekov dropped their speed again, and they were floating just a few centimeters per minute faster than the mysterious beacon. And they were closing in. Kirk transferred manual control of the grapple to his fingertip panels, ready to override the computer if it failed to snag the beacon on the first pass.

Chekov looked as though he wanted to say something, but there wasn't much he could say. With Kirk in command, they were going to grab this beacon one way or another.

On his console, Kirk watched the video zoom in and out as the computer made minute adjustments to the robotic arms. The clamps were aimed directly at the tubelike device, but Kirk couldn't see any place on the smooth surface for the clamps to grab ahold. So he decided that they would have to go for the antenna array, even if it meant breaking them off. He took manual control, his eyes riveted on the video output.

"Keptin," said Chekov, noting his actions, "twelve seconds to impact. Ten, nine, eight—"

As his pilot counted down, Kirk lifted the robotic claws and imagined that the stalk of antennas were actually a Romulan's throat, principally the one who had dragged them all the way out here for nothing. Even before Chekov reached "two," Kirk pushed the claws forward and grabbed the Romulan beacon by its top-knot of tiny dishes. A few of them snapped off and floated away, but it was a clean grab otherwise.

"Got it!"

"Yes, sir," answered Chekov with a sigh of relief. "I am slowing to match the speed of surrounding asteroids—we can coast for a while. Is there room to bring it in?"

"I think so." At his console, Kirk issued the commands to withdraw the grapple and its captured prey, and he nodded with satisfaction when all of it snapped into place inside the cargo bay. He closed the outer hatch and said, "Let's take a look."

While the shuttlecraft drifted through the Duperre Asteroid Belt like just another piece of space junk, Kirk and Chekov made their way to the back of the vessel and opened the rear hatch. Kirk jumped into the hold, grabbed the meter-long beacon, and ripped it away from the robotic claws. He felt no sorrow that the beacon would never be used again to lure fools into this dangerous place.

"It's Romulan, all right," said the Russian, studying the engravings along a center band. "Do you want to try to get it open?"

"Make sure it's not booby-trapped first."

Chekov fetched a tricorder from the locker and spent a good minute scanning the device. "There are no explosive dewices—only a small energy source. It is safe."

"Let's rip it open." Kirk grabbed an ultrasonic tork wrench from the locker and attacked the band around the middle. After removing four screws, he gripped the top of the beacon and lifted it up for Chekov to grab the bottom. "You turn counterclockwise," he ordered.

With the two of them straining in opposite directions, the device popped open, and a sheet of neon-pink paper fluttered out of the inner circuitry and landed at Kirk's feet. From the garish graphics printed on the sheet, it appeared to be an advertisement for some sort of recreational lounge.

With a frown, Kirk picked up the sheet and studied it. There was a message scrawled on the back, so he turned the page over and read it aloud: "Dear *Enterprise,* thank you for coming. If you want to see the boy, Hasmek, alive again, leave an unmanned shuttlecraft near these coordinates and proceed to the Tarquolese System. Come to the Bayool Cafe on the third moon of the third planet. If you have done as instructed, the boy and his companion will be safe and waiting."

Kirk's jaw hung open as he stared at Chekov. "It's a *ransom* note!"

"I've heard of that place," said Chekov. "It's run by Orions."

Captain Kirk stuck the sheet into his jacket and rubbed his aching temples. "The next time somebody invites me to a wedding, I'm declining."

Spock sat in a wicker chair on the porch of the lodge, feeling the warmth of the sun on his heavily bandaged skin. The joyous sound of children playing filled the air, and he watched their exuberant game of tag as it flowed from one end of the compound to the other. He cringed slightly to see Teska laughing and shrieking with the others, but her training and *koon-ut-la* were now hopelessly delayed. She might as well enjoy her childish pleasures for a few more days, because there was nothing he could do about the *koon-ut-la* until the *Enterprise* returned.

Like the Rigelians, Spock now wore black clothing over his bandages, and a casual passerby would never know that two Vulcans had taken up residence with the Heart Clan. Nor would a passerby know

181

that the man sitting in the chair had been near death forty-eight hours earlier.

Spock was still far from robust, but he could walk with his wooden crutch, and the skin grafts were healing at an accelerated pace. He wished Dr. McCoy could spend some time in the Heart Clan's infirmary—not only would he improve his medical knowledge but also his bedside manner. It would have been impossible to receive finer and more compassionate care than he had received from the Heart Clan's healer, Korinna, and her volunteer staff. He was making remarkable improvements every hour, and he could feel the strength returning to his limbs.

Then why did he have such an illogical sense of unease?

Part of the reason had to do with a middle-aged man who was repairing the door on the craft building across the commons. Hemopar obviously felt Spock's scrutiny, because he kept peering over his shoulder at the patient. They had not spoken since Spock had confronted Hemopar for lying on the witness stand. As no one else from the Heart Clan had attended the inquest, Spock doubted if any of them knew that they harbored a liar in their midst.

He decided that it was vital to know Hemopar's intentions. In particular, was the man more loyal to Hanua and the Heart Clan or to Madame Vitra? Spock felt as if he had regained enough strength to confront Hemopar again, and there was no sense procrastinating over it. His and Teska's lives depended upon the trustworthiness of the Heart Clan, and he didn't trust this man.

When Hemopar looked up from his work again, he not only found Spock staring at him, but also waving. The Rigelian looked around furtively, as if he were hoping that Spock was waving at somebody else, but there could be no doubt. With shoulders slumped, Hemopar put down his hammer and walked slowly across the clearing, looking like a condemned man going to the gallows.

His head was bowed as he approached Spock, and he avoided looking him in the eyes. Before Spock could speak, two other members of the clan walked out the entrance of the lodge and nodded politely to Spock and Hemopar, and the Vulcan realized that the porch was not the place to have a private conversation.

"Would you help me walk to the latrine?" he asked Hemopar.

The man nodded, biting his lower lip. He went to Spock's side and lifted him gently out of his chair. Although Hemopar was slight, he possessed the same wiry strength common to most Vulcans and Rigelians.

It took them a while to shuffle around to the side of the lodge, as it was a substantial longhouse built of brick and mortar, almost eighty meters long. The building easily housed the twenty-nine members of the Heart Clan in whatever sleeping arrangements they wished, and it could have housed double that number.

"This is far enough," said Spock, edging toward a tree stump.

Hemopar lowered him onto the stump. "You don't really have to go to the latrine, do you?"

"No, but I must speak with you."

The Rigelian nodded with resignation. "I am prepared to leave the clan. After you tell them what I did, it will be expected."

"I have not told them," replied Spock, "and I have no intention of doing so."

Hemopar blinked at him in amazement. "I may be directly responsible for your wounds."

"That is not entirely accurate, but you are directly responsible for a murderer evading punishment. Why did you lie on the witness stand?"

"I *had* to." Hemopar looked around sheepishly to see if anyone had heard him. But it was the middle of the day, and the adults of the clan were occupied. The children were still charging through the compound, but they showed little interest in the conversation of two middle-aged men.

Hemopar twisted his hands with agitation. "We are desperate for that trade agreement, and Denker was trying to destroy it."

"Correction," said Spock. "Ambassador Denker was merely trying to make sure that the agreement wasn't signed under false pretenses. He did not want to falsify the report to the Federation."

Hemopar laughed derisively and motioned to the lush forest, which surrounded and protected the buildings of the commune like a nest protects its eggs. "Look around you. We are secondary to nature, and all Rigelians know that. It rose up and cut us down, and now we accept it as our superior. We have no quarries, mines, power plants, or pollution—but we have no economy either. We have a few industrialists like Madame Vitra, but most of us are poor."

"That is why you sell your children into marriage," remarked Spock.

Hemopar stared at him and swallowed. "You know about that?"

"It is obvious," said Spock. "Given your group marriages and your natural multiplicative proclivities, your communes must produce more children than they can support. On the *Enterprise,* Hanua mentioned that your clan had recently split, and she seemed remorseful about it. I see no children here between the ages of twelve and fifteen. I must assume that children marrying adults is a way of life on Rigel V."

Hemopar looked down at the ground. "It's a way to prevent inbreeding, and we consider it unnatural to go without sex. The purpose is always to form new clans of younger people with older—"

"And the older people 'buy' the younger ones," said Spock, completing his thought. "When you lied for Madame Vitra, you were protecting both her primary business and a secret that you all share. The visitors' lodges—"

"Yes, yes," muttered Hemopar, pacing nervously. "And what are you going to do about it?"

Spock looked up. "I am in no position to do anything. However, if you do not end those practices, which are patently illegal under Federation law, you will not get your trade agreement. Perhaps Rigel V will even be expelled from the Federation."

"But if we had the trade agreement, we could begin to change those practices!"

"You must admit to them first," said Spock, "before you can begin to change them."

Hemopar sat dejectedly on the ground. "You're right—as long as we're hiding it, we'll never change it. I made a mistake at the inquest when I lied for Madame Vitra, but I was confused. We had just come back from Earth, and it seemed so hopeless! I thought I was protecting our future."

"Of more immediate concern to me," said Spock, "is whether you will betray us again to Madame Vitra."

"No, no!" answered Hemopar, shaking his head vehemently. "I'm done with her. I swear to you, Captain Spock, I won't do anything to bring you harm."

"I have heard you lie before," said Spock matter-of-factly.

The Rigelian rose to his feet and looked earnestly at the Vulcan. "By the primary number, you've heard me lie for the last time, Captain Spock. I am in your debt twice—for lying against the girl, and for your kindness in not telling the others. A debt of two requires extraordinary service, and you will get it from me."

"I will settle for advice," said Spock. "You know Vitra—will she come after us?"

Hemopar's lips thinned. "Yes, she will. Perhaps not right away, because she had to appear before the Assembly after our trip to Earth. But sooner or later, she will get a full report about the fire, and she will know that you are still alive. She will think of the Heart Clan."

"Then we must leave," said Spock, "we are endangering all of you by remaining here."

"We don't look at it that way," said Hemopar. "We are honored by your presence. We wish you and Teska would stay—marry into our clan."

Spock raised an eyebrow. "That is a generous sentiment, but I must decline."

"Our loss," said Hemopar with a bow.

Hanua came charging around the corner of the lodge, a look of concern on her face, and Spock realized that she was searching for him. "One thing, Hemopar—"

"Anything."

"Bring me my belongings," whispered Spock, "especially the phasers."

The Rigelian nodded as Hanua and Teska charged into their midst. "Captain Spock, you are not supposed to be wandering around. You're supposed to be sitting still."

"I am sitting still," said Spock, glancing at his tree stump. "Just not in the place you left me."

"You are supposed to be where Hanua leaves you," countered Teska, crossing her arms. Then she glared at Hemopar. "And you are supposed to be fixing that door."

"Yes," he nodded, hurrying off. "I will remember our conversation, Captain Spock!"

Spock nodded appreciatively. "As will I."

With Hanua gripping his arm protectively, Spock barely had to walk as she maneuvered him into the lodge. She steered them past the outer lounge and through the curtains into the corridor that separated the sleeping compartments. In this sturdy lodge, the compartments were actual rooms with walls and windows. The room he had been sleeping in was midway down the corridor on the left, and Hanua steered him into it.

"Lie on the bed," she ordered, "on your side with your wounded arm up." Spock did as ordered.

Hanua shut the curtains behind him and turned to Spock with a no-nonsense look on her face. "You need to begin your rehabilitation. Korrina has left it to me, with certain guidelines."

Spock nodded appreciatively. "You have been very helpful."

"Just doing my job," she said, kneeling by his bed. Hanua unloosened his black robe and pulled it gently off his wounded shoulder and weakened arm. She checked his shoulder, and gently worked his arm back and forth. As she did, she brushed very close to his face and chest, and Spock could smell a fresh flowery scent on her skin and hair. He began to pull away.

"Relax, Captain Spock," she said with a calming smile. "We believe that the *entire* body must be exercised for optimum health. Furthermore, our studies show that sexually active persons are happier and recover more quickly from injuries. This is part of your therapy."

"I think not," said Spock, pulling his robe back over his shoulder.

Her smile became bittersweet. "Isn't it possible

for you to enjoy *anything* without analyzing it to death? Can't you accept the fact that we are here to give comfort and love to each other, not to live alone and withhold our love. You know I want you to stay with us, but I accept the fact that your marriage is to your shipmates. However, you must accept the fact that you are an empty man, denying yourself more than you deny others."

With that summation, the slim woman turned on her heel and marched out of his sleeping compartment.

Spock let out his breath and rolled onto his back. He gazed at the rough swirls in the plaster on the ceiling, thinking that Hanua had not told him anything he didn't already know. With rare exceptions, he had never been able to truly give of himself, even in the limited ways that were allowed to Vulcans. He had always stood apart, uncompromising, unyielding. In the final analysis, only his long-term friendship with Jim Kirk and his loyalty to his shipmates had demonstrated selflessness on his part. It wasn't much by Rigelian standards, but Spock took comfort in the fact that he had good friends.

A human saying came to mind: *A man is judged by the friends he keeps.*

His human friends. With all their emotional displays, they were practically Vulcans compared to the Heart Clan. No, despite their good intentions, the Rigelians were too erratic and unpredictable to give him the foundation of logic he needed in his life. It would be more logical to devote himself to Teska, who needed him more than anyone. Perhaps Teska had come into his life at this moment to give him the focal point he needed.

All of that was conjecture, but one thing was certain—he and Teska could not stay with the Heart Clan any longer than was absolutely necessary. As soon as he was capable of travel, they had to leave.

Chapter Twelve

CAPTAIN KIRK PACED the bridge of the *Enterprise,* glancing at his assembled brain trust: Uhura, Scotty, Chekov, and Dr. McCoy. It was either look at them or look at that blasted field of asteroids in the viewscreen, which only reminded him that he was getting shaken down for a ransom.

"Ambassador Sarek has authorized us to give up a shuttlecraft," he muttered, shaking his head at the injustice of it. "We have to erase all Starfleet records and codes from its computer but leave it operational. In fact, we are to follow the instructions in the ransom note to the letter, as long as no one is put in danger."

Kirk slammed his fist into his palm. "I still hate to give up a shuttlecraft, even our smallest one. I've decided that it's not enough to erase the computer banks—I want to hear suggestions on how we can *sabotage* the shuttlecraft, so they'll be stuck in the middle of nowhere. I want them to wish they had never *seen* that shuttlecraft!"

Scotty shrugged. "We could rig a plasma device to the impulse engines."

"No, nothing that would blow it up," said Kirk. "With luck, maybe we can retrieve the craft after it's been disabled. I'm sure they'll do a scan of everything before they try to fly it, so I don't think any kind of obvious booby-trap would work."

"How about a computer virus," suggested Uhura. "It could gradually take over the shuttlecraft's computer, then shut it down."

"I thought of that, too," answered Kirk with a sigh. "The trouble is, we've only got a few minutes, not enough time to write a virus program. If we delay, the kidnappers, who are probably hiding out in the asteroid belt, will know that we're up to something. If I'm asking for too much and should just forget it, let me know."

McCoy chuckled and scratched his chin.

"Yes, Bones?" said Kirk testily. "Feel free to jump in anytime."

The doctor rocked on his heels and grinned. "Maybe we need a *biological* booby-trap. It just so happens I have some embryos."

"Embryos?" asked Chekov doubtfully.

The doctor nodded. "I ordered them for a recent study I was working on. They reproduce awfully fast, and you never know when you might need some tribbles."

"Tribbles?" asked Kirk, horrified. "Bones, you've been keeping *tribbles* on this ship?"

"Just a couple of embryos," said McCoy. "As long as they were kept in stasis, they weren't going to do anything. Anyway, it would take two minutes to hide a few embryos and a little grain for food. If the kidnappers come to get the shuttlecraft quickly, a life-form scan will show up negative. But you know what that craft will be like in forty-eight hours— complete chaos."

Kirk nodded with satisfaction. "Do it, Bones. Scotty, you erase the computers, but leave them operational—we want them to get far away."

"Aye, sir," said the engineer with a chuckle.

"I can pilot the shuttlecraft into the asteroid belt from here," said Chekov, tapping his console. "And leave it drifting."

"All right, I want to depart in half an hour." Captain Kirk reached into his tunic, pulled out the pink handbill he had taken from the Romulan beacon, and unfolded it. He turned it over and stuck his finger into the scrawled words. "We've got a date at the Bayool Cafe, Tarquolese System, third moon of the third planet."

Spock sat on his stump at the side of the lodge, watching the late afternoon shadows march from the base of the forest across the compound. The breeze had a bracing coolness to it that contrasted with the warmth of the bluish sunlight. His wooden crutch lay in his lap, and he was hobbling around with more proficiency all the time. Since Hanua had told him not to sit on the stump, he had turned it into his own private station in the commune. Everyone knew that when he was sitting on his stump, he was disobeying orders, so they mostly left him alone.

All except Teska, of course. The seven-year-old was striding purposefully toward him with a stern look on her face. More and more, she was acting as if *she* were the adult and he the child, and Spock was trying to be patient, considering the circumstances.

Teska stopped, put her hands on her hips, and looked crossly at him. "Hanua says you are refusing your treatments. Espera came to give you a massage this morning, and you turned her away!"

Spock cleared his throat. "Yes, I find the massage therapy fascinating, but I believe I am recovering well without it."

"You are not improved enough that you can ignore the healer's orders," insisted Teska.

Spock rose to his feet and towered over Teska. "I am considerably improved. In fact, I am capable of travel, and we will leave tomorrow at first light."

Teska's confident expression dissolved into wide-eyed shock. She stared at her uncle and shook her head in disbelief. "No, I do not want to go. I want to stay here!"

Spock cocked his eyebrow. "Impossible. You may be attracted to this lifestyle and these people, but you are not a Rigelian. You have a destiny ahead of you, and it is not here."

"I have got *your* destiny ahead of me," she countered. "These are *your* choices, not mine. If you really cared about me, Uncle, you would let me stay here, where I want to be!"

"I see," said Spock, collapsing back onto the stump. He was neither prepared nor strong enough to battle such total illogic, such a total breakdown of Vulcan identity. He tried to tell himself that the girl had been through a traumatic experience, and she might still be suffering from mind-meld identification with Denker. Or perhaps she had been unduly influenced by the Heart Clan, who could be persuasive. Whatever the cause of this rebellion, he had to stand firm.

"Teska," he said slowly, "you have forgotten who you are. Perhaps someday you can abandon your own race, but you are not old enough to make that decision. Also consider that our presence here is a danger to the commune—Vitra and Mondral could easily locate us. There is no logical basis for this discussion. We are leaving tomorrow to go back to Ancient Grace and, if possible, to fulfill your *koon-ut-la.*"

Teska's jaw set with determination, and Spock could see the thoughts churning behind her dark intelligent eyes. She didn't answer but merely tossed her head and walked away.

Spock let out a sigh. He had been thinking that telling Teska the news would be easy compared to telling Hanua, but now he had a certain amount of trepidation. Perhaps it would be better to tell the Rigelians in the morning, just before he and Teska left. If he told them now, they were liable to become very sentimental and melodramatic, and he didn't want any going-away parties.

The Vulcan heard some branches rustle, and he

turned to see a figure crouching in the brush at the edge of the clearing. He was about to call out in alarm, when the figure stood up and revealed himself to be Hemopar. The slim middle-aged Rigelian ran to Spock, carrying a cloth bag over his shoulder.

Hemopar crouched beside the Vulcan, looking around furtively. "I was about to come over to you when I saw your niece approach."

"Then you heard our conversation," said Spock.

"Yes, but I won't say anything. I agree with you— you should leave in the morning." Hemopar dropped the cloth bag in Spock's lap. "Here are your belongings, but I could only get *two* of the phaser weapons. Hanua holds the third one."

"Two is sufficient," said Spock.

"I'm making a cane for you, too," added Hemopar with a smile. "It's almost done."

"Thank you." Spock untied the string to open the cloth bag the Rigelian had given him. The two hand-held phasers were the most reassuring objects he found inside, although he was oddly relieved to have back his tiny numerology book, *The Doctrine of Lollo*. The two triangular coins would be useful if they had to spend the night in a visitors' lodge, but two other objects were of dubious use—his melted wrist communicator and the personal-health device given to him at the hospital in Ancient Grace.

"You may have this," he said, handing the health gauge to Hemopar.

The Rigelian looked at the device with curiosity and stuck it in his own purse. "Thank you, Captain Spock. There are two of you, two phasers, two coins—you are in balance."

Spock raised an eyebrow. "I am depending upon you to say nothing until after we have left."

"Don't worry about me," answered Hemopar. "I haven't really met that many gentlemen, Captain Spock, but you are indeed a gentleman. It's been a pleasure to serve you."

"Thank you," answered Spock. He was still concerned about Hemopar's loyalty, but he was not about to discourage the man's admiration. Hemopar backed away, smiling at Spock, apparently pleased to have been of assistance.

The Vulcan looked up at the twilight sky, which had deepened into a royal blue shot with streaks of crimson. Rigel V was physically beautiful, by anyone's definition, but that couldn't hide the ugliness under its surface. It also couldn't explain Teska's enormous attraction to the place, because she knew everything that Ambassador Denker had known. She knew the planet's dark side, yet it made no difference.

The seven-year-old was not herself, and he hoped it wasn't too late to undo the damage.

As the *Enterprise* rounded the sulfurous mustard-gray planet of Yquitra in the Tarquolese System, Chekov slowed to one-quarter impulse. Captain Kirk jumped off the captain's chair and began counting moons, each one larger than the one before it. The third moon in distance from Yquitra was the size of most planets, and from the haze around the sphere, it seemed to have a weak atmosphere. But there was no sign of life except for an artificial bubble on the polar ice cap.

"That's got to be it," said Kirk. "Is there air inside that dome?"

"Aye, Captain," said Scotty from the science station. "Heat, too. They built the town over thermal geysers, and I'm picking up several thousand life-forms."

"Can we transport through the dome?"

"That shouldna be a problem."

"Captain," said Uhura at the comm station, "I'm receiving various low-range frequencies—they seem to be advertisements."

Kirk strode toward her, waving the handbill. "Anything about the Bayool Cafe?"

She listened for a few moments, then suppressed a grin. "Yes, Captain—there is nightly entertainment."

Kirk shrugged and looked at Dr. McCoy. "I suppose you want to go down with me."

"Wouldn't miss it," replied the doctor with a smile. "But did somebody say this place was run by Orions?"

"That's what I heard," answered Chekov, "somewhere or other."

"We're beyond Federation space," said Kirk, "so let's be careful. Uhura, have two armed security officers meet us in the transporter room."

"Aye, sir. I'll send coordinates for the cafe to the transporter room."

"Scotty, you have the bridge, and be ready to beam us back at the first sign of trouble."

"Aye, sir."

Kirk started for the door. "All right, Doctor, it looks like you get some more shore leave. But I want to get in, get the boy, and get out. The last time we hung around for a drink, look what happened. We've followed that ridiculous ransom note to the letter, so there shouldn't be a problem."

"Famous last words," grumbled McCoy.

As they exited from the turbolift and strode down the corridor to the transporter room, they nearly ran into two hulking security officers coming from another direction. The officers snapped to attention and let the captain and the doctor pass.

"Be ready for anything," said Kirk. "Phasers set to stun."

"Yes, sir!" answered the officers, checking their weapons.

The four men strode purposefully into the transporter room, where Kyle stood at the transporter controls.

"Get us down and back quickly, if you would."

"Yes, sir!" he said confidently. "The coordinates are laid in, and I have orders to get you back at the first sign of trouble."

Kirk nodded as Bones climbed onto the transporter platform after him, followed by the security officers with drawn phasers. Kirk nodded and the crewman plied the controls and sent their molecules spinning through an artificial bubble on the third moon of the third planet of the Tarquolese System.

Knowing the pugnacious attitude of Orions, Kirk braced himself for action, but they transported into an empty courtyard surrounded by picturesque white buildings. Gurgling fountains and cheerful cobblestones decorated the plaza, and the meticulous buildings had a fairy-tale quality to them. No one was in sight, except for two old people with green skin shuffling slowly across the plaza.

Kirk and McCoy glanced quizzically at one another, then at the security men, one of whom motioned with his phaser toward a building. The captain followed his gaze and spotted a nondescript establishment with a tasteful sign in the window which read *Bayool Cafe*. It looked like a sidewalk cafe, with a handful of tables and chairs situated outside the door. No one was taking in the artificially strong sunlight, as magnified by the dome, and the cafe looked as deserted as the rest of the town.

"Put away your weapons," Kirk told his security officers, as he led the way toward the sedate cafe. McCoy strode along beside him, and he could tell from the doctor's expression that this was not at all what he expected.

Kirk strode to the door and opened it, causing a tiny bell to tinkle, and he stepped cautiously into a cafe that was cheerful and clean. There were alien antiques, artwork, and pottery decorating the walls, plus a number of sturdy tables and chairs; the smell of pastries baking and tea brewing filled the air. There were a half dozen patrons inside the Bayool Cafe, seated at different tables and apparently ignoring each other. All of the patrons had wrinkled green skin and stark white hair, and they paid little attention to the intruders.

"My God, Jim," whispered McCoy, "it's an old-folks' home."

"And a nice one at that. Too bad we don't qualify," said Kirk. "It looks like it's only for Orions."

The captain strolled across what appeared to be a

dance floor, and his movements tripped some sort of sensor—a curtain rose on a small stage to his right, and several handsome young Orions stood there, their healthy pallor and dark hair contrasting sharply with the wizened old people sitting in the audience.

"Welcome to the Bayool Cafe," said the bandleader with a wide smile. "Are there any requests? We can play anything." Kirk looked around to see if the bandleader was talking to him or somebody else.

McCoy stepped beside him, aiming his medical tricorder at the musical combo. "They're not real, Jim. They're animatronic robots. I bet they *can* play anything."

"All right," said the bandleader cheerfully. "How about 'The Bayool Stomp!'"

"No!" groaned one of the patrons, slumping into his cup of tea.

"Not that song!" a little boy shrieked. The little boy had dark hair and pointed ears.

"Hasmek?" asked Kirk.

The boy whirled around in shock and fell down. He stared at the humans, then screamed over the music, "Master Pardek! Master Pardek!"

A pair of swinging doors flew open, and a stout Romulan walked out, eating a sandwich. "What are you yelling about now?"

At the sight of the intruders, he stopped and stared. Then he ran up to Kirk. "You've come, Captain! Excellent!" He turned to the boy. "This is Captain Kirk—he's come to *rescue* us!"

The boy jumped off the stage, ran over, and bowed his head respectfully. "Thank you, Captain!"

"You're, uh, welcome," said Kirk. He looked at the robotic musicians, who were blithely sawing away at their instruments. "Let's go outside where we can talk."

Kirk led the way toward the door, but one of the old Orions stepped in front of him and grabbed his jacket with quivering hands. "Take me, too!" he begged. "Don't leave me here."

Kirk gently pried his hands off. "We're only taking these people today. I'm sure your family will be coming back for you."

The Orion spit on the floor. *"They* put me here! Why would they come back for me? *You* take me with you."

"I can't." Kirk tried to get around the old man, but he was very insistent, again grabbing his jacket. Even an aged Orion was strong compared to a human, and Kirk was nearly jerked off his feet.

An eager security officer drew his weapon. "Release him, sir, and step back!" he ordered.

While the robotic combo played sprightly music in the background, the Orion turned to the human and snarled, "Go ahead and *kill* me! You'd be doing me a favor!"

Suddenly another Orion jumped up, grabbed his chair, and smashed it over the security man's head. He collapsed to the ground, his weapon clattering across the dance floor.

Kirk shoved the Orion with all his might, but when the old man did nothing but stagger back a step, the captain knew he was in trouble. Kirk grabbed Pardek and the boy and pushed them out the door. "Let's get out of here!" he cried.

One of the Orions dove for the fallen phaser, and the other security man tackled him. As they wrestled on the ground, an aged Orion woman jumped on McCoy and tried to bite the doctor's ear. "Ouch, damn!" he yelped. He reached behind and tried to lift the woman away from his back.

"Hold still!" Kirk managed to pry the woman off just as another Orion grabbed him, punched him in the face, and sent him sprawling across a table.

To the happy strains of "The Bayool Stomp," the barroom brawl proceeded in full swing for several exhausting moments. Finally Kirk managed to send his attacker flying and buy himself enough time to draw his own phaser. After checking to make sure it was set to stun, he picked off the rampaging Orions one by one, until they lay still on the dance floor.

The band played on, and the bandleader crowed, "That's great dancing!"

Panting with exhaustion, McCoy stared at Kirk. "Whatever happened to shuffleboard?"

"Come on," said Kirk. He and McCoy picked up the injured officers and dragged them out into the courtyard, where Hasmek and Pardek were dutifully waiting.

Kirk gave the older Romulan a suspicious look. "When we have a moment, I'd like to hear about how you wound up in this place."

"Our pilot and the crew of the scout ship were treacherous," said Pardek. "They demanded more money for the risks they were taking, and I couldn't pay. So they said they would collect from the Federation. Did you give them a shuttlecraft?"

"Yes, and a few extra goodies." Kirk wiped a

trickle of blood from the corner of his mouth. "I hope you won't mind that we've had some delays at our end, too. But as soon as I drop you two off at Vulcan, we'll get everything squared away."

He tapped his wrist communicator. "Kirk to *Enterprise*—six to beam up."

Teska lay awake in her bed until the sounds of talking died down throughout the entire lodge. She knew she wasn't the only one awake, as she had been exchanging hand signals with her friend, Falona, on the other side of the room all night long. By now, they had to be the only two people awake in the entire compound.

The young Vulcan climbed out of bed and waved once more to her accomplice, then she pulled a sack of clothing, food, and tools out from under her bed.

Falona crept over to her and whispered, "Shall I go get it?"

"Yes." While her friend slipped away to Hanua's compartment, which she shared with Espera, Rassero, and others, Teska made sure that she had enough food and a complete change of black clothing. She made no effort to take the Vulcan clothing she had worn on her arrival on Rigel V, as Denker's bloodstains were still visible on it. Let Spock keep it.

Falona returned, making less noise than the breeze in the shutters, and she slipped something cold and hard into Teska's hand. The girl looked at the phaser and squeezed her friend's arm. They touched foreheads together, which was their special sign of friendship, then Teska grabbed her bag and ~~turned~~ toward the door.

They were extra quiet slipping past Spock's compartment, but Teska knew that her uncle was sleeping soundly these nights, as his weakened body hoarded strength for healing. Within a few seconds, they stood in the starlight at the edge of the forest, where they were able to converse freely.

"Where will you go? What will you do?" asked Falona excitedly.

Teska checked to make sure that her phaser was safely tucked away under her clothing. "The first thing I will do is hide until my uncle leaves Rigel V. He may stay an extra few days because I am missing, but he will eventually have to go with the *Enterprise*. Once he is gone, I can come back and live with the Heart Clan. It would be more logical to marry *you* than some boy I don't even know."

The young Rigelian squealed with excitement. "How will you know when he's gone?"

Teska grinned. *"You* will tell me, by flying your red kite. I can see that kite from a great distance, and when you fly it I will know he is gone."

"Great!" Falona clapped her hands, then she looked thoughtful. "But what else will you do? Just hide?"

"No," said Teska gravely, "I will eliminate the threat of Madame Vitra and Mondral, if I can."

Falona nodded somberly. "They deserve to die."

"Do not reveal where I've gone." Teska mussed her own hair so that she would look more like a Rigelian.

"Never," promised Falona. "They may torture me, or sell me—I'll never tell."

They touched foreheads one more time, and Teska

pulled a thin flashlight from her bag. She turned it on and waded into the dense forest, which swallowed her bobbing light in a matter of seconds.

For most of the night, Teska stuck to the woods, moving slowly, searching out every vine or fallen log with her light before she had a chance to stumble over it. She heard rustling in the ferns and trees, which she tried to ignore. Sometimes she followed the noises with her light, but she was never fast enough to see anything but quivering leaves.

Teska had heard of boarlike creatures in the forest that might attack when cornered, but large predators were mainly confined to wilderness areas. The adults in the clan often admonished the children not to roam the forest at night; as there were few places to go, this wasn't a difficult rule to obey. Teska fought down her fear by clasping the phaser under her clothing.

When she was certain that she wasn't being followed by anyone, Teska skirted toward the main path leading to the eastbound transporter. It was the only transporter she knew about, although she wasn't entirely certain if traveling east was in her best interests.

If escape was her primary concern, then traveling east might be wise, as she could exit at any point to elude her pursuers. However, if vengeance was her primary mission, then she should travel west—and wait by an eastbound transporter to intercept Vitra and Mondral. If Spock was correct, then sooner or later they would be coming for the Vulcans, and they wouldn't be expecting an ambush. If Teska had learned one thing living among humans on Earth, it was that a good defense was a good offense.

The girl had time to consider her options as she strolled along the path in the starlight. Despite the ruts in the dirt footpath, she extinguished her flashlight so as not to give herself away. She didn't think that Rigelians traveled much by night, but they were an unpredictable lot.

They were almost childlike in their naiveté and lack of initiative, thought the Vulcan. In some respects, they needed people like Madame Vitra, if her more unscrupulous tendencies could be curbed.

Once again the Rigelians found themselves at a fork in the road, Teska thought as she passed the ruins where the commune ran a gift shop. If these people wanted to reach out to the Federation, they had to become more like the Federation, while remaining independent and distinct, as the Vulcans had done. Most importantly, the Rigelians had to accept common ethics.

She would show them the way, thought Teska. They *needed* her, much more than Vulcans needed her. Rigel V would be her workshop, as Starfleet had been Spock's workshop. Why couldn't he see how important this place was to her? He had also deserted his homeworld, and that decision had turned out to be beneficial to both worlds, as her decision would be.

It was her youth, thought Teska, but she had already been exposed to three different cultures in her short lifetime, so she wasn't a typical seven-year-old. She could recognize the healthy as well as the destructive tendencies in each culture and act accordingly.

While Teska was thinking to herself, a hulking figure jumped out of the trees and wrapped his arms around her. Teska fought the impulse to scream, and she bit him, gnawing into an old glove instead of skin. The man ripped his hand out of her mouth and squeezed her tightly, forcing the air out of her lungs.

"This one's feisty," he growled with a laugh.

"She's a little small," muttered an accomplice, who was no more than a shadow in the forest.

"She'll fetch something though," said her attacker. Before Teska could get her breath, he wrapped a rope around her arms, pinning them tightly to her side.

"Put her with the others," said the man in the woods. "We have our number."

The man jerked Teska off her feet, tucked her under his arm, and carried her off like a rolled-up rug. Before she could even cry out, he slapped his gloved hand over her mouth. "You'll shut up, unless you want trouble."

Teska shut up, but she couldn't stop herself from shivering.

Chapter Thirteen

SPOCK BOLTED UPRIGHT in bed and sat perfectly still, fighting the prickling sensations that ran along his newly healed skin. *Something* had awoken him, but he wasn't sure what it was—a noise outside, someone stirring in bed, or perhaps his own troubled thoughts. He listened, but there were no unusual sounds in the quiet lodge or the commune, and Spock concluded that his treatments had made his nerves as prickly as his skin.

He gazed out the window at a sky that was so black and sprinkled with stars that it reminded him of space, his true home. Despite the obvious dangers of space, it was a closed environment; people couldn't walk across kilometers of forest to kill a person, as they could here. By the wisps of fog on the ground and the coolness of the air, Spock judged it to be fairly close to morning. He might as well stay awake, Spock decided, because the sooner he and Teska were packed and gone, the better.

The Vulcan had decided that once they got back to the City of Ancient Grace, he would demand transportation off Rigel V. Without a working comm device, there was no reason for them to stay on the planet and make Captain Kirk's job even harder. For all Spock knew, the captain might have already returned to the planet and could be looking for them now. He wondered why no one had made the logical decision to seek them at the Heart Clan.

With a grimace, Spock stood and stretched his aching limbs, especially his right leg, which remained the most tender. He could feel his strength returning with every passing day, but that didn't negate the fact that he would be slowed on the trail. He hoped that Teska would not cause trouble on the journey—at some point, she had to return to the rule of reason.

He dressed in his uniform, ignoring the pain when he maneuvered his right arm through the sleeve of his jacket. Spock gathered up his bag of belongings and put one of the phasers in his belt, but he decided to put aside the crutch in favor of the sturdy cane Hemopar had given him. As an afterthought, Spock threw his black clothing into his bag; he hated traveling incognito, but there was always the possibility that he and Teska would need to blend into the general populace.

Satisfied that he had everything he needed, Spock stepped out into the corridor and hobbled on his cane to the rear of the lodge, where the female children slept dormitory-style. He went to Teska's bed, thinking that she must be buried deep in her covers, but when he rummaged through the blankets, he found no one. Teska was gone!

A bed squeaked in another part of the room, and Spock whirled around to find the remaining girls lying quietly, apparently asleep. He supposed that Teska might have gone outside to use the latrine, but he had been awake for several minutes and had heard no one leave. He quickly reached the conclusion that Teska had run away rather than leave with him in the morning.

In the unlikely event she was still nearby, Spock limped out the front door and stood in the coolness of the early morning, watching wisps of fog swirl around the tree trunks. He heard no footsteps and found no sign of Teska. He fought the temptation to call her name, knowing that she wouldn't respond. In Teska's mind, running away was logical, and she would be aggressive about it. She was gone, and finding her would not be easy, especially for him in his current condition.

Spock limped back into the lodge and found the compartment that Hanua shared with three others. He found her bed and gently shook her shoulder.

Without even opening her eyes, Hanua draped an arm around his neck and tried to pull him closer for a kiss. When he resisted, she opened her eyes and stared at him for a moment before a drowsy smile spread across her face.

"I was hoping you'd come," she whispered.

"I have not come for that," he answered, trying to keep his voice low. "I was going to leave."

"To leave?" Hanua sat up and noticed his uniform for the first time. "Well, at least you had the decency to say goodbye."

"Do you know where Teska is?"

She frowned. "Isn't she in her bed?"

"No."

Hanua stood, her naked body silhouetted briefly in the starlight before she pulled on her black tunic and pants. "Come on," she whispered, grabbing his elbow and helping him into the corridor.

After Hanua made sure with her own eyes that Teska was gone, she dragged Falona out of bed and took her outside, where she could raise her voice. Spock had never seen the woman so angry.

"Where's Teska?" she demanded of Falona.

The girl looked down. "I don't know."

Hanua grabbed her by the peak of her ear and twisted hard. "Where is she?"

"Ow!" yelped Falona. "I don't know where! Only where she could be—"

"Where could she be?" asked Spock.

"Hiding. I don't know where."

Hanua let go of the girl's ear, but she continued to glare at the child. "How long ago did she leave?"

"Hours ago, after everyone fell asleep," said Falona, rubbing her ear.

"I've told you these woods are not safe at night!" snapped Hanua.

"*I* didn't go into them!" replied Falona with impeccable logic. "Can I go back to bed now?"

"No." Hanua crossed her arms. "What did Teska take with her? You might as well tell me, because I'll find out sooner or later."

The girl looked down and kicked the dirt with her bare toe. "Just some clothes and stuff."

"What stuff?" pressed Hanua.

"A flashlight, some cooking utensils, and—"

"And what?"

"One of those phaser things."

Hanua glared at the girl, and Spock interjected, "I have two of the phasers, so it must have been the one you were keeping. What is so dangerous in the woods at night?"

The Rigelian woman still looked cross, but she motioned to Falona. "Go back to bed. I'll deal with you in the morning." The girl ran off before she could change her mind.

"I am surprised by your strong reaction," said Spock. "What is there to fear in the woods at night?"

Hanua frowned. "I doubt if there's anything to fear, but there are people who . . . who sometimes take children. Usually runaways, children who don't have a proper clan."

Spock leaned on his cane. "For the purpose of marrying them to adults?"

"Yes," said Hanua, rubbing her eyes. "So what happened? You told her you were going to leave, and she did this."

"We must find her," said Spock.

Hanua laughed derisively and waved at the vast expanse of darkened forest. "Be my guest. In the morning, maybe we can follow her trail, but not now. Do you have any idea where she would go?"

"None. Perhaps we should question Falona more closely."

"Oh, we will," agreed Hanua, "but maybe Teska wasn't headed to a specific place. She doesn't know this area and our customs."

The woman sighed. "At first light, we'll form a search party, and we'll send out word to the surrounding clans. If she's hiding, I hope she found a good place."

Shaking her head, Hanua strode back into the lodge, leaving Spock standing alone in the early Rigelian morning. He surveyed the circle of dark trees all around him, hearing and seeing nothing unusual. After a moment he limped around to the side of the lodge in what he knew was a futile effort.

Spock finally sat on his tree stump and assessed the situation. In trying to protect the girl, he had placed her in danger. Because she was running from him, he couldn't help her even if he were healthy. He had alienated himself from Teska and failed to judge how deeply she had been affected by her experiences on Rigel V. He had lost her in more ways than one.

The brutish Rigelian finally set Teska on the ground, but he tied her hands together with rope and led her like a pack animal. She expected to be taken to one of the solar transporters, so she was surprised when her captors hacked their way through the forest with their long knives, making their own path to some unknown destination. From their grunted conversation, she deduced that the men had hidden themselves on the path hoping for this exact occurrence—a child wandering by, unaware of the danger. They talked about reimbursing her clan, so in their minds they had done nothing wrong in seizing her.

Teska debated whether to tell them who she really was—whether doing so would gain her freedom or more trouble. From the surly demeanor of the big man who had grabbed her, she finally decided that not speaking was the best course of action. Only then could she avoid saying the wrong thing.

Thus far, they hadn't searched her and found her phaser, so Teska kept pushing it deeper into her clothing. Apparently they didn't expect a poor rural child to have such an exotic device, or anything of value. If they found it, she would be forced to reveal her identity as an off-worlder. Luckily, Teska was slight, and her clothes were too big, so there was no indication that she was armed. If she got her hands free, she could use the weapon, but she knew she would have to be aggressive—in all likelihood, she would only get one opportunity to stun her captors, and she would have to make the most of it.

As dawn crept into the forest, they reached a clearing where ten other boys and girls sat in a semicircle, eating hot cereal out of bowls. To Teska's surprise, all of them were older than her, and none of them were roped and tied as she was. But there were three other adults present—two women and one man—who were clearly guarding the youths to prevent escape. Like the other two, these adults carried long branch-hacking knives on their belts.

One of the captured boys looked up and smiled at Teska. "I'm glad you're here," he said, "now we can get going."

"Is that so?" answered Teska, trying not to sound like a Vulcan. "But I am hungry."

She held out her bound hands and looked plaintively at the men who had captured her. If they allowed her to eat, it might give her the opportunity she needed to stun them and escape. But she wondered about the likelihood of picking off all six of the adults, and perhaps the children as well. There had to be a few of them who didn't mind being dragged off to another life, away from their rural clans, and they might try to stop her, too.

The Rigelian looked doubtfully at her and touched the hilt of his knife. "You won't give us any trouble will you."

"No," she lied.

He drew his knife and deftly cut her ropes. "All right, get yourself a bowl."

Teska did as she was told, and one of the women spooned some cereal into it from a silver pouch. "What's your name?" asked the woman.

Teska bit back her first response and said, "Lana of the Heart Clan."

"Not anymore," said one of the men with a smirk. "You just graduated."

"She's awfully young," said the woman doubtfully.

"That's what I told Pisko," muttered the other man, getting himself a bowl.

"Well," grumbled Pisko, "she's old enough to be wandering around by herself in the middle of the night."

He walked over to Teska and roughly gripped her

chin. "She's not homely, and there are some who like them young. Besides, now we've got eleven to take back. Mondral can decide what to do with her."

Teska blinked at the man, then looked down, trying not to reveal her interest in the subject of Mondral. She supposed that more than one person on Rigel V could have that name, but she had a suspicion that only one would be involved in kidnapping children to become mates for displaced city dwellers. Instinctively, she felt for her phaser to make sure that it was still hidden in the folds of her clothes. It was.

If going along with this scurvy band would bring her closer to Mondral and Madame Vitra, then she would do so. She would bide her time. They wouldn't expect death to come from a small kidnapped child.

Teska went swiftly to the circle of children and sat next to the boy who had spoken to her.

"You're not too young," he whispered to her. "Don't you want to get out of this stinking forest? Always clearing land, planting crops, making stupid crafts—I'm ready for the city!"

"I've been to the city," said Teska. Then she added, "With my clan."

"Which city?"

"Ancient Grace."

"Oh, that's not a big city," scoffed the boy. "A big city is like the capital, Nine Hills. I hope that's where we go."

"Me, too," said Teska with all sincerity. Nine Hills sounded like a good place to get revenge and then hide.

"I'm Tonopar," said the boy.

"Lana," answered the Vulcan. She wondered if this fate would someday befall her friend Falona and the other children of the Heart Clan.

After their simple breakfast, the children were forced to their feet to begin another trek through the forest. Once again, they avoided the regular paths and took obscure trails or made their own. Teska didn't have the slightest idea where they were among the vast towering trees, but the Rigelians never consulted a compass. As they plowed ahead, they seemed to have an uncanny sense of direction. If their telepathic abilities were impaired in some respects, they were acute in others.

The youths were allowed to talk in low voices as they tromped through the forest, and Teska listened to their similar histories. About half of them, including the boy Tonopar, were from the Dusk Clan, and the others had been secured from different rural clans. Only she had been kidnapped, and only because the slavers were in a hurry to get their prime combination—six girls and five boys—and be on their way home. None of the youths knew their destination, and the adults were close-mouthed and businesslike, reminding her of Vulcans.

By midday the terrain changed, and they found themselves trudging up and down marshy, muddy hills where there had been recent rains. They saw large animals at a distance, herd beasts, and Teska tried not to look too curious about them.

The ragtag band was climbing up a steep knoll and was fairly spread out when Teska realized that there was only one adult in the rear—one adult between her and freedom. She could stun him with the phaser and be gone before the others realized it. In all likelihood this would be her last chance to get away before walking into the lion's den.

She couldn't be sure how long her weapon would remain undiscovered, because at some point, she would have to change clothes or take a bath. If she had to take off her clothes, she would have to use the phaser then and there, no matter what the circumstances.

The Vulcan was about to make her move when a high-pitched sound split the air overhead. She looked up to see a large black shuttlecraft come streaking through the cerulean sky, headed toward the top of the knoll. The craft had no markings and looked like a repainted Federation personnel carrier. It vanished into a ring of clouds at the top of the peak, and the adults finally broke into smiles and cheers.

"Move it along," ordered Pisko behind her.

The moment of escape was past, and the mysterious shuttlecraft was interesting enough that Teska moved along as ordered. A shuttlecraft had to be valuable on Rigel V, maybe valuable enough to be piloted by Mondral himself.

The novelty of the craft had caused most of the young people to hurry to the top of the knoll, and they arrived in time to see the shuttlecraft drop into an extinct volcanic crater about fifty meters across, surrounded by a wall of lava rock about three meters high. It was like a natural landing pad and fortress at the same time, and Teska began to despair that she could escape from the crater even though she had a weapon.

The girl skidded down the sharp black gravel, clutching the phaser for safekeeping under her shirt. She fought down the crushing feeling that she had wasted her only chance of escape.

Suddenly, the idea of boarding that big black shuttlecraft sounded like suicide.

The port hatch of the craft lifted like a gull wing, and a muscular Rigelian dressed in black jumped out. It was Mondral! He waved impatiently to his confederates. "Come on, we're running late!"

Now Teska's heart began to hammer, and she gripped the phaser with both hands. But how could she stage an ambush on Mondral—he would recognize her on sight! Her only chance was to lower her head, sneak past him, and wait for another opportunity when she wasn't surrounded by armed cutthroats and walls of rock. Maybe she would have a better chance of escape after they reached their destination in the city.

As Teska had been lagging behind, several of the youths had boarded the craft ahead of her. Tonopar was almost at the hatch, and she ran to catch up with him. She didn't want to enter alone, because Mondral was checking his merchandise as it strolled past, looking pleased, displeased, or noncommittal.

Teska ran up, grabbed Tonopar's arm and giggled excitedly. She wanted to look and sound like a fun-loving Rigelian—anything but a Vulcan. The boy smiled at her, pleased that she was enjoying herself.

"I hope we go to the same clan," he said.

She gazed at Tonopar, which kept her face away from Mondral, and she giggled again as if he were telling her something funny. Suddenly a strong hand landed on her shoulder and dragged her backward, and Teska gripped her phaser, ready to use it. Unfortunately, she hadn't had an opportunity to change the setting to kill—it was still set on stun.

Mondral shook her by the scruff of the neck, but he wasn't looking at her—he was looking at Pisko and the others. "This one's too small," he complained. "Throw her back and catch her again in a couple of years."

He flung Teska to the ground, and the phaser tumbled out of her grasp and landed on the black gravel in plain sight. Mondral stared at it. "What have you got there?"

"Just my brush," she said, scrambling for the metallic object. She clutched it in her lap, trying to find the trigger with her thumb.

Now Mondral's gaze shifted to the girl, and he looked even more suspicious. "Do I know you?"

His eyes widened with the shock of recognition, and his hand went to his belt. Before he could grab his knife, Teska lifted the phaser and fired a blue streak into his abdomen, and Mondral toppled over with a groan. Teska jumped to her feet just as Pisko lunged for her, and she staggered backward, sprawling across Mondral's unconscious body.

As Pisko drew his knife, she hastily aimed the phaser and fired. But her aim was off, and she only nicked his arm, which wasn't enough to stun him.

He kept coming, along with the other adults, and Teska had no choice but to jump to her feet and run into the shuttlecraft.

Tonopar stood in the doorway looking shocked, and Teska shoved him into the craft, screaming, "Get out of my way!"

There were eight young people inside, and they just stared at the mad seven-year-old as she brandished a phaser and slapped buttons on the pilot's console until she found one that shut the outer hatch. A woman with a knife tried to slip through the descending door, and Teska drilled her in the chest with the phaser, knocking her backward. The hatch slammed shut with a resounding thud, and the adults began to beat on the hull and windows with their fists, shouting vile words at her.

"Hey," muttered Tonopar, "what are you doing?"

"Hijacking this ship," answered Teska.

With a scowl, a strapping young woman jumped to her feet and rushed Teska, who immediately shot her with the phaser. As her unconscious body crumpled to the deck, the others began to back away from the girl. Now she was relieved that her phaser was set on stun.

"Stay in your seats!" she ordered, having to shout over the adults who were pounding on the hull. "I am not a Rigelian, I am a Vulcan." As she was wielding an alien weapon and had just commandeered a shuttlecraft, nobody cared to contradict her.

"Can you *fly* this ship?" asked Tonopar with amazement.

"No," admitted Teska glumly. Then she realized

that *she* couldn't fly a shuttlecraft, but Spock could—and she had recently mind-melded with him. She still possessed his knowledge, if only she could concentrate and access the pertinent information.

"I lied," she said, slipping into the pilot's seat. "I *do* know how to fly it, but I must concentrate. If anybody bothers me, I will fly us straight into a mountain!"

The others were still dumbfounded by the sight of the woman lying unconscious on the deck and the furious adults swarming around the craft, banging on windows. Teska knew they would stop that noise once she powered up the thrusters, but she had to act quickly. The girl put the phaser in her lap and took a deep breath, then she closed her eyes and laid her tiny hands on the controls.

In her mind, she envisioned exactly what she wanted to do—start the thrusters, lift off, engage impulse engines, and fly a safe distance away where she could land and let the others off. Teska envisioned the flight pattern of the shuttlecraft as if it were already happening, and she opened her eyes to see that her fingers were plying the controls. The thrusters popped on.

To startled gasps from the children, the shuttle-craft lifted smoothly off the ground. Teska was now submerged, and an experienced Starfleet officer sat in her place, deftly flying the shuttlecraft as he had hundreds of times before, every movement sure and swift. The crater faded away beneath them as they roared over the hilly terrain.

"By all the numbers!" cried Tonopar. "You *can* fly it!"

"Obviously," replied the Vulcan with a cocked eyebrow.

A moment later the pilot checked her readouts and saw that they were already ten kilometers away from the crater, so she banked the craft into a tight circle and began to look for a clearing among the trees and hills. She spotted a herd of four-legged beasts watering in a broad valley, and she swerved toward them, sending them scattering in all directions. With no wasted movement or fuel, she dropped the shuttlecraft onto the mushy ground and killed the engines.

"Let me out!" shouted someone in the back.

Teska blinked and shook her head, snapping out of her trance. She looked down at her hands, which seemed to belong to someone else, then gazed at the unfamiliar terrain outside the window. She had flown the ship! They were somewhere else!

She had to think about which button to push to open the hatch, but she finally found it. As the hatch lifted, she picked up her phaser and waved it at her reluctant passengers. "All right, get out. Tonopar, help the stunned girl off."

She didn't have to tell them twice, as the young Rigelians piled out of the shuttlecraft and ran for their lives. Teska assumed they were running in the right direction and would eventually find their way back to the crater. Or maybe some of them would take this opportunity to return to their homes, having satisfied their thirst for adventure.

Tonopar helped the unconscious girl off the ship, and he looked back at Teska with awe. "That was great! Is there anything I can do to help you?"

"Go to the Heart Clan," she answered, "and tell them that I am all right."

"I'll never forget this," he said with a grin. "Good combinations to you!"

"Thank you."

For several moments Teska sat in the pilot's seat and studied the controls. What was she going to do with a giant black shuttlecraft? She could fly it, that was clear, but her weariness and disorientation warned her that doing so took a tremendous psychic toll. Besides, if she was trying to hide from people, a big black shuttlecraft was rather conspicuous. In addition, stealing was wrong, even from the likes of Mondral and Madame Vitra.

She would have to abandon the craft, and this was as good a place as any. With ten kilometers between her and the slavers, she had enough time to get away, but she didn't want them coming after her in the shuttlecraft. Stealing was wrong, but sabotage was defensible under the circumstances.

Teska rose from the pilot's chair and walked to the back of the craft. She checked her phaser and adjusted the setting from stun to disruption, then she aimed the weapon at the control panel and cut loose with a blue beam that melted instruments and sent smoke and sparks shooting into the air. Holding her nose, she dashed past the noxious fumes and into the clean air.

There were no signs of the other children, who

undoubtedly would not feel comfortable hanging around Teska. It was odd, but her experience with the slavers, followed by the ease with which she had flown the shuttlecraft, made her appreciate being a Vulcan. What other race was capable of such a thing? And like it or not, Spock was not only her family, but he lived inside her mind. She could run to the ends of the universe, and she would never escape him, or what they were. Vulcans.

Teska looked up at the azure sky with its mighty sun and golden wisps of clouds. Rigel V was a beautiful place, and she felt drawn to it, but it wasn't her home. In that instant, the girl knew that she had been rash to desert Spock for her own selfish purposes. He had nearly died risking his life to save her, and she had repaid him with treachery. Now she was at least twenty-five kilometers away from him, with Mondral and his thugs between them, and she didn't even know in which direction to travel.

Despite her training, a tear rolled down Teska's smooth cheek, and she wiped it away. With a determined look on her face, she picked a direction and began to walk.

Spock, Hanua, and Rassero stood on the path between the commune and the eastbound solar transporter, studying broken branches and fresh footprints in the dirt. Spock was no woodsman, but even he could see a clear trail of slashed branches and footprints leading off into the forest.

Rassero shook his head grimly. "There was definitely a struggle here. You can see where her footprints stopped and these other footprints stepped all over hers. I'd say they were waiting for her . . . for somebody. After they grabbed her, they headed off in that direction. Even though we tolerate these people, they know enough to stick to the back paths and forests when they travel. Nobody wants to see them and be reminded of what they're doing."

Hanua balled her hands into fists and shook with rage. "We've got to stop this foul custom! I'm terribly sorry, Captain Spock. We didn't warn either one of you as well as we should have."

But Spock was too busy examining the trampled foliage to acknowledge Hanua's comment. Finally, he turned his attention to Rassero. "Then in your opinion, she was seized by slavers and taken to one of your cities. There can be no other explanation?"

"None," answered Rassero. "That's what happened to her. We can follow their trail, but they have many hours' head start. I don't want to get your hopes up."

"I understand," said Spock, leaning on his cane. "However, she has a phaser—she may be able to defend herself."

Rassero put his fingers to his lips and whistled, and two more Rigelians who had been searching the woods came to his call. "Come on," he said, "let's follow their trail."

"Wait." The Vulcan took his extra phaser out of his pocket and handed it to Hanua. "It is set to stun. Use it if you must."

She nodded, and without any further discussion,

Hanua, Rassero, and the other two Rigelians waded into the dense vegetation.

Spock wanted to accompany them, but he was exhausted from walking a few kilometers on a level path with a cane. He tried not to think about what had happened to his young charge—to do so was pointless. She had made a mistake, perhaps more than one, but she didn't deserve this. If the *Enterprise* would only return, perhaps they would have the personnel and resources to find Teska, but a wounded Vulcan and a handful of Rigelians on foot did not offer much hope.

At this point, Spock didn't even care about Teska's *koon-ut-la* and all the grandiose plans they had for reunification between Vulcans and Romulans. He didn't even care if Teska stayed with the Heart Clan or returned with him to Vulcan.

He only wanted her to be safe.

Mondral steeled himself as he turned on the hand-held transmitter and tuned it to Madame Vitra's private frequency. He wasn't sure how he could tell her what he had to tell her, except to blurt it out. She might personally fly out to the country to disembowel him, but he had to tell her. His comrades had wandered far away, leaving him sitting by himself on a rock in the crater. *Cowards.*

He sent out the hailing code and waited, hoping she would be in a meeting and not in her office in Nine Hills. But this was not Mondral's lucky day. She answered the hail immediately.

"Vitra," she purred. "State your business."

"It's Mondral."

"Why are you calling me?" she demanded. "You should be on your way here with the shipment."

"We've had a problem with the shipment."

"What problem? I heard we had a full count."

Mondral cleared his throat. He could love her, fight her battles, and kill people for her, but he still feared her as much as anyone. Perhaps he should tell her the good news first. "That little Vulcan girl—we've seen her."

"What!" barked Vitra. "Did you capture her? Kill her?"

"No," said Mondral in a rush, "she pulled a phaser on me and stunned me, then she stole our shuttlecraft, with most of the shipment on it. She got clean away."

There was silence on the other end, and he could imagine the rage creeping across Vitra's face. Finally she said, "I hope you've been drinking, and you're trying to get out of trouble by making up outrageous stories. A little girl did *not* steal our personnel shuttlecraft and lose our shipment!"

"Yes, she did. She flew it off better than any pilot I've ever seen. We have no idea where it is, or where eight of our recruits went."

"You *moron!* That's what I get for pulling you off the line. You're no better than *they* are!"

Mondral's jaws tightened. "Don't worry, I'll kill her as soon as I find her. I'm putting everything on hold and going after her right now."

"No, wait! I'm coming there myself," declared Vitra. "I don't trust you to do it right. Where are you?"

"The crater. Remember to bring the tracker—the homing device may still be active."

"I'll bring more people, too. Vitra out."

When she cut the connection, there was a squeal of static in his ear, and Mondral scowled and hurled the transmitter to the ground.

Chapter Fourteen

SPOCK LIMPED ALONG the path toward the eastbound solar transporter, unsure how far he would actually walk. His right side was stiff and sore, and his progress was annoyingly slow. He debated whether he should proceed with his original plan to return to Ancient Grace, where his shipmates were likely to look for him, or stay near the commune. He didn't want to leave the Heart Clan in case the search party found Teska or needed his help.

Logically, however, it was doubtful how much help he could give to able-bodied Rigelians who knew the countryside far better. Before this experience, Spock had never quite understood what the term "moral support" had meant, but now he knew—an inability to do anything but offer encouragement.

"Hullo!" came a man's voice from afar.

Spock turned and looked back down the trail to see a figure, who waved and started jogging toward him. The Vulcan lifted his cane and waved back, although he wasn't sure who it was.

As the figure trotted closer, Spock recognized him as Hemopar, which was a relief. He leaned on his cane and waited for the middle-aged man to join him.

"Captain Spock," said Hemopar glumly, "I just heard what happened to Teska. It's a terrible shame."

"It is most unfortunate," agreed Spock.

"But I see you're getting along all right on the cane."

"Acceptably," answered Spock. "The cane is sturdy, but I am not."

Hemopar clicked his tongue with concern. "I want you to know, if there's anything I can do—"

Spock cocked his head thoughtfully. "I do have a need. With my communicator broken, the *Enterprise* has no way to find me, so they would probably go to Ancient Grace. With Teska missing, I cannot go there, but you could. You could even get word to Starfleet about what happened—you know all about the inquest."

Hemopar cringed. "You had to bring that up, didn't you? All right, I'll go to Ancient Grace to look for your people. I agree that you should stay here. Teska is a resourceful child, and I think you'll see her again soon."

"Perhaps," said Spock guardedly.

Hemopar shook his head. "You know, your communicator isn't the only thing that's broken. That health gauge you gave me doesn't seem to work at all. If I'm going to Ancient Grace, I guess I might as well take it back to the hospital and get a new one," he mused.

"But your first priority . . ."

". . . is to find your friends. Yes, I know," Hemopar grinned. "You go back and relax, Captain Spock, I'll get word to them."

"One moment." Spock reached into his bag and took out his two triangular coins. "You may need these."

"Thank you." With a wave, Hemopar headed down the trail at a brisk pace.

As Spock watched Hemopar charge up a hill, he decided that perhaps he should conserve his strength, rather than traipse up and down the trail. He spotted a fallen log by the side of the path that was about the right height to sit upon, and he lowered himself carefully, feeling about 210 years old.

The Vulcan glanced back and saw Hemopar disappear over the rise and around a bend in the trail. Spock continued gazing down the path for no other reason than that he was too tired to look elsewhere. Suddenly he saw a strange flash of light and heard a scream from that direction.

Spock's leg wouldn't allow him to bolt immediately to his feet, so he rose slowly, wondering if he was hallucinating. Then he clearly heard voices— shouting.

He scurried about ten meters into the forest and dropped to his stomach in the sticky ferns, listening.

The Vulcan heard what sounded like chopping noises, but the sounds faded away quickly. Without birdsong, the Rigelian forest was deceptively quiet.

Spock didn't want to move from his hiding place, but he had to know what had happened on the trail ahead of him. Stoically, he rose to his feet, putting as much weight as he could on his cane, and shuffled forward. Traversing the vines and undergrowth was extremely difficult, and it was hard to be quiet as he knocked away branches with his cane. So Spock drew his phaser and held it in his weak right hand.

He crept up the hill, hoping that he wasn't walking into some kind of ambush, as Teska and then Hemopar apparently had. But he took consolation in the fact that if he couldn't see his foe in the lush vegetation, they couldn't see him either. As he reached the top of the rise, Spock again crouched down to rest his aching muscles and listen for stirring, but the forest remained eerily quiet. There wasn't even a breeze to disturb the leaves. Finally satisfied that he was either alone or pitted against a very quiet foe, Spock rose up on his aching legs and crept forward.

At the bottom of the hill, Spock estimated that he had gone as far as Hemopar could have gone before he heard the screams and saw the flash of light. He was parallel to the trail and could see most of it, and no one was there. So Spock came out of hiding and made his way back to the path, which looked deserted as far as he could see in either direction.

Remembering the detective work Hanua and Rassero had employed while searching for signs of

Teska, Spock looked for footprints and broken branches. He knew he didn't have far to look when he found not only footprints but also a scorched spot of earth. Some dirt had been hastily kicked over the scorchmarks, but it didn't cover them enough to hide them. Branches at the side of the trail appeared not only hacked but trampled.

Leveling his phaser, Spock walked along a trail of decimated vegetation that a five-year-old could have followed. He didn't go far, about twenty meters, before he saw a dark form lying on the ground amid the humus and vines. Spock approached the still figure cautiously, even though he had an idea of what he would find.

Hemopar lay on a bed of bright green leaves and dark green blood, his eyes wide open and half his chest vaporized by a phaser blast. He had apparently been shot on the trail and dragged back here. But why? There was little need to feel for a pulse, but Spock did so anyway. As expected, there was none, but he found the health device given to him at the Ancient Grace hospital—it was clutched in Hemopar's dead fingers.

Dispassionately, Spock assessed the situation. Hemopar had been summarily executed on the trail, which didn't sound like the way the slavers operated. It was, however, typical of the ruthlessness of Madame Vitra and Mondral. But why would they kill Hemopar, who had been their accomplice at the inquest only a few days ago? Could it have been a case of mistaken identity?

Spock bent down and pulled the health gauge out

of Hemopar's stiff fingers. He had never tried to operate the device, but he clearly recalled when the helmeted guard at the hospital had given it to him. At first, he feared it was a weapon, because it was about the size and shape of a phaser. Only after Prefect Oblek had assured him that it was harmless did he take it.

Without thinking about it, Spock had given the device to Hemopar, who found it to be nonfunctional. Now Hemopar was dead.

The Vulcan still possessed considerable strength in his left hand, so he gripped the device in his weaker right hand and pressed his fingers along the seam that separated the two halves of the device. Pressing and twisting at the same time, he snapped the device open and scrutinized the internal components. It was obvious why it wasn't working. A metallic object about the size of a coin was fused to two contact points, which had shorted out the device.

He took out the second, smaller object and pried it open with his fingernail. It, too, contained something remarkable. Among the miniature circuits he identified a transceiver assembly and a krellide power cell—it was a transmitter. If it were a homing device, that would explain how the first band of assassins had tracked them so quickly after they left Ancient Grace, and it also explained why Hemopar was dead. Had Spock kept the device, their status would more than likely be reversed.

Spock considered throwing the treacherous device away, but then he realized that perhaps it could be modified to send a signal to the *Enterprise*. Unfortunately, he had no time at the moment to test his theory. A band of murderers was at large in these woods, and they would be headed to the commune of the Heart Clan.

Spock had to warn the clan of the danger, but its members were spread out all over the area, searching for Teska or attending to their chores. He couldn't run, and in his cranberry uniform, he stood out among the black-clad Rigelians even more than he stood out on the bridge of the *Enterprise*.

But Spock remembered that he still had his black clothing in his bag, so he stripped down where he was, checked his wounds, and put on the Rigelian clothing. To do otherwise would make him a sure target. In order to get back as quickly as possible, he had to risk traveling on the main trail, so he struck out for the commune, hobbling as fast as he could.

"He's not here, Keptin," reported a puzzled Chekov.

Captain Kirk rose from his command chair and stared at the azure and olive-colored planet that was filling the viewscreen of the *Enterprise*. "Not here? This is Rigel V, isn't it?"

"Yes, sir, but Keptin Spock's communicator is not working, at least not in this hemisphere. We could always search for him on the other side of the planet."

"He's not going to be on the other side of the planet," said Kirk, sounding more confident than he felt. So far, this had been the Murphy's Law of missions, and the bad luck apparently wasn't going to stop now. "Any way to isolate his life-form readings?"

Scotty shook his head. "Not here, sir. Our sensors can't tell the difference between a Vulcan and a Rigelian. Without his communicator to find him, Mr. Spock is just another Scotsman in a kilt."

"Then we'll beam down to Ancient Grace," declared Kirk, heading for the door. "We have a security team on standby—tell them to meet me in the transporter room."

"Sir!" said Uhura, stopping him in his tracks. "I don't know if it's related, but there's an automated distress signal coming from a large shuttlecraft."

"I see it," said Scotty, "a wee bit shy of two hundred kilometers from Ancient Grace."

Chekov added, "I don't think the Rigelians have many wessels like that."

"Send the coordinates to the transporter room," ordered Kirk. "I'll beam down with security and take a look. Scotty, you have the bridge."

"Aye, sir."

Minutes later Kirk stepped upon the transporter pad with four security officers. Two were women; the other two were the men who had seen action on the Orion retirement colony.

"Phasers on stun." Kirk looked around glumly. "My tricorder officer is missing. Will somebody volunteer to take readings?"

"I will," said a bald-headed Deltan female. She holstered her phaser and detached her tricorder from her belt.

"Thank you, Lieutenant. All right, beam us down."

Moments later they materialized inside a boggy hollow where the mud and weeds squished under their feet. It was late afternoon, and a wind was blowing along with dozens of dust devils that scooted around and kicked up soggy leaves. The sky was gray, and the abandoned shuttlecraft looked like just another boulder in this rugged terrain.

The Deltan lieutenant studied her tricorder. "Life-form readings ninety meters to the northwest—four of them."

Kirk looked around, but he didn't see anybody. Still he began to back toward the hulking shuttlecraft mired in the mud. He didn't know why he was being so cautious, except that he expected his luck to keep getting worse. It did, as a slight drizzle began to fall from the gray sky.

"Fall back to the shuttlecraft," he ordered. "We can use it for cover."

One of the male officers made it to the craft first, and he peeked inside. "Wow, somebody took a phaser to the instrument panel. They did a job on it, too."

The mention of a phaser weapon made everybody duck involuntarily, which was a good thing because at that moment, two phaser beams streaked over their heads and scorched the side of the shuttlecraft.

Kirk dove to the ground, landing on his stomach and knocking most of his wind out. "I'm too old for this." He groaned. He rolled over and saw two of his landing party on the ground with him, one more inside the craft, and another one running behind the shuttlecraft. Despite two more phaser blasts ripping the air, all of them made it safely to cover.

Kirk tapped his wrist communicator and yelled, "Scotty, beam us up!"

By the time the next volley of phaser fire streaked across the meadow, the five members of the landing party had dissolved into tiny nebulas of light.

Teska sat forlornly on a rock and finally admitted to herself that she was lost. To be accurate, she hadn't known where she was since her capture, so it was redundant to say she was lost. Without knowing it, she might have flown closer to the Heart Clan when she escaped in the shuttlecraft, because one stretch of pristine hills, woods, and meadows certainly looked much like another. There were no landmarks, unless you could memorize a bush. On top of that, the sky was cloudy, and a cold drizzle was beginning to fall.

How did the Rigelians manage simply to walk from one place to another, unerringly, without maps or compasses? She had managed to walk in an approximately straight line by using the old trick of picking a tree in the distance and walking toward it, then picking another one, and so on. But she was guessing at a direction. Her logic really must have broken down. How could she ever think she would get away with hiding in the forest for days or weeks on end? She couldn't even walk through it without getting woefully lost.

Nevertheless, Teska had a rational plan for finding her way back to the commune, and it had a reasonable chance of success. Unfortunately, it also had a real element of risk.

Just as she had used Spock's experience to pilot that shuttlecraft, she ought to be able to tap into Ambassador Denker's innate sense of direction. In doing so, she might also tap into unknown parts of his memories and desires that could distract her and cause her problems. She had finally gotten control over most of her emotions, after suffering what her uncle had correctly called a breakdown, and the last thing she wanted was to feel those frightening urges of revenge again. Punishing Mondral and Madame Vitra was no longer her primary goal—she just wanted to find Spock and get to safety.

But safety seemed remote when one was lost in a wilderness, without a clue as to which way to turn. It would soon be night as well, and she wouldn't even be able to pick out trees and walk toward them. Deep down she *knew* that Denker would be able to find his way from here to the Heart Clan without any trouble. It wouldn't even be an issue. She could almost feel his strong personality trying to exert itself again, and she worried about inviting him back.

But she wanted to return to the Heart Clan, precisely because she feared that Mondral would go there next looking for her. And it wasn't right for the Heart Clan to suffer when Madame Vitra only wanted her. The needs of the many outweighed the needs of the few.

The young Vulcan closed her eyes and invited Ambassador Denker back into her consciousness.

* * *

As the rain began to fall even harder, Falona stood at the window of the schoolhouse, watching the drops splash in the puddles. The children were supposed to be seated at their desks doing homework, but their teacher had excused herself to help unload a cart of grain. The commune was short-handed today with so many people out searching for Teska.

The young Rigelian felt terrible, both for getting into trouble and for giving her friend bad advice. What was she thinking when she let Teska go off by herself in the middle of the night? She knew about the men who took children—they had been here only a few weeks ago and had taken several of her older siblings. But they had expected that to happen. For some reason, she thought that things would be different for an off-worlder, that Teska would be immune to the seamier side of Rigelians' lives. But on a dark path, they wouldn't know she was any different.

Falona sniffed, fighting back tears that blurred the rainy scene in front of her. When it rained and no one was playing or working outside, the commune did not seem so cheerful. In the mud, it seemed like what it was—a poverty-stricken rural village.

She noticed a tall man in black clothing crossing the courtyard, headed toward the school. At first she thought it was Rassero, because he was so broad-shouldered. But there was no gray in his hair, and the suit he wore, although black, was of a finer cut and material than anyone in the Heart Clan wore. She pressed her face against the windowpane and looked closer; finally she recognized him—Mondral, the champion of Madame Vitra!

Falona whirled around, frightened. She wanted to shout a warning, but all of her classmates were dutifully working at their desks or whispering in childish voices. Besides, it wasn't illegal for an outsider to come walking into the commune or even visit the school. Perhaps she was mistaken about who it was, thought Falona; she had better check again. The girl looked back out the window, but the dark-suited figure was gone.

Then she heard a door open, and she froze. Footsteps sounded in the corridor, coming closer, and the children who were whispering sat up straight at their desks and tried to look busy. Everyone hurried to get their work done; they assumed that their teacher was returning. Falona was afraid that she would have to run for it, but there was only one doorway into the room, and a broad-shouldered figure suddenly filled it.

Mondral surveyed the surprised children as if he were judging animals at the stockyards. The children sat stiffly, confused by the face of a stranger. Falona rushed toward her seat, trying to look inconspicuous.

But her movement caught Mondral's eye, and he looked at her and smiled. "I know you from the trip to Earth. How are you?"

"I'm fine," she answered. "Our teacher will be back soon."

Mondral snorted a laugh. "Perhaps, perhaps not. Where is the little Vulcan girl?"

Falona tried to disappear into her chair, but her siblings didn't help matters when they all turned to stare at her. Yes, said their eyes, she was the expert on the little Vulcan girl.

The big man strode across the room and stopped in front of Falona's desk. "I said, where is the Vulcan girl?"

"I don't know," admitted Falona, looking helplessly at the man. "She ran away!"

"Oh, did she? And she hasn't come back yet?"

Falona shook her head.

"And I suppose Hanua is out looking for her?"

The girl nodded, grateful to have him answer for her.

Mondral smiled again, but it wasn't a pleasant smile. "Well, we have a surprise for *some* lucky little girl. Since it can't be Teska, it will have to be you."

"I don't want a surprise," said Falona, looking down.

"That's too bad." Mondral reached across the desk, grabbed Falona by the arm, and rudely yanked her to her feet. Then he reached across the aisle and grabbed one of her little brothers, Dalafro. As they both screamed and squirmed trying to get away, he dragged them toward the door.

"The rest of you are good students," he shouted, "so you can remember this! Tell your parents that we have these two, plus two adults, and we'll trade them for the Vulcan girl. Understand?"

They sat in their seats, looking shocked.

"Understand?" barked Mondral angrily.

A dozen heads bobbed up and down. "Good,"

said the thug. "We'll send word after nightfall on a meeting place."

With his clamplike grip on the children's arms, Mondral pushed them out the door, down the hallway, and into the rain.

As the trail grew muddier and the sky darker, Spock had to walk even more slowly. He had just passed the place where Teska had been abducted, and now he was headed toward the ruins where the Heart Clan kept their store. Spock heard a shout behind him, and he turned to see Hanua, Rassero, and two more Rigelians headed his way.

He could tell from their weary downcast expressions that they hadn't found Teska, which was just as well under the circumstances. Spock didn't want the girl to be forced into prostitution, but it was better than being dead. He leaned on his cane and waited for them.

"We found their camp!" said Hanua, panting from exhaustion. "But we couldn't keep going in the dark and the rain."

"Understood," said Spock, "but that is now the least of our problems. I found Hemopar's dead body."

"What?" snapped Rassero. "You're joking."

"I never joke. Hemopar is dead, and I have reason to believe that he was mistaken for me. The only logical explanation is that Madame Vitra has sent assassins after Teska and me."

"No!" Hanua gasped. "They may be in the compound!"

Spock nodded grimly. "Most likely. This is the reason I wanted to leave as soon as possible."

"We must hurry!" Hanua grabbed Rassero's arm and pushed him down the trail.

"Wait!" called Spock. "We need help. One of you has to go to a prefect or a neighboring clan, and I will try to contact the *Enterprise*. Does anybody have any small tools?"

Rassero answered, "There is a tool kit in the ruins where we keep our shop, for repairing jewelry. Look in the storage chest, under the awning."

"I will run to the Hedges," offered the youngest Rigelian in the group. "They have a prefect and a citizens' brigade."

"Hurry," said Hanua. The young Rigelian waded into the forest, as Rassero and the fourth Rigelian jogged down the trail toward the commune.

Spock and Hanua exchanged glances, and he could see a mixture of anger and concern in her dark eyes. "Do you still have your phaser?" he asked.

"Yes. I tried it to make sure it works." She looked at him, nodded gravely, and dashed off after the others.

Hobbling on his cane, Spock followed them as long as he could, but they were soon out of sight. As he walked, he wondered if there was anything he could have done differently to divert this tragedy. Short of not beaming down to Rigel V in the first place, he couldn't think of any overt errors. If Teska had been standing somewhere else that night, their visit would have been short and uneventful. Now they were embroiled in a scandal which was bound to have repercussions for all of Rigel V, not to mention the lives that were being destroyed.

Of all the Vulcanish races, he decided, the Rigelians were the least willing to confront their violent tendencies. The Romulans were ruthless conquerors who gave in to their bloodlust and authoritarian streak, while the Vulcans suppressed all emotions in an attempt to suppress the violent ones. The Rigelians converted their burning blood into sexual pleasure, as they tried to convince themselves they were living in paradise. And maybe their planet was a kind of paradise, but judging from what Spock had seen, it certainly wasn't populated by angels.

By the time Spock reached the ruins where the Heart Clan sold their crafts, he could barely see the white pillars for the black clouds and long shadows. He had a suspicion that this night would be even more eventful than the last. He ducked into the ruins, knowing he had to work swiftly if he was going to be successful.

He found the storage trunk behind the portico, opened it, and removed the colorful awning. To his relief, he found not only a complete jeweler's kit, including a loupe, but a small flashlight as well. He had the tools to modify the frequency of the homing device to match a Starfleet communicator; he only hoped that his weak right hand was up to the task of such exacting work.

Taking care not to reinjure his wounded leg, Spock hunkered down in the bleached bones of the ancient building and began to disassemble the alien device.

Thirty minutes later his eyes were watering from

the strain, and he had no idea whether he had succeeded in altering the frequency. Without a receiver or test equipment to pick up the signal, he had to operate blindly. There was a strong possibility that he would alert Vitra's assassins instead of the *Enterprise,* and an even greater likelihood that the device was simply not working at all after his tinkering.

Spock snapped the case shut, and a moment later he heard footsteps running on the path, coming quickly toward him. Was it a coincidence, he wondered. Just in case it wasn't, Spock turned off the flashlight. Quietly, he dropped the light, jeweler's kit, and comm device into his bag, where they clinked against the other oddities he had collected during his stay on Rigel V.

Although he was better hidden sitting down, Spock decided he should stand, or he would have no mobility at all. Leaning against the wall for support, Spock rose to his feet. He wasn't going to fight off many assassins in his condition, but he drew his phaser, anyway, and he tried to remain perfectly still in the shadows of the ruins. For once, he was glad to be wearing black clothes.

Several sets of footsteps pounded to a stop on the path, and he heard muffled conversation. "Captain Spock!" somebody called cautiously.

Rigelians, thought Spock, but friend or foe? Since they came from the direction of the commune, Spock decided to take a risk. He stepped out of the shadows, his cane scraping on ancient tile. "I am here."

Three young Rigelians strode toward him, still

panting from their run, and he recognized Espera among them.

"Captain Spock!" said the young woman. "You must come back with us. Mondral has kidnapped two children and two adults from the clan, and he threatens to kill them unless we turn over you and Teska!"

He limped onto the path. "Has Teska returned?"

"No," she admitted.

"Then you have nothing to bargain with but me," said Spock.

The Vulcan gazed up at a sliver of cloudy sky visible between the dark treetops, but there was no sign of his comrades.

Once again, Kirk stood on the transporter platform of the *Enterprise*. Only this time he was surrounded by six security officers, including the barroom brawlers and the female Deltan, who already had her tricorder open. Sometime he would really have to take a few minutes to learn their names, thought Kirk. This trip, all members of the security team were armed with phaser rifles, and the captain held a phaser pistol.

"Phasers set to stun," he ordered, checking his own.

"Aye, sir," answered half a dozen voices at once.

"Shoot first, ask questions later," said Kirk.

Chapter Fifteen

CAPTAIN KIRK AND the security team beamed into the middle of the Rigelians' camp near the crippled shuttlecraft, and the black-suited thugs were taken by surprise. Kirk dove to the ground and rolled, avoiding the enemy's initial shots, but three phaser beams converged on the Deltan with the tricorder, vaporizing her in a blue fireball.

The remaining security officers cut loose with their phasers and dropped three of the four Rigelians, who collapsed into the mud with wet thuds. The fourth one tried to run for it, and Kirk lifted his phaser pistol and drilled him in the back. He careened into the black shuttlecraft with a loud clang and dropped to the ground.

"One casualty," said Kirk with a scowl, noting

that there was nothing left of the Deltan to bury. "Any other life-form readings?"

Another member of the team whipped open his tricorder and studied it. "No, sir, we're alone."

"Search them," ordered Kirk, "tie them up and give one of them a hypo. It's time for questions."

Hanua eyed Spock warily, and he felt uncomfortable under her accusatory gaze, as if he were supposed to feel guilty for what had happened. Even if he were capable of feeling guilt, he didn't think that response would be logical because the Rigelians were equally to blame. The two of them stood alone in the empty schoolroom from which Falona and another child had been abducted. This was a private meeting.

"So what are you going to do?" she demanded.

"I will offer myself to them in exchange for the members of your family," he replied. "It is all I can do under the circumstances."

Hanua paced with obvious agitation. "I don't want to do that, Captain Spock, but I don't know what else to do. Will they be satisfied with just you?"

"Unlikely," answered the Vulcan. "It is Teska who knows everything that Ambassador Denker knew. She is the one they fear."

"I just want to end this!" said Hanua, slamming her fist into her palm. "I want my children and my spouses back."

"Understood," said Spock. "Do we know where to exchange hostages?"

"Not yet. They said they would tell us after

nightfall, which could be any minute." The woman slumped onto one of the desks and lowered her head. Then she brushed back her unruly black hair. "It's not your fault—it's ours."

Spock hobbled over with his cane and put his hand on her shoulder. "I will make the sacrifice, but so must you. You must devote your energy to ending the abduction and sale of children on Rigel V."

"I will," she vowed. "It's long overdue. I will go to the Assembly myself and make the case that Denker would have made."

As Spock nodded his encouragement, they heard running footsteps, and Rassero burst into the room. "He's here! Mondral!"

Hanua jumped to her feet and dashed out of the room with Rassero, leaving Spock to limp after them. Since he was already lagging behind, the Vulcan decided to remain in the doorway of the schoolhouse, out of sight, while Hanua negotiated for their side.

He could see most of the clan gathered in the central courtyard, their gaze directed toward a portable spotlight that had been set up on the path. The bright light spilled across the compound, and a tall figure paced back and forth in front of it, like a panther in silhouette. No one spoke until he spoke:

"We have no trouble with the Heart Clan," declared Mondral. "But we know the Vulcans came here, and you gave them shelter. Turn them over to us, and we'll return the two children and the adults. Refuse, and your clan will be looking for new members to fill its number."

"But we don't have the Vulcan child!" shouted

someone. "Slavers took her to the city." Others yelled in agreement.

"She escaped from them!" answered Mondral. "Trust me, she is free to go wherever she wants, and I think she will come here."

Spock cocked his head at this news. If Teska had escaped, she was only safe from the lesser danger. He hoped she would return to Ancient Grace, where the prefect knew her and might be able to protect her.

Hanua stepped forward and shielded her eyes from the powerful light beam. "If you can't find the girl, how can we?"

"And how do I know she's not really here?" snapped Mondral. "We are talking in riddles. Do you want to see them alive again, or not?"

"Captain Spock has agreed to be exchanged for the hostages you now hold," said Hanua.

"Not enough. Your daughter told me that Teska *ran away* from Spock, so his presence won't mean that she'll cooperate."

"Then I'll come, too," declared Hanua. "You've already killed one of us—I won't let you kill any more. You can hold Spock and me until you find the girl."

The dark figure stopped pacing and stood silhouetted in the light. "Very well. In one hour, the two of you come alone to the ruins where you sell your pitiful crafts. We will free the others at that point. But we will only free Spock and Hanua when we have the girl, so you had better help us find her."

"One more thing," said Hanua. "I want Madame Vitra to be there."

"You're not making the demands," replied Mondral. "We are." He strode behind the spotlight and extinguished it, and there was nothing but darkness in the path.

Spock was about to step down from the schoolhouse doorway when he heard rustling in the bushes behind him. He whirled around, leveling his phaser, but he saw only the twitch of a branch. Then he heard more rustling, followed by footsteps running off, but he was hardly spry enough to give chase. Somebody had been there, watching the proceedings, but Spock assumed it was probably another one of Vitra's thugs. They definitely had the upper hand in this confrontation, and he hoped that he could talk some sense into them once he became their captive.

Spock sat down on the stoop of the schoolhouse door, opened his bag, and took out the tool kit and the homing device. Perhaps he would have a few minutes to try again to modify the frequency and contact the *Enterprise.*

"They claim not to know anything," muttered Captain Kirk, motioning to the four Rigelians he held prisoner. They sat bound and gagged on the ground in front of the shuttlecraft, giving him dirty looks. "All they'll say is that they were sent here by Mondral to guard Vitra's shuttlecraft."

Dr. McCoy scowled. "And you think I might have some truth serum? I'm a doctor, not an inquisitor."

"I thought you might have some ideas," said Kirk. "That's why I sent for you. Uhura talked to the prefect in Ancient Grace, and we know that Mondral and Vitra were acquitted of Denker's murder.

And there was an apparent attempt on Spock and Teska's lives before they disappeared. This is serious, Bones."

"Why don't you let this bunch go?"

"Let them go!" snapped Kirk. "They killed one of our crew and fired indiscriminately on us."

"But you would have to follow through in Rigelian courts," said the doctor, "and that doesn't sound like a good way to go."

McCoy put his hand on Kirk's shoulder and steered him away from the prisoners to whisper, "But if you let them go and *follow* them, maybe they will lead you to Mondral, or even Spock."

"How are we supposed to follow them through these woods at night?"

"I've got something that might help." The doctor reached into his medical kit and took out a hypo. "I've got trace amounts of a radioactive isotope in here, and you could detect it from a couple hundred meters away with any tricorder. One of them has a nasty bump on his head, and I could say that I was giving him something for the pain."

Kirk smiled and pulled his tricorder off his belt. "See, Bones, I knew you would have a clever idea. Go ahead and give it to him."

"Just get that stubborn Vulcan back, will you?"

"I'm trying."

By the wavering light of an oil lamp, Spock and Hanua walked alone on the dark trail, their destination the ruins. The captain had changed back into his cranberry-colored uniform, hoping it would have some impact on these foolish gangsters. He wanted them to realize that by threatening him they were threatening the entire Federation, and they would have more than just an injured Vulcan to deal with.

Because of Spock's slow pace, they had given themselves plenty of time to make the walk. Both Hanua and Spock insisted that no one else from the clan could follow them; they agreed that no more innocent people should be endangered over this matter.

Otherwise, the Rigelian woman remained cool toward Spock, exhibiting a number of emotions ranging from shame to grief. He knew that Hanua was a woman of good intentions; she had simply closed her eyes for too long and was now paying for her acquiescence. She had worked around the clock to nurse him back to health, and they might die together in a few minutes. He preferred not to leave Hanua, or this plane of existence, on an unpleasant note.

"I harbor no ill feelings toward you," said Spock.

She scoffed. "You don't harbor any feelings at all, do you?"

"I wish that were true," answered Spock. "I have learned to master my emotions, nothing more. These people are murderers, so I am concerned about our safety."

"So am I," admitted Hanua with a shiver. "Can I hold your hand?"

It was illogical, but Spock offered her his weak right hand, while he kept his left hand on his cane. He could imagine going through life with a competent intelligent woman like Hanua at his side. Perhaps she was right, and he had denied himself companionship for too long. But there was still time for him to change. He would live approximately 130 more years if he had a typical life expectancy. Of course, he had to survive this madness with Mondral and Vitra first, and the probability of doing so was not high.

"I am not going to turn Teska over to them," he said in a low voice.

"I wouldn't either," answered Hanua with a jut of her chin. "I'm not turning any more children over to anybody. The first thing we have to do is to make sure the innocents get home safely."

"Agreed," said Spock. "Do you still have your phaser?"

"Yes, but I presume they'll search us for weapons."

"We will not submit to a search until your family has been freed," declared Spock.

"And if they aren't freed? If we have to fight—"

"I cannot run to escape," said Spock, "but you can. I will lay down cover fire, and you escape with your family."

She squeezed his hand. "We are together, and our combination is good—one and one. We'll get out of this, Captain, and then I'm going to beat you at three-dimensional chess."

"I will look forward to it."

There was no more conversation between them as they moved cautiously down the dark path, surrounded by a golden aura from Hanua's lamp. At one point, Spock saw a pinpoint of light off in the forest; it faded quickly, and he assumed that it was one of Vitra's thugs, keeping lookout. They gave

Vitra's guards no reason to be alarmed as they shuffled along like two old people taking an evening stroll.

Hanua gripped his hand tighter when they rounded a bend in the path and caught sight of a light in the distance, shimmering within the remains of bone-colored pillars. That was their destination on this damp night, but Spock was in no hurry to get there.

"I need my hand," he said, pulling it out of her grasp and placing it on his phaser. "It might be better if we walked some distance apart."

Hanua smiled gamely. "I wish we could have met under different circumstances, Captain Spock."

"You will run, if necessary," he reminded her. "I will stay behind and cover you."

"Businesslike to the end." She put her hands on her hips and strode ahead of him. Spock would have preferred to take the lead, but he couldn't run to catch up. All he could do was limp along behind her and hope they could free the captives before something terrible happened.

When Hanua was about twenty meters away from the ruins, a broad-shouldered figure stepped into the ghostly light emanating from the bleached stones. "That's far enough. Lift your arms, so that my people may search you."

Spock was aware of movement in the dark forest all around him, and he was not about to relinquish his weapon so quickly.

"First we want to see our family!" demanded Hanua in no uncertain terms. To emphasize her point, she went ahead and drew her phaser. "Let them go, and I'll hand over my weapon."

"Now, Hanua," said the silhouetted figure, "I thought you were a pacifist. Put that thing down before you hurt someone."

"Release the children and spouses, or I will hurt someone—you!"

Mondral laughed and made a beckoning motion to the old ruins. Falona and little Dalafro staggered out, rubbing their eyes as if they had been blindfolded. When they saw Hanua, they shrieked, waved, and ran toward her.

To her credit, the Rigelian woman remained as calm and focused as a Vulcan. She kept her phaser trained on Mondral and gave her lamp to Falona instead of the hug the girl expected.

"Get your little brother home," ordered Hanua. "Don't wait for us, and don't stop for anything. Just keep going."

The girl nodded, held the lamp high, and grabbed her brother's chubby hand. They hustled past Spock, obeying Hanua's orders to the letter. Spock kept his hand on his phaser as he watched the golden light bob up and down the trail until it was swallowed up by darkness.

"Now the others," said Hanua.

Mondral shook his head. "Hold on, I thought this was a two-for-two trade. Nobody would trade two-for-four—it's not in balance."

"Let them go," demanded Spock. "At this point, it is *you* who are in no position to bargain."

"Right," said Mondral with a chuckle. "You are

thinking of your famous captain, who is wandering aimlessly in the wrong part of the forest even now. You are surrounded by *my* people, and I could cut you down in a flash. But I need you to bargain with Teska. That's all we want—one little girl in this great big galaxy. Who would miss her?"

"Let the others go," said Hanua, "and you will still have us."

"Oh, stop this bickering!" growled another voice. Madame Vitra stalked into the glow and leaned against a pillar, the light glinting off her black leather jumpsuit. "Why are we bargaining with *them?* They don't have what we want. Where is that obnoxious little Vulcan?"

"Right here!" squeaked a voice.

Everyone's eyes darted upward to the trees, where a bright phaser beam flashed into the ruins and sheered the pillar behind Madame Vitra's head in half. She screeched and dropped to the ground as the carved stone fell on top of her. Mondral drew his phaser and aimed for the tree, as did half a dozen others, but little Teska dropped from the branch as their beams converged in a horrific explosion.

Spock was thrown off his feet, and branches and leaves showered on top of him. There was nobody left standing, but that didn't stop Mondral and his thugs from leaping to their feet and shooting indiscriminately at everything that moved. In those next terrifying seconds, Vitra's thugs probably killed more of their own number than their foes. Through the smoke and burning branches, Spock could see neither Teska nor Hanua, but he hoped they were hugging the ground as he was.

A Rigelian ran past him, firing at someone on the ground, and Spock lashed his leg out to trip him. The Vulcan winced in pain as the man went down. As he rolled onto his back and fumbled for his weapon, Spock stunned him with his phaser blast.

Now he had given his position away, so he scrambled to his feet and struggled to run as fast as he could. As phaser blasts scorched his heels, he dove off the path and into the dense vegetation. He heard a blast over his head, and he looked back to see a thug standing behind him with a raised knife. Only the man didn't have a head anymore, just a burning stump where the phaser had caught him. The body crashed through the branches, and Spock had to push it aside as it crumpled on top of him.

The Vulcan peered through the smoke and chaos to see Teska charging down the trail, shooting wildly with a phaser set on full destruct. She was a menace, and she was starting to draw enemy fire. So Spock made a quick decision to lift his phaser and fire at her; his beam struck and dropped the girl a microsecond before other beams rent the empty air above her.

"Good shooting!" he heard someone yell.

The odd compliment seemed to bring a lull to the shadowy battlefield, but it was impossible to tell who had won the battle. The Rigelians would assume Teska was dead, not stunned, and Spock hoped that no one would inspect her body immediately. He clearly heard a woman shriek in pain, but he couldn't tell who she was. So he remained still, lying in the bushes beside a headless body.

"Spock!" he heard Mondral yell. "Spock, it's over!

The girl is dead, Hanua is dead, and Madame Vitra will soon be dead if I don't get her some help. Spock?"

The Vulcan lay still. He would not dissuade Mondral from thinking that he was dead.

"At least hold your fire while we attend to our wounded," growled the Rigelian. "My people, regroup at the ruins!"

Spock could see shadowy figures moving on the trail, as the shocked Rigelians staggered toward the aged stones. In the swaying light, he could see Mondral crouched over a fallen pillar, trying to move it, as several of his comrades rushed to his aid. Spock glanced behind him, hoping that no one was inspecting Teska's body, but the Rigelians were slouching toward the ruins as ordered. Teska lay in the path like a crumpled rag.

Then he heard a ghastly sound—a chorus of bloodthirsty shrieks, like monsters or madmen. The forest emptied in a swarm of black-suited Rigelians carrying pitchforks and scythes, and they descended upon Mondral and his men like an avenging horde.

Spock felt strong hands grip his shoulder and toss him over like a log. A scythe shrieked through the air, aimed at his throat, but it stopped a few centimeters short. A husky Rigelian woman stared at him, with bloodlust in her eyes. "You're wearing red—you're the Vulcan."

"Yes," he croaked.

She nodded and ran past him, looking for someone else to kill. Spock immediately staggered to his feet and ran for Teska's lifeless body. As black-suited figures surged around him, he crouched over the girl and protected her.

The charge was led by the young man from the Heart Clan, the one Hanua had sent to bring help. Phasers cut down a number of the farmers, but the citizens' brigade had overwhelming numbers and a mad bloodlust. Vitra's private army fell before the scythes like a field of grain.

A more terrifying shriek cut through the others, and he saw Madame Vitra lifted above the heads of the mob. She was still alive, if barely, and she managed to screech epithets at her attackers. Spock wondered if there was anything he could do to save her life, but the crowd was in a frenzy, exacting its own justice. As the farm implements descended, she screamed like something not even humanoid.

Suddenly Spock heard movement in the bushes beside him, and he turned to see a figure in the forest, staggering away from the carnage. With all the strength he could muster, Spock picked up Teska's limp body and rose to his feet. He hobbled down the path in pursuit of the escapee, and he got about twenty meters when a hulking figure leaped from the shadows and grabbed his throat. Both Teska and his phaser fell to the ground.

Mondral shook him like a doll and snarled in his face. "You've caused me enough trouble! I'll take care of you."

"I don't think so," came a familiar voice.

Spock opened his eyes to see Captain Kirk leap from the bushes, tackle Mondral, and wrestle him to the ground. He and Mondral rolled in the mud for several moments, trading punches. But finally the stronger and younger Mondral got on top of Kirk and pushed his face into the mud while he pulled a knife.

"Any . . . time!" Kirk gasped.

Spock lunged for Mondral's shoulder with his right hand, willing enough strength and accuracy to his fingers to shut off vital nerve impulses in Mondral's neck. He pinched hard, and the big Rigelian shuddered and fell over, unconscious.

"It is good to see you, Captain," said Spock, helping his friend to his feet.

Kirk gulped and rubbed his throat. "Good to see you, too, Spock. Scotty detected some phaser fire down here, but I thought it would be nothing, so I came by myself. It looks like we hit the jackpot. Should I even ask what's been going on?"

"There is a riot in progress." Spock bent down to pick up Teska. As he rose to his feet, there came a bloodcurdling scream from farther up the trail, followed by gales of laughter. "We should be leaving."

The captain lifted his wrist communicator. "Kirk to bridge. Three to beam up." He glanced at Mondral. "Make that *four* to beam up, and have security waiting."

At dawn, Spock materialized in the center of the Heart Clan's commune, and he was carrying a square box with a green bow on it. As he limped across the compound toward the infirmary, his feet squished in the soft mud, and shutters went up all over the lodge. The Rigelians were still edgy after the events of the night before, and Spock could hardly blame them. He waved at the watchful eyes as he climbed the steps and entered the infirmary.

A gray-garbed healer was on duty, and she hovered over a Rigelian male who looked badly burned. He was floating in the same tank that Spock had floated in a few days ago, and the Vulcan shook off the memory. All of the beds in the infirmary were occupied by wounded from the battle in the woods. The dead had been gathered elsewhere.

"Hanua?" he asked.

The healer put her finger to her lips and pointed to the far corner. Spock nodded and hobbled over to a bed where a dark-haired woman lay sleeping. Her right leg was elevated and was in a clear casing, and Spock could see the stitches where the leg had been reattached.

He expected simply to leave his gift and be gone. She would know who it was from. To his surprise, Hanua opened her eyes as he set the box on the table.

"A gift?" she rasped. "How sentimental of you, Captain Spock."

"I am glad to hear that reports of your death were exaggerated," said the Vulcan, sitting on a stool beside her.

"It will take more than Madame Vitra to stop me," said the woman. "You have a souvenir."

"I do?" asked Spock.

She nodded. "Mondral."

"Yes, we are taking him back to Earth where he has agreed to testify as to illegal activities here on Rigel V. The Federation will not have to guess anymore. If Rigel V does not make positive moves to end this practice, they may be forced to resign from the Federation."

"As soon as I'm well," promised Hanua, "I'm going to the Assembly. Things will change here—you will see."

"I hope so." Spock rose stiffly. "I must be going, because Teska still has her *koon-ut-la*. Remarkably, the boy is still willing."

"Who would not be willing to marry Teska?" said Hanua, managing a smile. "What's in the box?"

"A small gift for your convalescence," Spock replied.

"Open it, please."

Spock did as requested, and he pulled out a three-dimensional chess set and a bag of pieces shaped like starships. Carefully, he set the multilayered board game on the table.

"It is regrettable that I do not have time for a game," he said softly. "You were good competition."

"If you can ever stand more, come back," said the Rigelian with a smile. "Take care of that little one, Spock, and take care of yourself sometimes, too."

Spock nodded and spread his fingers in the Vulcan salute. "Live long and prosper, Hanua."

Chapter Sixteen

SPOCK STOOD ON A promontory at the top of a butte which overlooked Mount Seleya and the stark plains and spindly peaks which surrounded it. The Vulcan landscape was bathed in the golden glow of late afternoon, and a hot dusty wind stroked his face. On this remote spot, there was no sign of civilization except for a shuttlecraft landing port some kilometers away. At the base of the mountain stood the monoliths of the sacred grove.

A statuesque Vulcan woman stood beside him. She was dressed in a glittering silver gown with an ornate brush coiled in her luxurious black hair, and her breath came in fits and starts. Considering that she was suffering from the effects of *pon farr*, the young woman exhibited extraordinary control over her emotions, and her doting uncle was justly proud of her. It was all he could do not to beam.

Head of her class at the Vulcan Science Academy, a recognized expert in mind-meld techniques with numerous scholarly papers to her credit, now studying to be a medical doctor—Teska had accomplished all of this at an age when most Vulcans were just beginning their careers. Watching her grow and blossom from a precocious child into a leader of her people was a joy that Spock gladly permitted himself. Not only that, but she had finally grown into her regal ears, and she was beautiful.

As a bride, Teska was not only blushing but flushed. Although it was warm on the vast golden plain, she rubbed her arms as if she were freezing. "It is hard to believe that we stood here twenty-one years ago and were joined. Twenty-one years, and it seems like yesterday. I cannot wait to see him!"

"Only a few more minutes," said Spock with satisfaction. "Considering what we went through to get to your *koon-ut-la,* I wondered if this day would ever come."

Teska looked at him, her eyes moist with tears. "I have no control over my emotions at all, Uncle. I feel compelled to tell you how much I respect you. Is that permissible?"

Spock nodded. "Practically anything is permissible when you are going through *pon farr.*" She stepped toward him and awkwardly patted him on the shoulder, and he returned the simple gesture.

"You never gave up on me," she sniffed. "And I know I was not an easy child."

Spock shook his head. "I would disagree. Helping

you grow up was one of the most worthwhile things I ever did. It is I who am thankful to you."

Teska pulled away from him, dabbing a sleeve to her eyes. "I will look like a fool out there. I will not remember anything I am supposed to do or say."

"You have prepared all your life," said Spock. "Just speak from your heart and blood. But do not choose the wrong man—that causes problems."

"There is no possibility of that," she answered with a brave smile. "When I saw Hasmek again two years ago, I knew he was the one."

They heard footsteps on the old staircase that led to the plateau, and Sarek emerged through the open trapdoor, followed by Pardek. His father looked much as he always did, but the Romulan had grown stouter over the years and was huffing and puffing on the final steps.

Although there were reasons to be suspicious of Pardek, he had done an admirable job of raising Teska's betrothed, placing him in a secret Romulan colony that permitted outside teachings. From Spock's conversations with the young man, he seemed an open-minded, ambitious, adventurous sort. Teska planned to return to Rigel V and take her husband with her, so he could do archaeological research while she studied medicine with the Rigelians.

"All is in readiness," said Sarek with a somber face but a joyous lilt to his voice.

Pardek chuckled. "Yes, it is. Poor Hasmek is foaming at the mouth. We had to put him in the brig!"

The Romulan caught sight of Teska, who was also

doing a poor job of containing her emotions, and he looked down with embarrassment. "Uh, I didn't mean anything by that. In fact, this passion you have is most impressive. I hope that someday, when our races are reunited—"

"Let us not talk about such things today," cautioned Sarek. "Today we complete the bonding of Teska and Hasmek, and nothing else matters."

"Right!" said Pardek cheerfully. "It is just so amazing to me that something we did twenty-one years ago is coming to fruition today! It makes you believe in long-term planning."

"Will you be staying on Vulcan long?" asked Spock.

Pardek shook his head glumly. "No, I must return home to deal with the terrible infestation of tribbles. Do you know, that problem has also been going on for two decades now! We've had to abandon several of our colonies by the Neutral Zone. It's never-ending!"

Spock shook his head sympathetically. A mysterious infestation of tribbles had indeed decimated the Romulan Star Empire for two decades, doing more damage than any previous enemy. They seemed powerless against their tiny foe and were too proud to ask for help. No one knew how the infestation started, but Jim and McCoy used to chuckle whenever it was mentioned. Spock had tried to invite the good doctor to the wedding, but he couldn't locate him on such short notice.

Bells tinkled on the far bluffs, and they turned to see a long procession winding its way down Mount Selaya.

"It is time," declared Sarek.

In unison, the men turned toward Teska and caught their breath. She was suddenly radiant, composed, and proud—a formidable specimen of Vulcan womanhood.

"I am ready."

Pardek hurried down the stairs, and Sarek swept after him. Spock stood back to let Teska go first, and she paused to lay her fingertips briefly on his cheek. She didn't meld with him—it was simply a sign of affection. Spock nodded, grateful to have been a part of her life, and her mind.

As they descended from the promontory, they could see processions converging all across the stark mountain. There were a hundred bell ringers, carrying chimes and rows of perfectly tuned miniature bells. Then came the hooded, half-naked athletes, representing the array of Vulcan men from whom the bride could choose a champion to kill her intended mate. It was the female's right to choose and the male's lot to be chosen or die. The childhood bonding of the *koon-ut-la* had to be tested immediately, or the *koon-ut-kal-if-fee* could not be sanctified.

At the end of the procession came the litter of High Priestess T'Lar, borne aloft by a dozen acolytes. The thin aged woman sat regally in her chair, staring straight ahead, mustering her concentration on the task at hand. When the blood fever was upon two young people, she knew that anything could happen —including ritual fights to the death. Because this was the first recorded marriage between a Vulcan and a Romulan, it was historic, and T'Lar exhibited the proper solemnity.

The tiny group wound their way down the staircase to reach the reddish soil of Vulcan, and the men fell in behind Teska as she strode toward the sacred grove. Spock and Sarek were standing in for Teska's deceased parents, and Pardek was standing in for Hasmek's deceased parents—his presence with the bride's entourage showed that he would respect Teska's wishes even if she chose against Hasmek.

The procession wound their way into the sacred grove, which had spindly aged trees and was ringed with open columns supporting a narrow battlement. The fortresslike appearance of the grove warned everyone that combat took place here. A muscular man in a hood banged the great gong as the processions entered from various directions. In the center of the grove was a lava pit of colorful stones, which spit and bubbled sulfurous fumes into the air. A priestess threw incense upon the ever-burning flames, improving the fragrance.

Upon seeing his bride, Hasmek screamed like a wounded *le-matya,* and it took four of his best friends—confused but determined Romulans—to restrain him. By Surak, thought Spock, he *was* foaming at the mouth. The Romulans almost let him go when they caught sight of Teska, looking radiant, and they had to tackle him to the ground and hold him there, as he ranted. Hasmek wore a purple sash around his waist to let people know he was in *pon farr,* but it was hardly necessary.

Spock exchanged a glance with his father, and they were both thinking the same thing. This was a very strong reaction to the blood fever. Would Hasmek achieve control of himself when the ceremony started? Unlike Vulcan men, he had never witnessed a *koon-ut-kal-if-fee*. In truth, they had to depend upon the mastery of T'Lar, who had mindmelded with Teska and Hasmek at the same moment twenty-one years ago. She had implanted a drive that took over their entire bodies and brought them across space in a matter of days, unable to resist their longing.

The only sounds were shuffling feet, miniature bells, and Hasmek lying on the ground weeping. The bearers lowered T'Lar's litter to the stairs, and the High Priestess stepped off and climbed upward, dragging her white and crimson robes behind her. She ascended to the dais and looked over the crowd, which instantly quieted, except for Hasmek's poignant sobs.

Spock knew exactly what he was going through, as he realized that his bride could choose someone else—any man present—instead of him. That was a far worse thought than the knowledge that he could also die in combat.

T'Lar ignored the weeping groom and raised her hand in the Vulcan salute. "Our way of bonding comes down from the time of the beginning. It is our Vulcan heart and soul. He who denies the *koon-ut-kal-if-fee* denies the *plaktau* and the *pon farr,* and everything that is Vulcan."

Her expression softened slightly. "We have many off-worlders at this ceremony today. This is unusual but appropriate. However, there is one off-worlder I would like to see here, but he is no longer on this plane of existence. I would like to acknowledge the friendship of Captain James T. Kirk to the Vulcan people. May he live in our hearts and our minds forever."

She looked with satisfaction upon the distraught groom, who was still on his hands and knees, staring helplessly at her. "Your blood burns! This is good. Stand, Hasmek."

Suddenly calm, the young Romulan staggered to his feet, and his concerned friends backed away.

The High Priestess turned her attention to the bride. "Teska, do you burn?"

"I burn!" she shouted. "My eyes are flame, my heart is flame!"

Hasmek stepped toward her. "We meet at the appointed place."

"At the appointed hour," answered Teska, moving toward her mate. "We live in each other's thoughts—"

Spock looked down and hardly heard the rest of the ceremony. He was still thinking about the one person who was missing:

Jim.

About the Author

John Vornholt is the author of 26 books, half of them Star Trek novels for adults and children. He lives in Tucson, Arizona, with his wife and children.

If you'd like to send him e-mail, please send it to:

jbv@azstarnet.com

1252.01

COMING IN JULY!

STAR TREK®

VULCAN'S FORGE
by
Josepha Sherman and Susan Shwartz

Please turn the page for an excerpt from
Vulcan's Forge . . .

Intrepid II and Obsidian,
Day 4, Fifth Week, Month of the Raging *Durak*,
Year 2296

Lieutenant Duchamps, staring at the sight of Obsidian growing ever larger in the viewscreen, pursed his lips in a silent whistle. "Would you look at that. . . ."

Captain Spock, who had been studying the viewscreen as well, glanced quickly at the helmsman. "Lieutenant?"

Duchamps, predictably, went back into too-formal mode at this sudden attention. "The surface of Obsidian, sir. I was thinking how well-named it is, sir. All those sheets of that black volcanic glass glittering in the sun. Sir."

"That black volcanic glass is, indeed, what constitutes the substance known as obsidian," Spock observed, though only someone extremely familiar with Vulcans—James Kirk, for instance—could have read any dry humor into his matter-of-fact voice. Getting to his feet, Spock added to Uhura, "I am leaving for the transporter room, Commander. You have the conn."

"Yes, sir."

He waited to see her seated in the command chair, knowing how important this new role was to her, then acknowledged Uhura's right to be there with the smallest of nods. She solemnly nodded back, aware that he had just offered her silent congratulations. But Uhura being Uhura, she added in quick mischief, "Now, don't forget to write!"

After so many years among humans, Spock knew perfectly well that this was meant as a good-natured, tongue-in-cheek farewell, but he obligingly retorted, "I see no reason why I should utilize so inappropriate a means of communication," and was secretly gratified to see Uhura's grin.

He was less gratified at the gasps of shock from the rest of the bridge crew. Did they not see the witticism as such? Or were they shocked that Uhura could dare be so familiar? Spock firmly blocked a twinge of very illogical nostalgia; illogical, he told himself, because the past was exactly that.

McCoy was waiting for him, for once silent on the subject of "having my molecules scattered all over Creation." With the doctor were several members of Security and a few specialists, such as the friendly, sensible Lieutenant Clayton, an agronomist, and the efficient young Lieutenant Diver, a geologist so new to Starfleet that her insignia still looked like they'd just come out of the box. Various other engineering and medical personnel would be following later. The heaviest of the doctor's supplies had already been beamed down with other equipment, but he stubbornly clung to the medical satchel—his "little black bag," as McCoy so anachronistically called it—slung over his shoulder.

"I decided to go," he told Spock unnecessarily. "That outrageously high rate of skin cancer and lethal mutations makes it a fascinating place."

That seemingly pure-science air, Spock mused, fooled no one. No doctor worthy of the title could turn away from so many hurting people.

"Besides," McCoy added acerbically, "someone's got to make sure you all wear your sunhats."

"Indeed. Energize," Spock commanded, and . . .

. . . was elsewhere, from the unpleasantly cool, relatively dim ship—cool and dim to Vulcan senses, at any rate—to the dazzlingly bright light and welcoming heat of Obsidian. The veils instantly slid down over Spock's eyes, then up again as his desert-born vision adapted, while the humans hastily adjusted their sun visors. He glanced about at this new world, seeing a flat, gravelly surface, tan-brown-gray stretching to the horizon of jagged, clearly volcanic peaks. A hot wind teased grit and sand into miniature spirals, and the sun glinted off shards of the black volcanic glass that had given this world its Federation name.

"Picturesque," someone commented wryly, but Spock ignored that. Humans, he knew, used sarcasm to cover uneasiness. Or perhaps it was discomfort; perhaps they felt the higher level of ionization in the air as he did, prickling at their skin.

No matter. One accepted what could not be changed. They had, at David Rabin's request, beamed down to these coordinates a distance away from the city: "The locals are uneasy enough as it is without a sudden 'invasion' in their midst."

Logical. And there was the Federation detail he had been told to expect, at its head a sturdy, familiar figure: David Rabin. He stepped forward, clad in a standard Federation hot-weather outfit save for his decidedly non-standard-issue headgear of some loose, flowing material caught by a circle of corded rope. Sensible, Spock thought, to adapt what was clearly an effective local solution to the problem of sun-stroke.

"Rabin of Arabia," McCoy muttered, but Spock let that pass. Captain Rabin, grinning widely, was offering him the split-fingered Vulcan Greeting of the Raised Hand and saying, "Live long and prosper."

There could be no response but one. Spock returned the salutation and replied simply, "Shalom."

This time McCoy had nothing to say.

It was only a short drive to the outpost. "Solar-powered vehicles, of course," Rabin noted. "No shortage of solar power on this world! The locals don't really mind our getting around like this as long as we don't bring any vehicles into Kalara or frighten the *chuchaki*—those camel-oid critters over there."

Spock forbore to criticize the taxonomy.

Kalara, he mused, looked very much the standard desert city to be found on many low-tech, and some high-tech, worlds. Mud brick really was the most practical organic building material, and thick walls and high windows provided quite efficient passive air cooling. Kalara was, of course, an oasis town; he didn't need to see the oasis to extrapolate that conclusion. No desert city came into being without a steady, reliable source of water and, therefore, a steady, reliable source of food. Spock noted the tips of some feathery green branches peeking over the high walls and nodded. Good planning for both economic and safety reasons to have some of that reliable water source be within the walls. Add to that the vast underground network of irrigation canals and wells, and these people were clearly doing a clever job of exploiting their meager resources.

Or would be, were it not for that treacherous sun.

And, judging from what Rabin had already warned, for that all too common problem in times of crisis: fanaticism.

It is illogical, he thought, for any one person or persons to claim to know a One True Path to enlightenment. And I must, he added honestly, include my own distant ancestors in that thought.

And, he reluctantly added, some Vulcans not so far removed in time.

"What's *that?*" McCoy exclaimed suddenly. "Hebrew graffiti?"

"Deuteronomy," Rabin replied succinctly, adding, "We're home, everybody."

They left the vehicles and entered the Federation outpost, and in the process made a jarring jump from timelessness to gleaming modernity. Spock paused only an instant at the shock of what to him was a wall of unwelcome coolness; around him, the humans were all breathing sighs of relief. McCoy put down his shoulder pack with a grunt. "Hot as Vulcan out there."

"Just about," Rabin agreed cheerfully, pulling off his native headgear. "And if you think this is bad, wait till Obsidian's summer. This sun, good old unstable Loki, will kill you quite efficiently.

"Please, everyone, relax for a bit. Drink something even if you don't feel thirsty. It's ridiculously easy to dehydrate here, especially when none of you are desert acclimated. Or rather," he added before Spock could comment, "when even the desert-born among you haven't been *in* any deserts for a while. While you're resting, I'll fill you in on what's been happening here."

Quickly and efficiently, Rabin set out the various problems—the failed hydroponics program, the beetles, the mysterious fires and spoiled supply dumps. When he was finished, Spock noted, "One, two or even three incidents might be considered no more than unpleasant coincidence. But taken as a whole, this series of incidents can logically only add up to deliberate sabotage."

"Which is what I was thinking," Rabin agreed. " 'One's accident, two's coincidence, three's enemy action,' or however the quote goes. The trouble is: Who *is* the enemy? Or rather, which one?"

Spock raised an eyebrow ever so slightly. "These are, if the records are indeed correct, a desert people with a relatively low level of technology."

"They are that. And before you ask, no, there's absolutely no trace of Romulan or any other off-world involvement."

"Then we need ask: Who of this world would have sufficient organization and initiative to work such an elaborate scheme of destruction?"

The human sighed. "Who, indeed? We've got a good many local dissidents; we both know how many nonconformists a desert can breed. But none of the local brand of agitators could ever band together long enough to mount a definite threat. They hate each other as much or maybe even more than they hate us."

"And in the desert?"

"Ah, Spock, old buddy, just how much manpower do you think I have? Much as I'd love to up and search all that vastness—"

"It would mean leaving the outpost unguarded. I understand."

"Besides," Rabin added thoughtfully, "I can't believe that any of the desert people, even the 'wild nomads,' as the folks in Kalara call the deep-desert tribes, would do anything to destroy precious resources, even those from off-world. They might destroy *us,* but not food or water."

"Logic," Spock retorted, "requires that someone is working this harm. Whether you find the subject pleasant or not, *someone* is 'poisoning the wells.'"

"Excuse me, sir," Lieutenant Clayton said, "but wouldn't it be relatively simple for the *Intrepid* to do a scan of the entire planet?"

"It could—"

"But that," Rabin cut in, "wouldn't work. The trouble is those 'wild nomads' are a pain in the . . . well, they're a nuisance to find by scanning because they tend to hide out against solar flares. And where they hide is in hollows shielded by rock that's difficult or downright impossible for scanners to penetrate. We have no idea how many nomads are out there, nor do the city folk. Oh, and if that wasn't enough," he added wryly, "the high level of ionization in the atmosphere, thank you very much Loki, provides a high amount of static to signal."

Spock moved to the banks of equipment set up to measure ionization, quickly scanning the data. "The levels do fluctuate within the percentages of possibility. A successful scan is unlikely but not improbable during the lower ranges of the scale. We will attempt one. I have a science officer who will regard this as a personal challenge." As do I, he added silently. A Vulcan could, after all, assemble the data far more swiftly than a human who— No. McCoy had quite wisely warned him against "micromanaging." He was not what he had been, Spock reminded himself severely. And only an emotional being longed for what had been and was no more.

Look for STAR TREK Fiction from Pocket Books

Star Trek: The Next Generation®

Star Trek: Deep Space Nine®

Star Trek®: Voyager™